D0874006

the thrill of horror

the thrill of horror

22 terrifying tales

edited by Hugh Lamb

Taplinger Publishing Company | New York

First published in the United States in 1975 by
TAPLINGER PUBLISHING CO., INC.
New York, New York

Library of Congress Catalog Card Number: 75-8200

ISBN 0-8008-7683-0

ACKNOWLEDGEMENTS

Grateful acknowledgement is made for permission to include the following copyright material:

"Only A Dream" by H. Rider Haggard. From *Smith and the Pharoahs* by H. Rider Haggard. Copyright 1921 by Longmans; Renewal 1949 by David McKay Co., Inc., and used with their permission.

"The Life-Buoy" by A. Erskine Ellis. Copyright © 1975 by A. Erskine Ellis. Published by permission of the author.

"How It Happened" by John Gawsworth. Reprinted by permission of the Estate of the late T. I. F. Armstrong.

" 'Calling Miss Marker' " by Joy Burnett. Copyright © 1975 by Joy Burnett. Published by permission of the author.

"The Shouting" by L. T. C. Rolt. Copyright © 1975 by Mrs. Sonia Rolt. Published by permission of Mrs. Sonia Rolt.

"The Happy Dancers" by Charles Birkin. Copyright © 1975 by Sir Charles Birkin. Published by permission of the author.

"Eyes for the Blind" by Frederick Cowles. Copyright 1936 by Frederick Cowles. Reprinted by permission of Mrs. Doris M. Cowles.

"Mr. Ash's Studio" by H. R. Wakefield. From *Strayers from Sheol* by H. R. Wakefield. Copyright © 1961 by Arkham House Publishers, Inc., and used with their permission.

"Montage of Death" by Robert Haining. Copyright © 1975 by Robert Haining. Published by permission of the author.

"The Skeleton at the Feast" by E. H. Visiak. Copyright 1912. Reprinted by permission of the Estate of the late E. H. Visiak.

"Medusan Madness" by E. H. Visiak. Copyright © 1975 by the Estate of the late E. H. Visiak, and published with their permission.

"Out of the Sea" by A. C. Benson. From *The Isles of Sunset*. Reprinted by permission of The Master and Fellows of Magdalene College, Cambridge, England.

"The Tudor Chimney" by A. N. L. Munby. From *The Alabaster Hand* by A. N. L. Munby. Reprinted by permission of Dennis Dobson Publishers.

"The Experiment" by M. R. James. Copyright 1931 by M. R. James. Reprinted by permission of N. J. R. James.

For my parents
two of the nicest people I know

Contents

Foreword

As readers of my previous anthologies will know, and new readers are about to find out, I compile my books with the aim of presenting only those stories that are both good and rare. I avoid like the plague those well-known tales that have been used again and again ('The Monkey's Paw', to name but a dozen!) which, while of excellent quality, are continually rammed down the poor old macabre enthusiast's throat.

Readers of ghost and horror stories—and there are none more faithful—will know from bitter experience the situation of being faced with a 'new' anthology, in which perhaps half the stories will already be in their possession, in other books.

The unfairness of this does not just extend to being forced to see the same old stuff again and again. To obtain those other stories they do not have, means paying today's book prices (which are no joke) and getting what amounts to half the value of their money.

They may rest assured that *The Thrill of Horror* contains only rare stories, either previously unpublished or else out of print for many years. It is obviously impossible to read everything, of course, but I have seen none of these tales anywhere, apart from their original publication.

I have cast my net fairly wide for this collection. There are tales included from established authors in the genre, others not so well known, and some just completely ignored. One or two stories are from authors more famous in other fields and their efforts at macabre fiction will come as a pleasant surprise to you.

First and foremost, I have been fortunate in locating a ghost story by M. R. James, not included in his collected volume and here making its first appearance in book form. It is the prize item in this anthology and I am proud to be able to present it. Four of the authors included are of special interest. H. Rider Haggard, famous for his adventure tales, is shown here in a very different light with a grim tale of the supernatural. The name of E. H. Visiak will be familiar to macabre enthusiasts from his classic novel *Medusa*; the man is not so well known and it was a personal pleasure for me to be able to research the author of that splendid novel. As well as his occasional novels, Visiak also wrote poems and a few short stories; I have been able to find a splendidly chilling example of both. Valery Bryusov has not been featured in a horror anthology before, though he will be familiar to readers of Russian short stories. His tale included here is a masterpiece, set on the borderline between sanity and madness. Finally, R. Murray Gilchrist, a strange, solitary man, probably unknown to most readers, but who produced a classic volume of eerie stories at the end of the last century. I have included a superb vignette from his forgotten collection.

Familiar names from the world of terror included here are William Hope Hodgson, Charles Birkin, H. R. Wakefield, John Gawsworth and A. N. L. Munby. Less well known are Dick Donovan and Sir T. G. Jackson, who both deserve wider recognition, and whose tales featured here are among the best of their kind.

Of the authors who I have had the privilege of introducing in my previous anthologies, I have again featured tales by some of the most popular. There is a chilling case of possession from L. A. Lewis, a prehistoric survival from Eleanor Scott, a haunted burial mound from Grant Allen, a horrifying psychical attack from Frederick Cowles, and a unique beast from the sea by A. C. Benson. The quality of these tales more than justifies the further use of the authors.

Once again, I am privileged to present a new author. Robert Haining, the younger brother of Peter Haining, Britain's most prolific macabre anthologist, here makes his first appearance in print with a deftly drawn picture of a diseased mind.

And finally, there are three previously unpublished tales from Joy Burnett, A. Erskine Ellis and L. T. C. Rolt who died recently. All three authors have been more than helpful in supplying me with their material, and, in the case of L. T. C. Rolt, writing a new ghost story for the first time in twenty-five years.

So, as some small repayment for the many hours of pleasure that macabre fiction has given me, I return some more forgotten tales to print. The door of fear is open—it remains for you to step through it and experience *The Thrill of Horror*. You may even enjoy it. . . .

*   *   *

As always, my grateful thanks are due to the various people who helped me with this collection. First, the staff of Sutton Public Library, ever helpful, patient and obliging—without them, this book would be considerably less than it is.

Then there are those authors—Charles Birkin, Joy Burnett, A. Erskine Ellis, the late L. T. C. Rolt and Robert Haining—who either kindly wrote new stories, or supplied me with old material, for this collection.

Other people who deserve thanks for their help, in one way or another, along the road, are Mrs Doris Cowles, Frank Physick, Mrs Helen Beere, Tony Godin, Gordon Plumb, Pamela Redknap of the N.B.L. and Peter Haining.

Once again, especial gratitude and affection to my wife, Susan, who helped me in more ways than she realises. And to my own 'monsters', my sons Richard and Andrew, who didn't help me in any way at all—apart from making the whole job worthwhile.

HUGH LAMB
Sutton, Surrey.

the thrill of horror

Only a Dream

by

H. RIDER HAGGARD

As a fitting start to this anthology of rare tales, I present an author not normally associated with the macabre.

H. Rider Haggard (1856–1925) went as a young man to South Africa, to become secretary to Sir H. E. G. Bulwer, Governor of Natal. While in South Africa, Haggard developed an interest in agriculture and on his return to England, studied rural conditions in the country. He was knighted in 1912 and the same year was appointed to the Dominions Royal Commission, in which capacity he travelled round the world for the next five years.

His literary career began with a success that has been hardly ever rivalled. Robert Louis Stevenson's Treasure Island *had just been published and was receiving wide public acclaim. Haggard did not think much of the book, whereas his brother thought it excellent. The resulting dispute led to his brother betting Haggard five shillings that, as he thought so poorly of the book, he should try writing one better. The outcome was the publication in 1885 of* King Solomon's Mines. *It was an immediate, unqualified success, owing much to its advertising campaign. Posters proclaiming it 'the most amazing book ever written' were put up at night, with predictable results.*

Rider Haggard followed this up with the equally successful fantasy novel She *(1887) and went on, with the entire African continent at his fictional disposal, to produce the finest series of adventure tales of his day.*

Though not usually thought of as a macabre writer, many of his books contain little gems of atmospheric writing, supernatural events and gruesome horrors. In his little-known collection of short stories Smith and the Pharaohs *(1920), Haggard devoted an entire story to the supernatural, with chilling results. The tale in question was 'Only A Dream' and I am glad to present it here, after an absence of many years from the macabre scene. It is interesting to think what the results might have been if H. Rider Haggard had devoted more of his energies to writing ghost stories, for this tale reveals him as a hitherto unrealised master of the genre.*

Footprints—footprints—the footprints of one dead. How ghastly they look as they fall before me! Up and down the long hall they go, and I follow them. *Pit, pat* they fall, those unearthly steps, and beneath them starts up that awful impress. I can see it grow upon the marble, a damp and dreadful thing.

Tread them down; tread them out; follow after them with muddy shoes, and cover them up. In vain. See how they rise through the mire! Who can tread out the footprints of the dead?

And so on, up and down the dim vista of the past, following the sound of the dead feet that wander so restlessly, stamping upon the impress that will not be stamped out. Rave on, wild wind, eternal voice of human misery; fall, dead footsteps, eternal echo of human memory; stamp, miry feet; stamp into forgetfulness that which will not be forgotten.

And so on, on to the end.

Pretty ideas these for a man about to be married, especially when they float into his brain at night like ominous clouds into a summer sky, and he is going to be married to-morrow. There is no mistake about it—the wedding, I mean. To be plain and matter-of-fact, why there stand the presents, or some of them, and very handsome presents they are, ranged in solemn rows upon the long table. It is a remarkable thing to observe when one is about to make a really satisfactory marriage how scores of unsuspected or forgotten friends crop up and send little tokens of their esteem. It was very different when I married my first wife, I remember, but then that marriage was not satisfactory—just a love-match, no more.

There they stand in solemn rows, as I have said, and inspire me with beautiful thoughts about the innate kindness of human nature, especially the human nature of our distant cousins. It is possible to grow almost poetical over a silver teapot when one is going to be married to-morrow. On how many future mornings shall I be confronted with that teapot? Probably for all my life; and on the other side of the teapot will be the cream jug, and the electro-plated urn will hiss away behind them both. Also, the chased sugar basin will be in front, full of sugar, and behind everything will be my second wife.

'My dear,' she will say, 'will you have another cup of tea?' and probably I shall have another cup.

Well, it is very curious to notice what ideas will come into a man's head sometimes. Sometimes something waves a magic wand over his being, and from the recesses of his soul dim things arise and walk. At unexpected moments they come, and he grows aware of the issues of his mysterious life, and his heart shakes and shivers like a lightning-shattered tree. In that drear light all earthly things seem far, and all unseen things draw near and take shape and awe him, and he knows not what is true and what is false, neither can he trace the edge that marks off the Spirit from the Life. Then it is that the footsteps echo, and the ghostly footprints will not be stamped out.

Pretty thoughts again! and how persistently they come! It is one o'clock and I will go to bed. The rain is falling in sheets outside. I can hear it lashing against the window panes, and the wind wails through the tall wet elms at the end of the garden. I could tell the voice of those elms anywhere; I know it as well as the voice of a friend. What a night it is; we sometimes get them in this part of England in October. It was just such a night when my first wife died, and that is three years ago. I remember how she sat up in her bed.

'Ah! those horrible elms,' she said; 'I wish you would have them cut down, Frank; they cry like a woman,' and I said I would, and just after that she died, poor dear. And so the old elms stand, and I like their music. It is a strange thing; I was half broken-hearted, for I loved her dearly, and she loved me with all her life and strength, and now—I am going to be married again.

'Frank, Frank, don't forget me!' Those were my wife's last words; and, indeed, though I am going to be married again to-morrow, I have not forgotten her. Nor shall I forget how Annie Guthrie (whom I am going to marry now) came to see her the day before she died. I know that Annie always liked me more or less, and I think that my dear wife guessed it. After she had kissed Annie and bid her a last good-bye, and the door had closed, she spoke quite suddenly: 'There goes your future wife, Frank,' she said; 'You should have married her at first instead of me; she is very handsome and very good, and she has two thousand a year; *she* would never have died of a nervous illness.' And she laughed a little, and then added:

'Oh, Frank dear, I wonder if you will think of me before you marry Annie Guthrie. Wherever I am I shall be thinking of you.'

And now that time which she foresaw has come, and Heaven knows that I have thought of her, poor dear. Ah! those footsteps of one dead that will echo through our lives, those woman's footprints on the marble flooring which will not be stamped out. Most of us have heard and seen them at some time or other, and I hear and see them very plainly to-night. Poor dead wife, I wonder if there are any doors in the land where you have gone through which you can creep out to look at me to-night? I hope that there are none. Death must indeed be a hell if the dead can see and feel and take measure of the forgetful faithlessness of their beloved. Well, I will go to bed and try to get a little rest. I am not so young or so strong as I was, and this wedding wears me out. I wish that the whole thing were done or had never been begun.

What was that? It was not the wind, for it never makes that sound here, and it was not the rain, since the rain has ceased its surging for a moment; nor was it the howling of a dog, for I keep none. It was more like the crying of a woman's voice; but what woman can be abroad on such a night or at such an hour—half-past one in the morning?

There it is again—a dreadful sound; it makes the blood turn chill, and yet has something familiar about it. It is a woman's voice calling round the house. There, she is at the window now, and rattling it, and, great heavens! she is calling me.

'Frank! Frank! Frank!' she calls.

I strive to stir and unshutter that window, but before I can get there she is knocking and calling at another.

Gone again, with her dreadful wail of 'Frank! Frank!' Now I hear her at the front door, and, half mad with a horrible fear, I run down the long, dark hall and unbar it. There is nothing there—nothing but the wild rush of the wind and the drip of the rain from the portico. But I can hear the wailing voice going round the house, past the patch of shrubbery. I close the door and listen. There, she has got through the little yard, and is at the back door now. Whoever it is, she must know the way about the house. Along the hall I go again, through a swing door, through the servants' hall, stumbling down some steps into the kitchen, where the embers of the fire are still alive in the grate, diffusing a little warmth and light into the dense gloom.

Whoever it is at the door is knocking now with her clenched hand against the hard wood, and it is wonderful, though she knocks so low, how the sound echoes through the empty kitchens.

There I stood and hesitated, trembling in every limb; I dared not open the door. No words of mine can convey the sense of utter desolation that over-powered me. I felt as though I were the only living man in the whole world.

'Frank! Frank!' cried the voice with the dreadful familiar ring in it. 'Open the door; I am so cold. I have so little time.'

My heart stood still, and yet my hands were constrained to obey. Slowly, slowly I lifted the latch and unbarred the door, and, as I did so, a great rush of air snatched it from my hands and swept it wide. The black clouds had broken a little overhead, and there was a patch of blue, rain-washed sky and with just a star or two glimmering in it fitfully. For a moment I could only see this bit of sky, but by degrees I made out the accustomed outline of the great trees swinging furiously against it, and the rigid line of the coping of the garden wall beneath them. Then a whirling leaf hit me smartly on the face, and instinctively I dropped my eyes on to something that as yet I could not distinguish—something small and black and wet.

'What are you?' I gasped. Somehow I seemed to feel that it was not a person—I could not say, *Who* are you?

'Don't you know me?' wailed the voice, with the far-off familiar ring about it. 'And I mayn't come in and show myself. I haven't the time. You were so long opening the door, Frank, and I am so cold—oh, so bitterly cold! Look there, the moon is coming out, and you will be able to see me. I suppose that you long to see me, as I have longed to see you.'

As the figure spoke, or rather wailed, a moonbeam struggled through the watery air and fell on it. It was short and shrunken, the figure of a tiny woman. Also it was dressed in black and wore a black covering over the whole head, shrouding it, after the fashion of a bridal veil. From every part of this veil and dress the water fell in heavy drops.

The figure bore a small basket on her left arm, and her hand—such a poor thin little hand—gleamed white in the moonlight. I noticed that on the third finger was a red line, showing that a wedding-ring had once been there. The other hand was stretched towards me as though in entreaty.

All this I saw in an instant, as it were, and as I saw it, horror seemed to grip me by the throat as though it were a living thing, for as the voice had been familiar, so was the form familiar, though the churchyard had received it long years ago. I could not speak—I could not even move.

'Oh, don't you know me yet?' wailed the voice; 'and I have come from so far to see you, and I cannot stop. Look, look,' and she began to pluck feverishly with her poor thin hand at the black veil that enshrouded her. At last it came off, and, as in a dream, I saw what in a dim frozen way I had expected to see—the white face and pale yellow hair of my dead wife. Unable to speak or to stir, I gazed and gazed. There was no mistake about it, it was she, ay, even as I had last seen her, white with the whiteness of death, with purple circles round her eyes and the grave-cloth yet beneath her chin. Only her eyes were wide open and fixed upon my face; and a lock of the soft yellow hair had broken loose, and the wind tossed it.

'You know me now, Frank—don't you, Frank? It has been so hard to come to see you, and so cold! But you are going to be married to-morrow, Frank; and I promised—oh, a long time ago—to think of you when you were going to be married wherever I was, and I have kept my promise, and I have come from whence I am and brought a present with me. It was bitter to die so young! I was so young to die and leave you, but I had to go. Take it—take it; be quick, I cannot stay any longer. *I could not give you my life, Frank, so I have brought you my death—take it!*'

The figure thrust the basket into my hand, and as it did so the rain came up again, and began to obscure the moonlight.

'I must go, I must go,' went on the dreadful, familiar voice, in a cry of despair. 'Oh, why were you so long opening the door? I wanted to talk to you before you married Annie; and now I shall never see you again—never! never! *never!* I have lost you for ever! ever! *ever!*'

As the last wailing notes died away the wind came down with a rush and a whirl and the sweep as of a thousand wings, and threw me back into the house, bringing the door to with a crash after me.

I staggered into the kitchen, the basket in my hand, and set it on the table. Just then some embers of the fire fell in, and a faint little flame rose and glimmered on the bright dishes on the dresser, even revealing a tin candlestick, with a box of matches by it. I was well-nigh mad with the darkness and fear, and, seizing the matches, I struck one, and held it to the candle. Presently it caught, and I glanced round the room. It was just as usual, just as the servants had left it, and above the mantelpiece the eight-day clock ticked away solemnly. While I looked at it it struck two, and in a dim fashion I was thankful for its friendly sound.

Then I looked at the basket. It was of very fine white plaited work with black bands running up it, and a chequered black-and-white handle. I knew it well. I have never seen another like it. I bought it years ago at Madeira, and gave it to my poor wife. Ultimately it was washed overboard in a gale in the Irish Channel. I remember that it was full of newspapers and library books, and I had to pay for them. Many and many is the time that I have seen that identical basket standing there on that very kitchen table, for my dear wife always used it to put flowers in, and the shortest cut from that part of the garden where her roses grew was through the kitchen. She used to gather the flowers, and then come in and place her basket on the table, just where it stood now, and order the dinner.

All this passed through my mind in a few seconds as I stood there with the candle in my hand, feeling indeed half dead, and yet with my mind painfully alive, I began to wonder if I had gone asleep, and was the victim of a nightmare. No such thing. I wish it had only been a nightmare. A mouse ran out along the dresser and jumped on to the floor, making quite a crash in the silence.

What was in the basket? I feared to look, and yet some power within me forced me to it. I drew near to the table and stood for a moment listening to the sound of my own heart. Then I stretched out my hand and slowly raised the lid of the basket.

'I could not give you my life, so I have brought you my death!' Those were her words. What could she mean—what could it all mean? I must know or I should go mad. There it lay, whatever it was, wrapped up in linen.

Ah, heaven help me! It was a small bleached human skull!

A dream! After all, only a dream by the fire, but what a dream. And I am to be married to-morrow.

Can I be married to-morrow?

The Meerschaum Pipe

by

L. A. LEWIS

One of the tales that aroused most comment in A Wave of Fear *was 'The Child' by L. A. Lewis, from his 1934 collection* Tales of the Grotesque. *I have been asked to include another of his stories; here it is.*

Chambers' Twentieth Century Dictionary defines 'meerschaum' as 'a fine light whitish clay, making excellent tobacco pipes—once supposed to be petrified sea scum'. Something else is certain to be petrified at the end of this story—you.

November 17th.

Never having tried keeping a diary before, it will be amusing to see whether I have enough mental energy to go on with it. At all events my new-found leisure will not give me the excuse of being too busy. The only question about it is—shall I find anything worth recording in this quiet, country existence? Well, it pleases me to begin with such a trifle as my own enjoyment in this property I have bought, and, after all, I am writing for myself and not for others.

My ability to retire and settle down at the early age of forty is a cause of gratitude to the Gods of Chance, who gave me such rapid commercial success in the 'slump' years when so many others were feeling the pinch. I just happened to strike the right propositions all the time, and now I can play the Squire in my new 'domain' and look forward to the idyllic life which next summer will bring, fishing and pottering about these beautiful, unspoilt backwaters. Not that I despise the country and its pursuits in winter—being country-bred—particularly in this fine old house. I shall find all the entertainment I need for the long evenings sorting through the books and all the lumber with which it is stocked, and by next winter I hope to have made friends who will come round for billiards or cards.

Perhaps I may marry again, for 'Heronay' should possess a hostess, but I fear I could never bring to another union the zeal of my first romantic attachment so quickly ended in one of the London air raids.

I feel myself lucky to have got 'Heronay' at such a bargain price, and suppose it would have cost me a good few thousands more, but for the bad name it derives from its former occupant. After standing empty, however, for so many years, the dilapidation was great, and I could see how the agents jumped at my offer.

It is rather strange how a house can continue to bear an ill repute from the misdemeanours of a tenant, even years after his or her death, though no doubt this place holds very gruesome associations for many of the local residents. One can excuse Harper his crimes on the ground of his undeniable lunacy, but his 'reign of terror', conducted from here, must have been a ghastly period for the neighbourhood, especially in view of the shocking mutilations he always practised. Still, he died long ago in Broadmoor, and it is thought that the ground was cleared of all his victims. I have had the exterior entirely re-faced, and I think 'Heronay' may now claim to be purged of his influence.

Well, I seem to be rambling on—a good start for the diary, anyway, if I can keep it up! Now I will close for to-day, and spend the rest of the evening looking over my new possessions.

November 18th.

A bright day for the time of year, crisp and frosty. Had a call from the Vicar, who asked, among other things, if I proposed to join the local Hunt. Told him that I was no horseman, but hoped to do a bit of shooting when more completely settled. He then touched on the poor maniac, my predecessor, and I asked him if he thought the dreadful record of the place would affect my welcome in the village. He replied that he was sure the people in the other big houses would soon forget Harper when they realised the hospitality of the new owner and saw how the whole estate had been cleansed of its former unkempt appearance. The villagers, though, would take longer to accept me to their confidence, and I must not be surprised if tradesmen refused to deliver goods after dark, as the grounds of 'Heronay' were popularly supposed to be haunted. He made his exit, after inviting me to dinner next week, when he promised I should meet some of my new neighbours at the Vicarage. I shall welcome the change from solitude, although my evenings here will not be dull while I have so many of Harper's belongings to look through. He appears to have had no next-of-kin, which accounts for all the furniture being sold with the house. Before his dementia overtook him he must have been a man of refinement. His library is a book-lover's paradise, and his personal knick-knacks and ornaments mostly of quite intrinsic value. While rummaging in the drawers of the study desk last night I found a remarkably fine meerschaum pipe, which he must have smoked for many years, to judge by the degree of colouration of the bowl. It has an amber mouth-piece set in gold, and is, in fact, quite an ornament. I intend to clean it up and give it a place of honour on the mantel-shelf. My man can polish it when he starts on the china. As an ex-army batman, polishing is a hobby with him.

Incidentally, I must consider engaging a staff of servants now that I am about to meet new people. Jobson can manage quite well in a flat, as he has done for so long during my City career, but we shall need more than occasional daily help, if we are to entertain as I hope to be entertained. That's all for to-day. I shall consult the local registry—if any—in the morning.

November 19th.

An irritating set-back to-day. Called on Miss Simms the post-mistress, who acts as domestic registrar, and she promised to send round some applicants for my household jobs. Left her, thinking the matter as good as settled, and stayed at home till lunch-time, but nobody called. Now she has rung up to say that she 'can find no one suitable at the moment'. On reflection, I thought her a bit evasive during the interview, and am inclined to suspect the cause is all this superstitious rubbish the Vicar mentioned. Suppose I shall have to get servants from elsewhere, but it is very ridiculous. My alterations have given the place quite a modern appearance, and there is nothing sinister about the grounds at night. Evidently the local proletariat keep dwelling on the secret burials that used to take place, and imagination has done the rest.

Spent the earlier part of the evening thinking things over, and planning for the future. I must seriously consider taking another wife. She might solve the servant problem more readily, and a hostess is really essential for entertaining married guests; but I don't fancy the notion a bit. Mary's memory is still too fresh even after all these years. . . . Perhaps a lady housekeeper?

Jobson has made a splendid job of the meerschaum, which looks, as I said before, definitely ornamental. I have a great fancy for this class of pipe myself, though I have never achieved such superb 'colour' in any of my own. I am, in fact, tempted to sterilize the stem of this one and see how it tastes. It should prove a ripe smoke. It has never occurred to me before to smoke another man's pipe—much less that of a homicidal maniac—but I think washing the mouthpiece with lysol and scouring the bowl-stem with a hot wire should destroy any possible germs. . . .

November 20th.

I carried out my intention before retiring last night, and so enjoyed my smoke that I felt disinclined for writing up any more of this diary. With a load of my favourite tobacco, and a good fire in the study, the time passed like lightning. Really speaking, I think I must have dozed, though the meerschaum was still burning well when I saw by the clock that it was well past my usual bedtime. To-day I feel rather unrested, though I was sleeping soundly when Jobson called me. Most likely I have spent too much time indoors lately browsing among the relics of Harper's tenancy. When I am getting daily fresh air and exercise I never dream—but I am under the impression that my sleep was disturbed last night, though I cannot recall any details. I shall take a walk round the grounds now and blow the cobwebs away before lunch. . .

Later.

My morning walk very beneficial and brightened by parading my new acquisition. Saw the Vicar and Dr Corbett, the local G.P., passing my drive gates, and they complimented me on the 'colour' of it. As they made no reference to Harper I took it they did not recognize it as his, and I did not choose to enlighten them. My ramble took me to a strip of waste ground enclosed by a shrubbery and a walk where I am told, two of Harper's victims were buried—their trunks at least. It seemed an ideal spot for a murder, and I could almost enter into his distorted point of view—at least as far as the spice of secrecy was concerned.

There must be a grim fascination in committing a crime that rouses the countryside and then watching the police go off on false scents. Harper went about his butchery for months without attracting the least suspicion. Evidently he can have shown no outward symptom of insanity between the attacks, and must have exercised amazing caution in executing his horrible tasks; yet his dementia was of an extreme kind, as was shown by the distorted artistry of his mutilations.

Employed the afternoon and evening in a fruitless journey to the County town—twenty miles away—in search of domestics. Interviewed several candidates who happened to be at the Registry Office, but as soon as I mentioned my address they made various excuses not to accept service with me. The popular aversion to 'Heronay' is very widespread, it seems, and it looks as if I shall have to engage my staff in London. Most annoying.

Found some newspaper cuttings in the course of my evening's exploring among Harper's belongings. They all related to his criminal career, and I could picture him gloating over the horror which his monstrous 'recreation' was instilling in the public mind. Having been abroad at the time I was not well up in the history of this butcher, and so took the trouble to read the cuttings through. Apparently he was actuated by no personal motives but from a general lust to kill, and his victims were invariably women. The most revolting feature of the murders was his habit of severing the head and limbs with a sharp hatchet and leaving them on the scene for identification, while carrying away the trunk for addition to a sort of museum which is supposed to have been kept in some room of the house.

The subsequent interring seems only to have been affected when decomposition rendered it necessary, as the police deduced from the remains.

November 21st.

Another disturbed night, judging by this morning's lassitude—though again I have no clear recollection of my dreams beyond the feeling that they were of a distressing and even frightening nature. Also I am convinced that I did—for me—quite an unprecedented thing. I noticed earth stains on my feet when getting into my bath, and Jobson found more of them on the bed-linen, from which it is clear that I must have walked in my sleep. I have always regarded this as a sign of mental unbalance, so told Jobson I had gone down to the garden, fancying I heard an intruder. He must have wondered why I did not wear my slippers, but is too well trained to offer such criticism. I have never had a day's illness in my life, and I do not like this symptom of nerve trouble—especially as I spent most of yesterday out-of-doors. I shall spend to-day on the links and get my lunch at the Club House.

Later.

A splendid game of golf with a member to whom the Secretary introduced me, and another round, by myself, in the afternoon. I should sleep well to-night. Meanwhile a sensation has arisen in the village by the discovery of a dead body in Arningham Woods. It appears to be a case of murder, the victim being a young girl from a gypsy encampment nearby. The postman told me that her throat had been cut and that one of the hands, severed at the wrist, was missing.

The last I take to be a piece of village gossip originating in Harper's dismembering proclivities. I understand the affair is regarded as probably a crime of jealousy and that the police are looking for a young basket-maker who left the camp this morning.

Enough diary for to-day. Just half an hour's smoke, and I shall not want any rocking.

November 22nd.

Once more a shockingly restless night—this time caused by definite nightmares. Though I fell asleep at once and do not remember awakening until Jobson brought my tea, I feel as if I had been 'on the tiles'. Most of the time I seemed to be pacing endless corridors and clambering up and down stairs burdened by some weighty object which I was trying to conceal. What it was I cannot remember, except that it seemed both precious and repulsive simultaneously, and that I was in a panic in case anyone find me with it. I examined my feet on rising for any traces of sleep-walking, but could find no such evidence. One thing, however, puzzled me—namely, that I appeared to be wearing different pyjamas from those in which I went to bed. Still, most of my sleeping-suits resemble each other, being all black silk and varying only in the braiding, so I may have been mistaken. Somnambulism apart, though, if these exhausting dreams continue I must ask Corbett for a tonic. It will be a good opportunity to mention the matter if I can persuade him to a round of golf this afternoon.

Later.

I was wrong, it would seem, to start this diary wondering if I
should find enough to write about in so rural a spot. The murder
of the gypsy girl has now been followed by the mysterious disappearance of a cottager's daughter. By a coincidence she is one of
the prospective maids I interviewed two days ago, and, although
in service in the County town, was spending the week-end here
with her family.

Apparently she went out for a solitary walk late last evening
and she has not been seen since, nor has she returned to her
employer's residence. The discovery of blood-stains in a little-used
lane near the village has, of course, given rise to a crop of ugly
rumours, but as none of the girl's clothing or belongings has come
to light I see no reason to connect the two facts. Quite probably a
case of elopement. . . .

I was about to close my diary for the day when Jobson entered
my study in a great state of agitation. He had been taking a moonlight walk in the grounds near one of the boundary walls when he
noticed some unusual object in a tussock of grass. Stooping to
examine it, he saw, to his horror, that it was a human hand! As he
finished describing the finding of it he produced the horrible
thing from a roll of newspaper and laid it on my desk, when,
overcoming my natural revulsion, I inspected it under a powerful
reading-lamp. Though no student of anatomy, I judged it to be
the hand of a woman, partly, I dare say, on account of the cheap
and gaudy rings which adorned two of the fingers. These baubles
seemed, in a vague way, familiar, and I supposed that I had seen
their wearer at some time in the village. Naturally, I rang up the
police without loss of time, and have spent the last hour talking
with the Inspector—a very capable man who, as a young member
of the force, was instrumental in Harper's arrest. He not only
confirmed the rumour of the gypsy's hand having been cut off, but
positively identified it with Jobson's grim 'find'. He thinks that
the basket-maker, an unsuccessful suitor, must have taken the
hand as a keepsake and then, fearing to keep so terrible a re-
minder, have thrown it over my wall in his flight. This theory
gives them a clue to the direction in which he was travelling, and
the Inspector spoke hopefully of an early arrest.

November 26th.

The events of the past few days have occupied my mind to the exclusion of all other matters. My diary has been neglected, and I must recapitulate. So far from rustic uneventfulness, I seem to have landed myself in the middle of a Grand Guignol play.

A fresh series of crimes identical with those of my perverted predecessor has broken out in the neighbourhood, and the surrounding country is teeming with police, press men, and morbid sightseers. By having the gates locked I have been able to keep most of them off this property, but I caught two reporters astride the wall near Harper's 'cemetery' yesterday, and had Jobson turn them away. The village is in a state of siege, as no woman will venture out after dark, and even by daylight they go in twos and threes. A rumour that Harper had not died at Broadmoor, but had escaped, rapidly gained ground, and I found myself wondering if this were the case. The police, however, assure me that he died years ago and that so far from any such escape being 'hushed up' a warning would be broadcast to all districts. Hard upon the heels of Jobson's discovery of the hand came news of a second mutilation during the ensuing night. The head, arms and legs of Dr Corbett's cook were found lying on a tombstone in the churchyard. The torso was missing. The night after, another woman's head and limbs were left neatly piled by the roadside not far from the Assembly Rooms. They must have been placed there in the early morning hours, as a local dance held there was not over till well after midnight. It is very disturbing to have this dangerous lunatic on one's doorstep, apart from the noisy crowd of sightseers who came to pry around—and even picnic on!—the sites of his crimes. To add to all this discord (and perhaps resulting from it) my own health is causing me serious anxiety. It seems impossible for me to get a decent night's rest even with the sedative that Corbett prescribed. My sleep is constantly broken by the most hideous nightmares, in one of which, last night, I even dreamt that I was accompanying Harper on one of his nocturnal escapades. The beginning of the dream remains utterly chaotic, but I distinctly remember standing in a field over the corpse of a woman whom he had dismembered.

Though I could not see the man distinctly he seemed to be constantly at my side compelling me to busy myself hiding the traces of his handiwork. As often, I believe, happens in dreams when we do things as a matter of course that are completely foreign to our nature, I felt myself lacking all volition to resist Harper's influence and, in fact, quite entering into the spirit of his requirements. I buried the woman's clothes in a ditch, covering them carefully with earth and dead bracken, and arranged parts of the body on a gate, balancing the head on one post and hanging the limbs in a row on the bars. The rest of the nightmare is like a fogged photographic plate, save that I repeated my former impression of tramping great distances with a heavy burden—in this instance a nude female torso.

Such ghastly dreams must indicate some kind of ill-health, and if Corbett cannot stop them I shall consult a specialist.

Later.

Jobson has just come back from the village with fresh news which, to me at any rate, appears horribly significant. Another woman's head and limbs have been found, balanced on a gate dividing two nearby pastures. Jobson's description corresponds unpleasantly with my dream. Is it possible that I am somehow spiritually *en rapport* with Harper's ghost through the medium of a common dwelling-place? I have never imagined myself in the least 'psychic'. And then, how explain the finding of an actual corpse (or, at any rate, parts of one) in view of Harper's decease? No: obviously a different maniac, but with similar tendencies, must be at large, and I do not see why the 'aura' of Harper's possessions should bring me in touch with *him*—unless, perhaps, there is some malignant 'elemental' native to these parts which prompts the killings and which may, to some extent, influence anybody living locally. But this is too wild a speculation. I have never believed in such things. Jobson, by the way, found a telegram for him at the Post Office telling him of a sister's illness. He is a sterling friend and servant, so I told him that he must of course, take a few days off to see her. He demurred at first on the ground that I should be unable to get local help, but I could see he really wanted to go. He has accordingly left to catch a late train, and I have the house to myself.

November 27th.

Another outrage last night, and another nightmare for me! This time it is Miss Simms, the post-mistress, whose remains were found on her own counter by her daily help, who arrives to make early tea at seven o'clock. The unfortunate woman can have had no chance to resist her attacker as, though she had neighbours on both sides, no outcry was heard. The trunk, as usual, had been carried off. Whether my nightmare had, again, any connection with this crime I cannot recall. I am only aware of the sensation, to which I have now grown accustomed, of carrying things about and of being a fugitive. Towards morning however, I had an amazingly vivid dream to the effect that I came down the stairs from an upper floor at present disused, entered the bathroom and carefully washed my hands and feet, without, for some reason, turning on the light. This recollection came back as soon as I opened my eyes, and, being convinced that I had been guilty of actual sleep-walking on at least one previous occasion, I went at once to the bathroom to look for traces of my suspected earlier visit. But nothing turned out to be disarranged, and I was left in doubt until, after preparing and eating a light breakfast, I decided to explore the upstairs rooms.

One of the first things to catch my eye was a black tassel, similar to those of my pyjama girdles, projecting from under a locked door. I remembered having seen the key to this door hanging in a cupboard under the main staircase, but on going to get it found it had disappeared, and I am now forced to a conclusion that I hate to face. Apart from the evidence of somnambulism, which, in itself, I resent as a weakness, I cannot overlook the connection between my dreams and the nightly butchery that is being enacted.

Is it conceivable that, in my sleeping state, I have been actually present at one or more of these murders, and even—dreadful thought!—handled the dismembered cadavers? My whole mind shrinks from this theory; but it is otherwise hard to explain the subconscious urge to wash, the locking up of a (possibly *stained*) pyjama-suit, and the hiding of the keys. Good God! I must be under hypnotic suggestion, and if I am seen and recognized in this state I shall be thought guilty of the actual crimes themselves!

It has occurred to me that my bad nights may be due to excessive smoking—for I have lately been inseparable from my—or rather Harper's—meerschaum. To test this I shall abstain from it to-night and make do with a couple of cigarettes.

November 28th.

It is finished. And the meerschaum pipe is burnt in the largest fire I could build into my grate! I only write this last page of my diary for the sake of my next-of-kin—to assure them that, whatever my own condition, there is no *hereditary* taint. The pipe alone was to blame. When my writing is done I shall go out into the grounds and shoot myself under God's clean daylit sky!

I stuck to my intention of smoking nothing stronger than cigarettes, and for the first time in a week passed the early hours of the night in untroubled repose. Later, however, the restlessness must have returned, for a falling log awoke me to find myself sitting by the study fire—smoking the meerschaum. As I came to full consciousness I experienced the sudden waning of an abstract horror—indefinable but intense. It passed so quickly, though, that within a few seconds I doubted its very existence. Everything seemed normal, the room was still comfortably warm, and I felt too wide awake to seek my bed at once. Instead I said aloud and quite cheerfully, 'Well, if my sleep-walking only brings me down here for a smoke, there's no great harm done', and as the meerschaum was drawing satisfactorily I decided to sit up and finish it. If only I had suspected and burned the damnable thing then! An habitual smoker always derives a soothing effect from puffing at a pipe, and it was the marked superiority of the meerschaum in this respect that had attached me to it so strongly. Now, within a few moments, so pleasant a drowsiness crept over me that I heaped more logs on the fire, determined to finish the night where I sat rather than risk finally arousing myself by a journey back to bed. But if sleep came back—and it did, heavily—it was not the revitalizing, dreamless slumber that I wanted, but a fantastic string of the disjointed nightmare scenes in which I was constantly hunted from place to place by unseen pursuers and carrying in my arms a naked torso. At length these visions gave way to a sort of silent, oppressive darkness, and that, in turn, to pictures of my own earlier life, so that I shook off the menace of the former and looked happily at sane and wholesome things.

I forgot that Mary had long been dead, and thought that she lay beside me in our old room at Hampstead. She was asleep, to judge by her quietness, and I had just awakened; but she lay very still in my arms. I bent my head forward and tried to touch her face with my lips—but it eluded me—and, with an effort, I opened my eyes. I was back in my own bed at 'Heronay', and, of course, there was no face on the pillow beside me.

Yet I did indeed hold something in my arms down under the bedclothes—something that felt like the body of a woman, *but was very cold and still*. I slid my feet out of the bed *sideways without turning back the sheet*.

The missing bunch of keys lay on my pedestal cupboard, but I shall not belatedly explore that upper room. I know too well what it contains.

The Life-Buoy

by

A. ERSKINE ELLIS

As a result of publication of my first anthology, I was invited to take part in a local author's exhibition organized by Sutton Public Library. I accepted and, shortly before the exhibition, received a catalogue produced for the occasion. One entry in particular caught my editorial eye. I reproduce it below in full (the italics are mine).

ELLIS, Arthur Erskine. Mr Ellis was born in Bangalore, India, but has lived locally for the past 22 years. He received his education at Kingswood School, Bath and St Edmund Hall, Oxford. In 1925 he was appointed the first biology master at Lancing College and in 1931 became Head of the Biology Department at Epsom College, a position he held until 1963. Besides distinguished contributions in the field of natural history, *he has also written some ghost stories.*

Unfortunately, Mr Ellis and I did not meet at the exhibition opening. I determined to contact him about his ghost stories but, as I was moving house at the time, had to defer writing. What I did not realise was that Mr Ellis had also read my name in the catalogue and had decided to contact me. The address he obtained from the library was my old one, but luckily the letter was forwarded and, on the day I moved, waiting for me on the mat of my new house was a letter from Mr Ellis enclosing some of his stories.

The result was that I am now able to present an unpublished story by Mr Ellis in this anthology. I only hope that you can share some of the pleasure it gave me when I first read it, sitting on bare boards and surrounded by tea chests, while two men feverishly ripped up the floor around me!

Leaning pipe in mouth on the engine-room rail, I was dreamily watching the rhythmic movement of the huge engines of the Canadian Pacific liner *Montauk*, on which I was returning to

Glasgow after a business visit to Ottawa. We had taken the pilot on board and were passing up the Firth of Clyde about half way through the first dog-watch. There was so dense a fog in the Firth that the shores on either side were invisible and the ship was steaming dead slow, her siren continually emitting its warning bellow.

All the way across the Atlantic I had been looking forward to the first sight of the beautiful coasts of this noble estuary, and had pictured to myself time and again the tall hills of Arran and Argyll, with the afternoon sun glinting on their rocky summits. Now the only visual evidence that Scotland stood where it did was a fleeting glimpse of Ailsa Craig looming dimly through the mist. For the rest, we might just as well have still been in mid-Atlantic. Disgusted with this state of affairs, I sought refuge in the engine-room, and was taking a fond farewell of the great, throbbing creature which to me was an all but sentient being.

Suddenly the engine-room telegraph clanged and the indicator pointed to 'Stop'. Almost at once the bell rang again and the pointer swung up to 'Full Speed Astern'. As the great vessel shuddered to a standstill, I ran up on deck to ascertain the cause of the sudden stoppage, fearing that a collision was imminent or we were about to run aground.

I was not in time to witness the accident, but it appeared that we had rammed and sunk a small motor-boat. When I reached the ship's side, two people, a man and a woman, were struggling in the water.

Two life-buoys were at once thrown overboard, one of which fell some distance from the two people, the other just between them. The woman caught hold of the buoy near her, and then took place the most revolting exhibition of selfish cowardice it has ever been my misfortune to witness. The man, instead of making for the other life-buoy some ten yards off, which he could well have done, seized the one the woman was clinging to and, after a struggle in which he repeatedly struck her, succeeded in loosening her hold and clung to it himself. As a matter of fact the life-buoy could easily have supported them both, but either the fellow was crazed with panic or else he deliberately sought to drown the woman. She sank almost at once, and although one of the ship's officers and a passenger plunged in after her, their gallant effort was unavailing.

Meanwhile a fishing-boat came on the scene, the fog having by now thinned considerably, and picked up the man who had so aroused the indignation of all who witnessed his dastardly action. Luckily for him he was not brought on board the liner, for popular feeling was running high, but was landed by the fishing-boat at Wemyss Bay. I noticed that the life-buoy was not returned to the *Montauk*, but was inadvertently taken away by the fishing-boat.

Business called me abroad again as soon as I returned to Glasgow, so I never read any account of the accident in the papers, and certainly had no premonition of involvement in the dramatic sequel.

Later that year I spent a fortnight at Govandale, a seaside resort within view of the hills of Argyll and the Kyles of Bute. Most of my time was spent boating and fishing, and I hired a small motor-boat from a fisherman, Angus McNicol. He had a hut at the top of the beach, in which he kept his boat-gear and nets, a key to which he lent me.

One morning, when I had gone down to the beach to take out the boat, it came on to rain so heavily that I took shelter in McNicol's hut, where I found the old fellow splitting open mussels for bait. After we had chatted for some minutes, I observed, hanging on a peg beside my head, a life-buoy with the name *S. S. Montauk* painted on it in bold, black letters. Being surprised to see this, I inquired of Angus how he happened to come by one of the liner's life-buoys, mentioning that I had recently made a voyage in that very ship.

'When was ye on the *Montauk*?' he asked.

'The last week in February,' I replied.

'Then maybe ye'll mind a motor-boat bein' sunk by the liner off Toward Point as she was comin' up the Clyde?'

'Indeed, I remember it only too clearly,' I answered. 'A woman was drowned, and the man who took her life-buoy from her was picked up by a passing fishing-boat.'

'Weel, it was ma fishin'-boat, and it was masel' that hauled the man aboard. But what was it ye said about his takin' the wumman's life-buoy? I didna ken that.'

'The wretch actually forced the woman to release her hold on the life-buoy and let her drown,' I replied hotly. 'That man is a dastardly murderer, and the best thing you could have done would have been to leave him to drown too.'

'D'ye tell me sae?' exclaimed the old fisherman. 'And yet she was his ain wedded wife, sae he telt me, and he was owercome wie grief at what had happened.'

'Overcome with fright, more likely,' I retorted and, the weather having improved, went out to the boat.

The following week, as I was walking back to my hotel after a day's fishing, I noticed a man coming towards me on the opposite side of the road, whose appearance was vaguely familiar. It was not till later, when I was wallowing in a hot bath, that I recollected his identity. Brief as was the glimpse I had caught of him at the time of the accident, I was positive that I had again seen the unpleasant creature whose boat had been rammed by the *Montauk*. Here he was, then, apparently staying in Govandale. I fervently hoped I should not meet him again, but I was destined to see him once more.

Next morning, when I went along to the hut, I found Angus McNicol standing outside the open door, contemplating the interior with an air of puzzled annoyance. He turned when he heard my footsteps on the shingle, and I saw that his customary friendly beam had given place to a wrathful scowl.

'What was ye up tae last nicht?' he growled. 'I didna think ye was the kind o' gentleman who would let the liquor hae the better o' him.'

'What on earth do you mean?' I replied, considerably nettled by his tone. 'I never touch strong drink.'

Looking past him into the hut, I saw what had so upset his equanimity. The place was in a sorry mess. It appeared to have been inundated by the sea, and tangles of seaweed were scattered over everything. The hut was sopping wet, and in the middle of the floor, covered with slimy green algae, lay the *Montauk*'s life-buoy.

'Great heavens above!' I cried, 'however did this happen? The tide cannot have reached as far as this.''

'No, and what's mair, the door was lockit,' replied Angus. 'Tae ma certain knowledge but twa folk hae a key to this hut, ye and masel', and I can tell ye *I* didna make this unco' mess.'

'Neither did I,' I assured him. 'When I put away my things last night, I left the hut in its normal condition and locked the door as usual. Some mischievous ruffian must have picked the lock, or got hold of a key to fit it.'

' 'Twill be an ill day for him if I get ma haunds on him, who-ever he is. He'll nae be worth muckle when I'm thro' wi' him,' and he dourly set about cleaning up his hut.

I fished in Loch Fyne that day, and on the way back was delayed by engine trouble. Half way through the Kyles the motor gave an expiring groan, and it was a good half hour before I got it started again, after being in some peril of drifting on the rocks. By the time I had tied up to the mooring buoy at Govandale it was almost dark. I hooked in the dinghy which Angus kept moored at hand for my use and sculled ashore. On nearing the beach, I observed someone sitting or crouching on the boat-slip, and concluded it was probably some belated angler, or perhaps Angus McNicol awaiting my return.

As I drew alongside the slip, this person rose up and made up the beach towards the hut with what seemed, so far as I could see in the dim light, a peculiarly awkward and lifeless gait. As I leapt out of the dinghy, this individual seemed to enter the hut, but when I had made fast the boat and walked up the beach, I found the door locked. 'A curious illusion,' I thought. 'The person must have passed close to the hut and gone up to the road, though I could have sworn he went in. I wonder whether he had anything to do with that almighty mess last night.'

So musing, I opened the door and was just about to deposit my fishing tackle in the hut when two things made me draw hastily back. The first was a strong smell of seawater. The second was something black and wet crouching on the floor.

I hastily slammed and locked the door and set off in search of Angus. As it chanced he was just coming along the road to see if I had returned, and also in the hope of waylaying the rogue who messed up his hut. I told him that I thought the culprit was actually hiding inside the hut, having contrived to enter in some mysterious manner, and promised to keep a close watch while he fetched a light and a weapon. Angus at once untied the dinghy and sculled out to the motor-boat, returning with the mast-head lantern, which he lit, and a stout spar.

'Ye tak the licht and open yon door,' he ordered, 'while I gie him a taste o' this,' brandishing the spar with a chuckle of grim satisfaction.

'Well, don't murder him,' I cautioned, and unlocked the door. As I flung it open, the lantern illuminated the inside of the hut so that we could see clearly what lay huddled on the floor. Angus took a step backwards and dropped his improvised club, while I nearly followed suit with the lamp.

The hut was littered with seaweed and soaked as before. In the middle of the floor, her waist encircled by the *Montauk's* life-buoy, sat or crouched a woman. Her clothes and her hair, which hung down over her face, were bedraggled and dripping wet, and there was that about her appearance which gave the impression that she was not alive.

We withdrew a few paces and considered our next move. I told Angus to call the nearest doctor, while I went to fetch my car from the hotel garage, as we should obviously require some conveyance to take the poor creature away, whether alive or dead. I accordingly locked the door once more and we set off on our respective errands.

When I returned with the car, there was not long to wait before Angus appeared in company with a Dr Stead, whom I had met once or twice at golf. We three walked down to the hut and I unlocked the door. The astonishment and mortification of Angus and myself can well be imagined, for there was no one in it! The place was still littered with wrack and soaking wet, and the life-buoy lay on the floor, but the woman had vanished. We looked all around the hut and searched the beach in the vicinity, but to no avail.

What the doctor thought of it all can be guessed, but he was too much of a gentleman to speak his mind. Whenever we met in future he would glance at me apprehensively, as though expecting me at any moment to suffer another 'attack'. As for Angus and myself, we retired for the night, sorely bewildered men.

The next day I did not go out fishing, but spent most of the morning and afternoon on the golf-course. After dinner I took a stroll down to the beach, to make sure the motor-boat was in good order for the morrow. I got Angus to attend to a few things, and then we sat for a while on the gunwhale of a boat smoking and discussing last night's inexplicable happenings. As it was beginning to grow cool and a squall was approaching across the Firth, I presently rose to depart. Just then we noticed a small Bermuda-rigged cutter entering the bay and idly stood to watch her come in. She was coming up close-hauled against the wind, and made a pleasing picture with the heather-clad hills as a background.

When the cutter had arrived almost opposite the spot where Angus and I were standing, and was quite close to the end of the jetty, the squall we had noticed approaching suddenly burst upon us. The two men aboard the yacht were taken unawares and were quite incapable of coping with the emergency. Angus yelled instructions at them, but they lost their heads completely and almost at once the boat capsized. One of the men clung to the rigging, while the other, whom I recognised with a nasty shock as the poltroon who had let his wife drown, struck out for the shore. He was manifestly not a strong swimmer, however, and soon got into difficulties.

Angus grabbed the *Montauk's* life-buoy off its peg and threw it as far as he could towards the man in the water, while I rushed down to the slip and pushed off in the dinghy. As I started to row, I heard a hoarse cry behind me, and turning my head saw the man struggling frantically with the life-buoy. He seemed to be finding some unaccountable difficulty in getting hold of it, so I called to him to get his arms over it and he would be quite safe.

I shall never forget the dreadful cry he gave: 'I can't, there's something in it, there's something in it! Oh my God, it's her!' and letting go of the life-buoy he sank like a stone. In a few strokes I reached the spot, and with much difficulty dragged him up from the bottom with a boathook, but it was too late. I took the other man off the capsized yacht and rowed quickly back.

Dr Stead was summoned and did all he could for the man who had sunk, but he was beyond aid. At the post mortem he was found to have died of heart failure, not drowning. His features were set in an expression of abject terror.

After the dead man had been removed, we looked about for the life-buoy, but it was nowhere to be seen. It could not possibly have drifted out of sight in so short a time, yet it was not seen again until some weeks later in another place.

The surviving yachtsman told us that his companion was a Mr Oliver Pothington, a Lanarkshire industrialist, and remarked that it was a sad coincidence that Mrs Pothington had been drowned not long ago, when the boat she and her husband were in was sunk in a fog in collision with a liner, only a few miles from that very spot. 'It seems almost as though there is some evil fate at work,' he added sententiously.

Angus McNicol was troubled with no more unwelcome visitants to his hut.

A few weeks later, the skipper of one of the Clyde paddle-steamers, on which I was crossing from Largs to Millport, sighted a strange object floating some fifty yards to starboard. On closer inspection this proved to be a life-buoy with someone clinging to it. A boat was lowered, and the sailors were horrified to find when they reached the life-buoy, that it supported the body of a woman, now little more than a skeleton, her arms tightly hooked over it in a vice-like grip. Painted on the buoy was the name *S.S. Montauk*.

It was found impossible to disengage the body from the life-buoy, so it was covered with a tarpaulin and taken as it was into Millport, where the buoy was cut away. The remains were identified from the clothing and jewelry as those of a Mrs Pothington, who had been drowned some months previously as the result of the motor-boat in which she and her husband were out for a cruise coming into collision with the liner *Montauk*. How her body came to be clinging to one of the liner's life-buoys is an unsolved mystery of the sea. Mrs Pothington was laid to rest beside her husband in Govandale cemetery.

A year later I was again on holiday at Govandale, so one Sunday morning I made a pilgrimage to the cemetery. There was little difficulty in finding the grave. Pious relatives had caused to be erected an imposing marble tombstone as a memorial to the deceased couple. Engraved below their names was a verse from the Scottish Psalter:

> Deliver me out of the mire,
>   from sinking do me keep;
> Free me from those that do me hate,
>   and from the waters deep.
> Let not the flood on me prevail,
>   whose water overflows;
> Nor deep me swallow, nor the pit
>   her mouth upon me close.

Framing the inscription was a most realistic carving of a life-buoy.

The Lady of Rosemount

by

SIR T. G. JACKSON

Sir Thomas Graham Jackson (1835–1924) was educated at Brighton College and Wadham College, Oxford. He was a Fellow of Wadham College from 1864 to 1880, when he was forced to give up the Fellowship on his marriage. An Associate of the Royal Academy, he has works at Oxford, Eton, Rugby, Harrow, Westminster, Inner Temple and the Draper's Hall, among others. As well as several publications on architecture, he also wrote Six Ghost Stories (1919), from which this story is taken.

He thought highly of the work of M. R. James and, like that author, first wrote his tales for 'the amusement of the home circle, without any idea of publication'. It is good that he changed his mind, for 'The Lady of Rosemount', though treading on very traditional ground, is a long tale building to a sharp climax, that fully deserves reprinting.

'And so, Charlton, you're going to spend part of the Long at Rosemount Abbey. I envy you. It's an awfully jolly old place, and you'll have a really good time.'

'Yes,' said Charlton, 'I am looking forward to it immensely. I have never seen it; you know it has only lately come to my uncle and they only moved into it last Christmas, I forgot that you knew it and had been there.'

'Oh! I don't know it very well,' said Edwards: 'I spent a few days there a year or two ago with the last owner. It will suit you down to the ground, for you are mad about old abbeys and ruins, and you'll find enough there to satisfy the whole Society of Antiquaries as well as yourself. When do you go?'

'Very soon. I must be at home for a week or so after we go down, and then I think my uncle will expect me at Rosemount. What are you going to do?'

'Well! I hardly know. Nothing very exciting. Perhaps take a

short run abroad a little later. But I shall have to read part of the Long, for I am in for Greats next term. By the way, it is just possible I may be somewhere in your direction, for I have friends near Rosemount who want me to spend part of the vac. down there.'

'All right,' said Charlton, 'don't forget to come over and see me. I hope I may still be there. Meanwhile, *au revoir*, old man, and good luck to you.'

Charlton remained some time at his window looking on the quad of his college. Term at Oxford was just over and the men were rapidly going down. Hansoms were waiting at the gate, scouts and messengers were clattering down the staircases with portmanteaux and other paraphernalia proper to youth, and piling them on the cabs, friends were shaking hands, and bidding good-bye. In a few hours the college would be empty, and solitude would descend upon it for four months, broken only by occasional visitors, native or transatlantic. The flight of the men would be followed by that of the Dons to all parts of Europe or beyond, the hive would be deserted, and the porter would reign supreme over a vast solitude, monarch of all he surveyed.

Charlton was not due to go down till the next morning. He dined in the junior common-room with three or four other men, the sole survivors of the crowd, and then retired to his rooms to finish his packing. That done, he sat on the window-seat looking into the quad. It was a brilliant night; the moonshine slept on the grass, and silvered the grey walls and mullioned windows opposite, while the chapel and hall were plunged in impenetrable shadow. Everything was as still as death; no sound from the outer world penetrated the enclosure, and for the busy hive of men within, there was now the silence of a desert. There is perhaps no place where silence and solitude can be more sensibly felt than the interior of an Oxford college in vacation time, and there was something in the scene that appealed to the temperament of the young man who regarded it.

Henry Charlton was an only child. His father had died when he was a lad, and his mother, broken down by grief, had foresworn society and lived a very retired life in the country. At Winchester and Oxford he naturally mixed with others and made acquaintances, but his home life was somewhat sombre and his society restricted. He grew up a self-contained, reserved lad, with few friendships, though those he formed were sincere and his attachments were strong. His temperament—poetical, and tinged with melancholy—naturally inclined to romance, and from his early youth he delighted in antiquarian pursuits, heraldic lore, and legend. At school and college he revelled in the ancient architecture by which he was surrounded. His tastes even carried him further, into the region of psychical research, and the dubious revelations of spiritualism; though a certain wholesome vein of scepticism saved him from plunging deeply into those mazes, whether of truth or imposture. As he sat at his window, the familiar scene put on an air of romance. The silence sank into his soul; the windows where a friendly light was wont to shine through red curtains, inviting a visit, were now blind and dark; mystery enveloped the well-known walls; they seemed a place for the dead, no longer a habitation for living men, of whom he might be the last survivor. At last, rising from his seat, and half laughing at his own romantic fancies, Henry Charlton went to bed.

A few weeks later he descended from the train at the little country station of Brickhill, in Northamptonshire, and while the porter was collecting his traps on a hand-barrow, he looked out for the carriage that was to meet him. 'Hallo! Harry, here you are,' said a voice behind him, and turning round he was warmly greeted by his cousin, Charley Wilmot. A car was waiting, into which he and his belongings were packed, and in five minutes they were off, bowling along one of the wide Northamptonshire roads, with a generous expanse of green-sward on each side between the hedges, and the hedgerow timber. The country was new to Henry Charlton, and he looked about him with interest. The estate of Rosemount had lately come unexpectedly by the death of a distant relation of his uncle, Sir Thomas Wilmot, and the family had hardly had time yet to settle down in their new home. His cousin Charley was full of the novelty of the situation, and the charms of the Abbey.

'I can tell you, it's a rattling old place,' said he, 'full of odd holes and corners, and there are the ruins of the church with all sorts of old things to be seen; but you'll have lots of time to look about and see it all, and here we are, and there's my dad waiting to welcome you at the hall-door.'

They had turned in at a lodge-gate, and passed up an avenue at the end of which Henry could see a hoary pile of stone gables, mullioned windows, massive chimneys, and a wide-arched portal, hospitably open, where Sir Thomas stood to welcome his nephew.

Some years had passed since Henry had seen his relatives, and he was glad to be with them again. A houseful of lively cousins rather younger than himself, had in former days afforded a welcome change from his own rather melancholy home, and he looked forward with pleasure to renewing the intimacy. His young cousin Charley was just at the end of his time at Eton, and was to go to university in October. The girls, Kate and Cissy, had shot up since he used to play with them in the nursery, and were now too old to be kissed. His uncle and aunt were as kind as ever, and after he had answered their inquiries about his mother, and given an account of his uneventful journey down, the whole party adjourned to the garden where tea awaited them under the trees, and then Henry for the first time saw something of the Abbey of Rosemount.

This ancient foundation, of *Sanctus Egidius in Monte Rosarum*, had been a Benedictine house, dating from the twelfth century, which at the Dissolution was granted to a royal favourite, who partly dismantled and partly converted it into a residence for himself. His descendants in the time of James I had pulled down a great part of the conventual buildings and substituted for the inconvenient cells of the monks a more comfortable structure in the style of that day. Many fragments of the Abbey, however, were incorporated into the later house. The refectory of the monks was kept, and formed the great hall of the mansion with its vaulted roof and traceried windows, in which there even remained some of the old storied glass. The Abbot's kitchen still furnished Sir Thomas's hospitable board, and among the offices and elsewhere were embedded parts of the domestic buildings. North of the refectory, according to the usual Benedictine plan. had been the cloister and beyond that the church, which lay at a slightly lower level, the lie of the ground inclining that way from the summit of the Mount of Roses on which the habitable part of the convent had been built. Of the cloister enough remained, though much broken and dilapidated, to show what it had been, but the greater part of the church was destroyed for the sake of its materials when the Jacobean house was built. A considerable part of the nave, however, was still standing, part of it even with its vaulted roof intact, and of the rest, enough of the lower part of the walls was left to show that the church had been of a fair size, though not on the scale of the larger establishments.

Henry Charlton, with the greedy eye of the born antiquary,

took in the general scheme of the Abbey with his tea and buttered toast under the shade of the elms that bounded the lawn on that side of the house. But he had to control his impatience to visit the ruins, for after tea his cousins insisted on a game of tennis, which lasted till it was time to dress for dinner, and after dinner it was too late and too dark for exploration.

They dined in the great hall, once the monks' refectory, but not too large for modern comfort, the Abbey having been one of the smaller houses of the Order, and the number of the brotherhood limited. Henry was enchanted and could not restrain the expression of his enthusiasm.

'Ah!' said his aunt, 'I remember your mother told me you were crazy about architecture and antiquities. Well, you'll have your fill of them here. For my part, I often sigh for a little more modern convenience.'

'But my dear aunt,' said Henry, 'there is so much to make up for little inconveniences in living in this lovely old place that they might be forgotten.'

'Why, what do you know about house-keeping?' said his aunt, 'I should like you to hear Mrs Baldwin, the housekeeper, on the subject. How she toils up one staircase only to have to go down another. The house, she says, is made up of stairs that are not wanted, and crooked passages that might have been straight, and it took the maids a fortnight to learn their way to the food-store.'

'It's of no use, mother,' said Charley, 'you'll never convince him. He would like to have those old monks back again, and to be one of them himself with a greasy cowl on his head and sandals on his naked feet, and nothing to eat but herbs washed down with water.'

'No, no!' said Henry, laughing, 'I don't want them back, for I like my present company too well. But I confess I like to call up in imagination the men who built and lived in these old walls, I believe I shall dream of them to-night.'

'Well, Harry,' said his uncle, 'you may dream of them as much as you please, so long as you don't bring them back to turn us out. And you shall have every opportunity, for you are to sleep in a bit of the old convent that the abbey builders of the modern house spared; and who knows but that the ghost of its former occupant may not take you at your word and come back to revisit his old quarters.'

Harry laughed as they rose from table, and said he trusted his visitor would not treat him as an intruder.

The long summer day had enabled them to finish dinner by daylight, and there was still light enough for the old painted glass to be seen. It was very fragmentary, and not one of the pictures was perfect. In one of the lights they could make out part of a female figure richly dressed; she had been holding something that was broken away, and beside her was the lower half of an unmistakable demon, with hairy legs and cloven hoof. The legend below ran thus, the last word being imperfect:

QVALITER DIABOLVS TENTAVIT COMITISSAM ALI . . .

The next light was still more imperfect, but there was part of the same female figure in violent action, with the fragment of a legend:

HIC COMITISSA TENTATA A DI . . .

Other parts evidently of the same story remained in the next window, but they were too fragmentary to be understood. In one light was a piece of a monk's figure and part of a legend:

HIC FRATER PAVLVS DAT COMI . . .

The last of all was tolerably perfect. It represented a female robed in black, and holding in her hand a little model of a church. She was on her knees prostrate before the Pope, who was seated and extended his hand in the act of benediction. The legend below said:

HIC COMITISSA A PAPA ABSOLVTA EST.

Henry was much interested and wanted to know the story of the sinful Countess; but none of the party could tell him, and indeed, none of them had till then paid much attention to the glass. Sir Thomas had once made a slight attempt to trace the identity of the Countess, but with little success, and had soon given up the search.

'There is an antiquarian problem for you to solve, Harry,' said he, 'but I don't know where you should look for the solution. The annals of Rosemount are very imperfect. In those within my reach I could find nothing bearing on the subject.'

'I am afraid, sir,' said Harry, 'if you failed I am not likely to succeed, for I am only a very humble antiquary, and should not know where to begin. It seems to me, however, that the story must have had something to do with the history of the Abbey, and that its fortunes were connected with the wicked Countess, or the monks would not have put her story in their windows.'

'Well, then, there you have a clue to follow up,' said his uncle, 'and now let us join the ladies.'

The room where Henry Charlton was to sleep was on the ground floor in one corner of the house, and looked out upon the cloister and the ruined abbey-church. It was, as his uncle had said, a relic of the domestic part of the Abbey, and when he had parted with his cousin Charley, who guided him thither, he looked round the apartment with the keenest interest. It was a fair-sized room, low-pitched, with a ceiling of massive black timbers, plastered between the joists. The wall was so thick that there was room for a little seat in the window recess on each side, which was reached by a step, for the window sill was rather high above the floor. Opposite the window yawned a wide fireplace with dogs for wood-logs, and a heap of wood ashes lying on the hearth. The walls were panelled with oak up to the ceiling, and the floor, where not covered with rugs, was of the same material polished brightly. But for the toilet appliances of modern civilisation the room was unaltered from the time when the last brother of the convent left it, never to return. Henry tried to picture to himself his predecessor in the apartment; he imagined him sitting at the table, reading or writing, or on his knees in prayer; on his simple shelf would have been his few books and manuscripts, borrowed from the convent library, to which he had to return them when they met in chapter once a year, under severe penalty in case of loss or damage. As he lay on his bed Henry tried to imagine what his own thoughts would have been had he himself been that ghostly personage five centuries ago; he fancied himself in the choir of the great church; he heard the sonorous Gregorian chanting by a score of deep manly voices, ringing in the vaulted roof, and echoing through the aisles; he saw the embroidered vestments, the lights that shone clearer and brighter as the shades of evening wrapped arcade and triforium in gloom and mystery, and turned to blackness the storied windows that lately gleamed with the hues of the sapphire, the ruby and the emerald. Pleased with these fancies he lay awake till the clock struck twelve and then insensibly the vision faded and he fell asleep.

His sleep was not untroubled. Several times he half awoke, only to drop off again and resume the thread of a tiresome dream that puzzled and worried him but led to no conclusion. When morning came, he awoke in earnest, and tried to piece together the fragments he could remember, but made little of them. He seemed to have seen the monk sitting at the table as he had pictured him in imagination the evening before. The monk was not reading but turning over some little bottles which he took from a leathern case, and he seemed to be waiting for some one or something. Then Henry in his dream fancied that some one did come and something did happen, but what it was he could not remember, and of the visitor he could recall nothing, except that he felt there was a personality present, but not so as to be seen and recognised; more an impression than a fact. He could remember, however, a hand stretched out towards the seated figure and the objects he was handling. More than this he could not distinctly recall, but the same figures recurred each time he fell asleep with slightly varied attitude, though with no greater distinctness. For the monk he could account by the thoughts that had been in his mind the night before, but for the incident in his dream, if so vague a matter could be called an incident, he could trace no suggestion in his own mind.

The bright summer morning and the merry party at breakfast soon drove the memory of the dream out of his head. After breakfast there were the horses and dogs to be seen, and the garden to be visited, and it was not till the afternoon that his cousins let him satisfy his longing to visit the ruins of the church and cloister. There they all went in a body. The cloister lawn was mown smoothly and well tended, and here and there barely rising above the green sward were the stones that marked the resting places of the brotherhood. Part of the cloister retained its traceried windows and vaulted roof, and on the walls were inscribed the names of abbots and monks whose bones lay beneath the pavement. At the end of the western walk a finely sculptured door led into the nave of the church, the oldest part of the building, built when the ruder Norman work was just melting into greater refinement. Henry was in raptures, and vowed that neither Fountains nor Rievaulx could show anything more perfect. The girls were delighted to find their favourite parts of the building appreciated, and led him from point to point, determined that he should miss nothing.

'And now,' said Cissy, 'you have to see the best bit of all, hasn't he, Kate? We don't show it to everybody for fear strangers might do mischief.'

So saying she pushed open a door in the side wall and led them into a chantry chapel built out between two of the great buttresses of the nave aisle. It was indeed a gem of architecture of the purest fourteenth-century Gothic and Henry stood entranced before its loveliness. The delicate traceries on wall and roof were carved with the finish of ivory, and though somewhat stained by weather, for the windows had lost their glass, had kept all their sharp precision. Part of the outer wall had given way, weeds and ivy had invaded and partly covered the floor, and a thick mass of vegetation was piled up under the windows against the masonry.

'What a pity to let this lovely place get into such a mess,' said Henry. 'I have never seen anything more beautiful.'

'Well,' said Charley, 'it wouldn't take long to clear all this rubbish away. Suppose we set to work and do it?'

So while the girls sat and looked on, the two men fetched some garden tools, and cut, hacked and pulled up the weeds and ivy and brambles, which they threw out by the breach in the wall, and soon made a partial clearance. Henry had begun on the mass that stood breast-high next the window, when a sudden exclamation made the others look at him. He was peering down into the mass of vegetation, of which he had removed the top layer, with an expression of amazement that drew the others to his side. Looking up at them out of the mass of ivy was a face, the face of a beautiful woman, her hair disposed in graceful masses, and bound by a slender coronet. It was evident that under the pile of vegetation was a tomb with an effigy that had long been hidden, and the very existence of which had been forgotten. When the rest of the vegetation had been cleared away there appeared an altar tomb on the top of which lay the alabaster figure of a woman. The sides bore escutcheons of heraldry and had evidently once been coloured. The figure was exquisitely modelled, the work of no mean sculptor; the hands were crossed on the breast, and the drapery magnificently composed. But with the head of the figure the artist had surpassed himself. It was a triumph of sculpture. The features were of perfect beauty, regular and classical, but there was something about it that went beyond beauty, something akin to life, something that seemed to respond to the gaze of the observer, and to attract him unconsciously whether he would or not. The group of discoverers hung over it in a sort of fascination for some minutes saying nothing. At last Kate, the elder girl, drew back with a slight shiver, and said 'Oh! What is it, what is the matter with me, I feel as if there was something wrong; it is too beautiful; I don't like it; come away, Cissy,' and she drew her sister out of the chapel, in a sort of tremor. Charley followed them, and Henry was left alone with his gaze still fixed on the lovely face. As he looked he seemed to read fresh meaning in the cold alabaster features. The mouth, though perfectly composed in rest, appeared to express a certain covert satire. The eyes were represented as open, and they seemed to regard him with a sort of amused curiosity. There was a kind of diablerie about the whole figure. It was a long time before he could remove his eyes from the face that seemed to understand and return his gaze, and it was not without a wrench that at last he turned away. The features of the image seemed to be burned into his brain, and to remain fixed there indelibly, whether pleasurably or not he could not decide, for mixed with a strange attraction and even fascination he was conscious of an undercurrent of terror, and even of aversion, as from something unclean. As he moved away, his eye caught an inscription in Gothic lettering round the edge of the slab on which the figure lay.

HIC JACET ALIANORA COMITISSA PECCATRIX
QVÆ OBIIT AÑO DÑI MCCCL CVIVS ANIMÆ
MISEREATVR DEVS.

He copied the epitaph in his notebook, remarking that it differed from the usual formula, and then closing the door of the chantry he followed his cousins back to the house.

'Well, here you are at last,' said Lady Wilmot, as Charley and his sisters emerged on the lawn. 'What a time you have been in the ruins, and the tea is getting cold. And what have you done with Harry?'

'Oh, mother,' cried Cissy, 'we have had such an adventure. You know that little chantry chapel we are so fond of; well, we thought it wanted tidying up, and so we cleared away the weeds and rubbish, and what do you think we found? Why, the most lovely statue you ever saw, and we left Harry looking at it as if he had fallen in love with it and could not tear himself away.'

'By Jove!' said Charley, 'just like old Pygmalion, who fell in love with a statue and got Venus to bring it to life for him.'

'Don't talk so, Charley,' said Kate, 'I am sure I don't want this stone lady to come to life. There is something uncanny about her,

I can't describe what, but I was very glad to get away from her.'

'Yes, mother,' said Cissy, 'Kate was quite frightened of the stone lady and dragged me away, just as I was longing to look at her, for you never saw anything so lovely in your life.'

'But there is one thing I noticed, father,' said Charley, 'that I think wants looking to. I noticed a bad crack in that fine vault over the chantry which looks dangerous, and I think Parsons should be sent to have a look at it.'

'Thank you, Charley,' said Sir Thomas, 'I should be sorry if anything happened to that part of the building, for archæologists tell me it's the most perfect thing of its kind in England. Parsons is busy on other matters for the next few days, but I will have it seen to next week. By the way, we shall have another visitor to-night. You remember Harry's college friend, Mr Edwards; I heard he was staying at the Johnstons and so I asked him to come here for a few days while Harry is with us, and here I think he comes across the lawn.'

Edwards had some previous acquaintance with the Wilmots, and was soon set down to tea with the rest, and engaged for lawn tennis afterwards, a game in which he had earned a great reputation.

Harry Charlton did not appear till the party were assembled in the drawing-room before dinner. On leaving the Abbey he was possessed by a disinclination for the lively society on the lawn. His nerves were in a strange flutter; he felt as if something unusual was impending, as if he had passed a barrier and shut the gate behind him, and had entered on a new life where strange experiences awaited him. He could not account for it. He tried to dismiss the finding of the statue as a mere antiquarian discovery, interesting both in history and in art; but it would not do. That face, with its enigmatical expression, haunted him, and would not be dismissed. He felt that this was not the end of the adventure; that in some mysterious way the dead woman of five centuries back had touched his life, and that more would come of it. To that something more he looked forward with the same indefinable mixture of attraction and repulsion which he had felt in the chapel while gazing at those pure alabaster features. He must be alone. He could not at present come back to the converse of ordinary life, and he set off on a swinging walk through field and wood-land to try and steady his nerves, so as to meet his friends in the evening with composure. A good ten-mile stretch did something to restore him to his usual spirits. He was pleased to find his friend Edwards, of whose coming he had not been told, and when he took his place at the dinner table next to his aunt there was nothing unusual in his manner.

The conversation during dinner naturally turned on the discovery that had been made in the Abbey that afternoon. It was singular that so remarkable a work of art should have been forgotten, and been overlooked by the Northamptonshire Archæological Society, which had so many enthusiastic antiquaries in its ranks. There had been meetings of the society in the ruins, papers about them had been read and published, plans had been made and illustrations drawn of various parts of the building, including the chantry itself, but there was no mention or indication given of the monument either in the text or in the plates. Strange that no one should ever have thought of looking into that tangle of brambles by which it was concealed, till that very day.

'I must go first thing to-morrow,' said Sir Thomas, 'to see your wonderful discovery. The next thing will be to find out who this pretty lady was.'

'That I think I can tell you, sir,' said Henry, who now spoke for almost the first time, 'and I think it helps to solve the mystery of the sinful Countess in the painted windows opposite, which puzzled us last night.'

All eyes were turned to the fragments of painted glass in the hall windows, as Henry continued.

'You see in the first window the devil is tempting the Countess ALI—, the rest of her name being lost. Well, on the tomb is an epitaph, which gives the missing part. She is the Countess Alianora; no further title is given. But whoever she was, the lady whose tomb we found is the same no doubt as the lady whose adventures were depicted in the windows.'

'Now I know,' broke in Kate, 'why I was frightened in the chapel. She was a wicked woman, and something told me so, and made me want to go away from her.'

'Well,' said Lady Wilmot, 'let us hope she mended her ways and ended her life well. You see, she went to Rome and was absolved by the Pope.'

'Yes, but I bet she did not get absolution for nothing,' said Charley. 'Just look at her in the last picture and you will see she has a church in her hand. Depend on it, she got her wicked deeds pardoned in return for her gifts to Rosemount Abbey; and I daresay she rebuilt a great part of it and among the rest her own chantry.'

'Charley,' said Edwards, 'you ought to be a lawyer; you make out such a good case for the prosecution.'

'At all events,' said Sir Thomas, 'Charley gives us a good lead for our research. I will look out the old deeds and try to find what connection, if any, there was between Rosemount Abbey and a Countess Alianora of some place unknown.'

The rest of the evening passed in the usual way. A few friends from neighbouring houses joined the party; there was a little impromptu dancing, and it was near midnight by the time they retired to rest. Henry had enjoyed himself like the rest, and forgot the adventure of the afternoon till he found himself once more alone in the monastic cell, looking out on the ruined Abbey. The recollection of his dream of the night before then for the first time recurred to him; he wondered whether it had any connection with his later experience in the chantry, but he could trace none whatever. The dream seemed merely one of those fanciful imaginings with which we are all familiar, devoid of any further meaning.

He was not, however, destined to repose quietly. This time his dream showed him the same monk, he recognised him by his coarse features and shaggy brows, but he was in the nave of a church, and in the massive round pillars and severe architecture of the arches and triforium, Henry knew the nave of Rosemount Abbey, not as now, in ruins, but vaulted and entire. It was nearly dark, and the choir behind the pulpitum was wrapped in gloom, in the midst of which twinkled a few lights before the high altar and the various saintly shrines. The monk held something small in his hand, and was evidently, as on the night before, waiting for somebody or something. At last Henry was aware that somebody had indeed come. A shadowy figure draped in black moved swiftly out from behind a pillar and approached the monk. What the figure was he tried in vain to discover. All he could see was that just as had happened on the night before, a hand was stretched out and took something from the monk, which it promptly hid in the drapery with which the figure was covered. The hand, however, was more clearly seen this time. It was a woman's hand, white and delicate, and a jewel sparkled on her finger. The scene caused Henry a dull terror, as of some unknown calamity, or as of some crime that he had witnessed, and he woke with a start and found himself in a cold sweat.

He got up and paced his apartment to and fro, and then looked out of the window. It was brilliant moonlight, throwing strong shadows of the broken walls across the quiet cloister garth where the monks of old lay quietly sleeping till the last dread summons should awake them. The light fell full on the ancient nave walls

'Where buttress and buttress alternately
Seemed framed of ebon and ivory'

and the light touched with the magic of mystery the delicate traceries of the chantry where lay the Countess Alianora. Her face flashed upon his memory, with its enigmatical expression, half attracting, half repelling, and an irresistible desire impelled him to see her again. His window was open and the ground only a few feet below. He dressed himself hastily, and clambered out. Everything was still; all nature seemed asleep, not a breath of wind moved the trees or stirred the grass as he slowly passed along the cloister: his mind was in a strange state of nervous excitement; he was almost in a trance as he advanced into the nave where the shadows of column and arch fell black on the broken pavement. He paused a moment at the gate which led into the chantry, and then entered as if in a dream, for everything seemed to him unreal, and he himself a mere phantom. At last he stood beside the tomb and looked down on the lovely countenance which had bewitched him in the afternoon. The moonlight fell upon it, investing it with an unearthly mystery and charm. Its beauty was indescribable: never had he conceived anything so lovely. The strange semi-satirical expression of which he had been conscious in the afternoon had disappeared; nothing could be read in the features but sweetness and allurement. A passionate impulse seized him, and he bent down and kissed her on the lips. Was it fancy or was it real, that soft lips of warm life seemed to meet his own? He knew not: a delirious ecstasy transported him, the scene faded before his eyes and he sank on the floor in a swoon.

How long he lay he never knew. When he came to himself the moon had set, and he was in darkness. An indefinable terror seized him. He struggled to his feet, burst out of the Abbey, fled to his rooms, scrambling in through the window, and threw himself panting on his bed.

Henry Charlton was the last to appear next morning at the breakfast-table. He was pale and out of spirits, and roused himself with difficulty to take part in the discussion as to what was to be done that day. After breakfast he pleaded a headache, and retired with a book to the library, while the others betook themselves to various amusements or employments. The girls were in the garden where they found old Donald the gardener, whose life had been spent at Rosemount, and in whose eyes the garden was as much his as his master's, and perhaps more so.

'Yes, missy,' he was saying, 'the weeds do grow terrible this fine weather, and as you was saying it is time we cleaned up a bit in the old Abbey. But I see the young gentlemen has been doing a bit theirselves, chucking all them briars and rubbish out on the grass just as I had mown and tidied it.'

'Why Donald,' said Cissy, 'you ought to have thanked them, for that chapel was in an awful mess, and they have saved you some trouble.'

'Well, miss, I suppose they pleased theirselves, but that's not where I should have meddled, no, no!' and so saying he moved away.

'But why not there,' said Kate, 'why not there of all places?'

'Oh! I say nothing about it,' said Donald. 'Only folk do say that there's them there as don't like to be disturbed.'

'Indeed; what do they say in the village about it?'

'Oh! ay! I say nothing. I don't meddle with things above me. And I shan't tell ye any more, miss, it's not good for young women to know.'

'But do you know, Donald,' said Cissy, 'what we found there?'

'What did you find, miss? Not her? Oh, Lord! She was found once before, and no good come of it. There, don't ask me any more about it. It's not good for young women to know.' So saying Donald wheeled his barrow away into another part of the garden.

'Father,' said Kate, to Sir Thomas who now came up. 'Donald knows all about the tomb and the statue, and he won't tell us anything, except that the people think it unlucky to meddle with it. Have you ever heard of any superstition about it.'

'Nothing at all,' said he. 'I have just been down to look at your discovery. The statue is a wonderful piece of work. I have never seen anything finer either here or in Italy. But the chapel is in a bad way and part of the roof threatens to fall. I have just sent word to Parsons to come to-morrow morning and attend to it.'

They were joined presently by Edwards and Charley, and the

day passed pleasantly enough, with the usual amusements of a country house in holiday time. Henry did not take much part with them. He was abstracted and inattentive, and altogether out of spirits. He had but a confused idea of what had happened the previous night, but there seemed still to linger on his lips that mystic, perhaps unhallowed kiss, and there still floated before his eyes the mocking enigma of that lovely countenance. He dreaded the approach of night, not knowing what it might bring, and did his best to divert his mind to other things, but without much success.

His friend Edwards was much concerned at the change in his behaviour, and asked Charley whether Henry had been upset in any way during his visit. He was assured that till yesterday afternoon Henry had been as happy and companionable as possible, and that it was only that morning that the change had come over him.

'But I can tell you one thing,' said Charley, 'I believe he was out of his room last night, for the flower beds show footmarks, and the creepers are torn outside his window, showing some one had been getting in and out, and there certainly has been no burglary in the house. Do you know whether he walks in his sleep?'

'I have never heard that he does,' said Edwards. 'We can't very well ask him whether anything is wrong, for he does not seem to invite inquiry, and has rather avoided us all day. But if it is a case of sleep-walking we might perhaps keep a look-out to-night to prevent his coming to mischief.'

'All right,' said Charley. 'My room is over his and looks out the same way. I'll try and keep awake till midnight, and will call you if I see anything of him.'

'That's well,' said Edwards, 'but we must be careful and not be seen, for it is dangerous to wake a somnambulist I believe.'

And so they departed to their several chambers.

The first part of the night passed peacefully enough with Henry. He had no dreams to trouble him, but towards midnight he began to turn uneasily in his bed, and to be oppressed by an uneasy feeling that he was not alone. He awoke to find the moon shining as brilliantly as on the previous night, and bringing into view every detail of the ancient buildings opposite. A dull sense of some sinister influence weighed upon him: some one was with him whom he could not see, whispering in his ear, '*You are mine;*

you are mine.' He could see no form, but to his mental vision was clearly visible the countenance of the figure in the chapel, now with the satirical, mocking expression more fully shown, and he felt himself drawn on he knew not whither. Again the mocking lips seemed to say, '*You are mine, you are mine.*' Half unconsciously he rose from his bed, and advanced towards the window. A faintly visible form seemed to move before him, he saw the features of the countess more plainly, and without knowing how he got there he found himself outside the room in the cloister garth, and entering the shade of the cloister. Something impalpable glided on before him, turning on him the face that attracted him though it mocked him, and which he could not but follow, though with an increasing feeling of terror and dislike. Still on his ear fell the words, '*You are mine, you are mine,*' and he was helpless to resist the spell that drew him on and on farther into the gloom of the ruined nave. And now the shape gathered consistency and he seemed to see the Countess Alianora standing facing him. On her features the same mocking smile, on her finger the jewel of his dream. '*You are mine,*' she seemed to say, '*mine, mine, you sealed it with a kiss,*' and she outstretched her arms; but as she stood before him in her marvellous and unearthly beauty, a change came over her; her face sank into ghastly furrows, her limbs shrivelled, and as she advanced upon him, a mass of loathly corruption, and stretched out her horrible arms to embrace him he uttered a dreadful scream as of a soul in torture, and sank fainting on the ground.

'Edwards, Edwards, come quick,' cried Charley, beating at his door. 'Harry is out of his room, and there is something with him, I don't know what it is, but hurry up or some mischief may happen.'

His friend was ready in a moment, and the two crept cautiously downstairs, and as the readiest way, not to disturb the household, got out into the cloister through the window of Harry's room. They noticed on the way that his bed had been slept in, and was tossed about in disorder. They took the way of the cloister by which Charley had seen Harry go, and had just reached the door that led into the nave when his unearthly scream of terror fell on their ears. They rushed into the church, crying, 'Harry, Harry, here we are, what is it, where are you?' and having no reply they searched as well as they could in the moonlight. They found him at last, stretched on the ground at the entrance to the fatal chantry chapel. At first they thought he was dead, but his pulse beat faintly, and they carried him out, still insensible, into the outer air. He showed some signs of life before long, but remained unconscious. The house was aroused and he was put to bed, and messengers were sent for the doctor. As they watched by his bedside, a thundering crash startled them; looking out of the window they saw a cloud of dust where the chantry had been, and next morning it was seen that the roof had fallen in, and destroyed it.

Harry Charlton lay many weeks with a brain fever. From his cries and ravings something was gathered of the horrors of that fatal night, but he would never be induced to tell the whole story after he recovered.

The fallen ruin was removed, and Sir Thomas hoped that the beautiful statue might have escaped. But strange to say, though every fragment of masonry was carefully examined and accounted for, no trace could be found of any alabaster figure nor of the tomb of the Comitissa Alianora.

How It Happened

by

JOHN GAWSWORTH

*Probably the only writer of macabre tales ever to make anybody an
Admiral was John Gawsworth (Terence Fytton Armstrong) who was
born in 1912 and died in obscure poverty in 1970. Gawsworth was
empowered to create Admirals and other ranks of privilege when he
inherited Redonda, a small island in the West Indies, from his friend
M. P. Shiel. Shiel had been crowned King of Redonda while a boy, by
his father and the Bishop of Antigua, and the island being unclaimed
by any government, had continued to be ruled by King Matthew. When
Gawsworth succeeded to the throne, he began to hold court in various
London pubs, in the midst of the circle of poets and authors whom he
published. One of his best and most representative collections of stories
by his author friends was* Strange Assembly *(1932), and indeed
Gawsworth's own poetry was collected into one edition published in
1948.*

*He went to Italy during the last years of his life and returned to
England, only to die shortly after. His most well known tale is 'The
Shifting Growth'; this little piece of horror which follows is not at all
so famous, but certainly should be. It is one of the grimmest pieces of
English macabre I have encountered.*

* * *

*The unhappy madman, Stanley Barton, is dead. Perhaps the reader
remembers his trial; perhaps, for such things are but nine days' wonders,
he does not.*

*All day long the wretched man would glare through the windows of his
cell, and it was noticed that his eyes always sought a small plantation
of fir trees that grew within their narrow horizon. Sometimes, especially
on very hot days, he became extremely violent, and the usual steps had
to be taken to prevent him from doing himself or his attendants an
injury.*

He died at length in the course of such a fit, leaving behind him the

*following account of his crime, which appears to offer sufficient interest to
the student of lunacy and criminology to deserve publication.*

Are you weak, man? No! I should like to ask you how the devil
you know. Have you ever been put to the test? Have you ever
had all the nerves and fibres in your body strained and twisted to
see if they would snap? Are you sure of that little cell on the left?
Are you confident of that tiny clot over the right eyebrow? I
think there may be a weakness there. I try you. G-r-r-u-p. Snap.
Ah! I thought so. Take him away to the asylum. He is a weak man.
Mind you, that was not how I went! No. For I was strong, oh!
so strong, all round. I had gone over them all from the top of my
skull to the soles of my feet, testing them one by one, and I found
them all taut and true. And presently I wrestled with Them, and
They broke them all at once, every one, all the big ones and the
little ones that didn't seem to matter until they were broken. And
then They put me in here, where I ought to be King, because mine
are broken every one, while the others have only lost one or two.
Sometimes theirs mend and then they go away, but the edges of
mine grate together and hurt me dreadfully and they cannot join.

Besides, I remember, and that would break them all again
anyhow.

It was my brother who did it, you know. He was the real
cause. You see I hated him right from the first. He was a few
years older than I was, and they called him 'Handsome'. He was
tall and fair, and the girls liked him. There was one girl who liked
him especially, a girl whom I *loved*. Her name was Margery and she
was very pretty. But I didn't mind her liking him. You see, I
could afford to wait; for, though I was small and dark, I knew
that I was the better man. Once, when Margery was there, I told
my brother so.

'Damn it,' he roared, 'he ought to have more pride than to hang
about when he's not wanted; oughtn't he, Margery?' and they
both laughed. 'Clear off,' he added, and they turned and walked
away from me.

We lived then in the depths of Surrey, and every night at half-
past eight my brother crossed the fields at the end of our garden,
and met Margery in the plantation of fir trees that topped the
horizon close by. I know he went every night because I used to
follow him and watch them at their games from a hiding-place up
a tree. I was agile, I tell you; as nimble as a cat.

Well one night shortly after my brother's rebuff I went there ahead of him. I had decided I didn't love Margery any more, she had laughed so unkindly at me. In the dusk she could not see who was coming, and hearing my footsteps she ran forward from the depths of the clump to greet me, mistaking me for my brother. She was a fool, and I didn't waste time, I stabbed her with the carving-knife I had brought from the dining-room sideboard and on my walk had hidden under my coat. She was really frightfully comic. She reminded me of the little pigs I used to see on Market Days. She squealed, sobbed quickly, and then toppled forward and lay still. I threw the knife into the bushes. 'My! Margery, how funny you look!' I said as I dragged her by the hair into the shadows and with a staple and hammer I had provided myself with—anticipating events—nailed her fast through the breast to my tree. And then I pulled her short jacket over her reddening blouse, so that the hooked-end of the iron could not be seen. I was enjoying myself. 'You won't laugh at me again, Margery?' I giggled, and I kicked her, and she was soft to my boot.

There wasn't very much time to lose because my brother would soon be coming, so I clambered up my tree to my cross-branch and tied a length of rope I had brought strongly to it. Then I made a large running noose at the end and a small loop higher up and hammered another staple into the trunk some three feet above the place where I had tied the rope to the branch. You see, I was quite sure that I was the better man and I knew what to do. I stayed up in the tree with the rope coiled in my hand and waited.

Soon my brother came along.

'Margery!' he called, 'Margery!'

I wanted to laugh—it was so funny. And then he must have seen her dress, for he cried out gladly and with relief in his voice, 'Why, there you are!' and stepped right under me. You wouldn't believe how simple it was! It was like throwing quoits at a fair. Plop! The noose fell over his head—a bull's eye! The running knot slid down tight on to his nape. I rose to my feet and, bracing my back against the trunk, with a heave pulled the small loop in the rope up to, and over, the staple. My brother below, kicked like billyho; his hands clutching at his neck, his legs beating the air. But the rope was strong and it held him. Oh, it was lovely! I was never so happy before. I slid down the tree and surveyed the pair. Margery was silent, her head had fallen forward and her arms hung limply; but my brother kicked and kicked. His eyes seemed to protrude. He grew purple and noises came from his throat.

'*He ought to have more pride than to hang about when he's not wanted, oughtn't he, Margery?*' I said.

But Margery did not seem to understand. The jerkings gave way to stillness, a lovely stillness. The burden on the rope swayed gently; its weight alone moving it. I looked at the rough footpath three feet beneath my brother's dangling feet.

'*Clear off*!' I said and whistled.

Then I turned and went away.

In The Mirror

by
VALERY BRYUSOV

Valery Bryusov (1873–1924) was a Russian author who went into self-imposed exile after the Revolution. His distaste for the new Russia was crystallised in his satiric fantasy 'The Republic of the Southern Cross', which tells of the gradual breakdown of an isolated self-sufficient community.

Described by one critic as 'an artificial production in the midst of the Russian literary world' he was an introspective and brooding writer. He said of his tales that 'they are written to show, in various ways, that there is no fixed boundary line between the world of reality and that of the imagination, between the dreaming and the waking world, life and fantasy; that what we commonly call imaginary may be the greatest reality of the world, and that which we call reality may be the most dreadful delirium.'

'In the Mirror' comes from Bryusov's only collection published in England, The Republic of the Southern Cross *(1918), and amply supports Bryusov's own analysis of his work. I leave you to sort out which half of the tale is the 'greatest reality' and which half 'the most dreadful delirium'.*

I have loved mirrors from my very earliest years. As an infant I wept and trembled as I looked into their transparently truthful depths. My favourite game as a child was to walk up and down the room or the garden, holding a mirror in front of me, gazing into its abyss, walking over the edge at every step, and breathless with giddiness and terror. Even as a girl I began to put mirrors all over my room, large and small ones, true and slightly distorted ones, some precise and others a little dull. I got into the habit of spending whole hours, whole days, in the midst of intercrossing worlds which ran one into the other, trembled, vanished, and then reappeared again. It became a singular passion of mine to give my body to these soundless distances, these echoless perspectives, these separate universes cutting across our own and existing, despite our consciousness, in the same place and at the same time with it. This protracted actuality, separated from us by the smooth surface of glass, drew me towards itself by a kind of intangible touch, dragged me forward, as to an abyss, a mystery.

I was drawn towards the apparition which always rose up before me when I came near a mirror and which strangely doubled my being. I strove to guess how this other woman was differentiated from myself, how it was possible that my right hand should be her left, and that all the fingers of this hand should change places, though certainly on one of them was—my wedding-ring.

My thoughts were confused when I attempted to probe this enigma, to solve it. In *this* world, where everybody could be touched, where voices were heard—I lived, actually; in *that* reflected world, which it was only possible to contemplate, was she, phantasmally. She was almost as myself and yet not at all myself; she repeated all my movements, but not one of these movements exactly coincided with those I made. She, that other, knew something I could not divine, she held a secret eternally hidden from my understanding.

But I noticed that each mirror had its own separate and special world. Put two mirrors in the very same place, one after the other, and there will arise two different universes. And in different mirrors there rose up before me different apparitions, all of them like me but never exactly like one another. In my small hand-mirror lived a naïve little girl with clear eyes, reminding me of my early youth. In my circular boudoir mirror was hidden a woman who knew all the diverse sweetness of caresses, shameless, free, beautiful, daring. In the oblong mirrors of the wardrobe door there always appeared a stern figure, imperious, cold, inexorable. I knew still other doubles of myself—in my dressing-glass, in my folding, gold-framed triptych, in the hanging mirror in the oaken frame, in the little neck mirror, and in many other mirrors which I treasured. To all the beings hiding themselves in these mirrors I gave the possibility and pretext to develop. According to the strange conditions of their world they must take the form of the person who stands before the glass but under this borrowed exterior they preserve their own personal characteristics.

There were some worlds of mirrors which I loved; others which I hated. In some of them I loved to walk up and down for

whole hours, losing myself in their attractive expanse. Others I
fled from. In my secret heart I did not love all my doubles. I knew
that they were all hostile toward me, if only for the fact that they
were forced to clothe themselves in my hated likeness. But some
of these mirror women I pitied. I forgave their hate and felt almost friendly to them. There were some whom I despised, and I
loved to laugh at their powerless fury; there were some whom I
mocked by my own independence and tortured by my power over
them. There were others, on the other hand, of whom I was
afraid, who were too strong for me and who dared in their turn
to mock at me, to command me. I hastened to get rid of the mirrors
where these women lived, I would not look in them, I hid them,
gave them away, even broke some in pieces. But every time I
destroyed a mirror I wept for whole days after, conscious of the
fact that I had broken to pieces a distinct universe. And reproach-
ful faces stared at me from the broken fragments of the world I
had destroyed.

The mirror with which my fate was to become linked I bought
one autumn at a sale of some sort. It was a large pier-glass,
swinging on screws. I was struck by the unusual clarity of its
reflection. The phantasmal actuality in it was changed by the
slightest inclination of the glass, but it was independent and vital
to the edges. When I examined this pier-glass at the sale the
woman who was reflected in it looked me in the eyes with a
kind of haughty challenge. I did not wish to give in to her, to
show that she had frightened me, so I bought the glass and ordered
it to be placed in my boudoir. As soon as I was alone in the room,
I immediately went up to the new mirror and fixed my eyes upon
my rival. But she did the same to me, and standing opposite one
another we began to transfix each other with our glance as if we
had been snakes. In the pupils of her eyes was my reflection, in
mine, hers. My heart sank and my head swam from her intent
gaze. But at length by an effort of will I tore my eyes away from
those other eyes, tipped the mirror with my foot so that it began
to swing, rocking the image of my rival pitifully to and fro, and
went out of the room.

From that hour our strife began. In the evening of the first day
of our meeting I did not dare to go near the new pier-glass;
I went to the theatre with my husband, laughed exaggeratedly, and
was apparently light-hearted. On the morrow, in the clear light of
a September day I went boldly into my boudoir alone and de-

liberately sat down directly in front of the mirror. At the same moment, she, the other woman, also came in at the door to meet me, crossed the room, and then she too sat down opposite me. Our eyes met. In hers I read hatred towards myself; in mine she read hatred towards her. Our second duel began, a duel of eyes—two unyielding glances, commanding, threatening, hypnotising. Each of us strove to conquer the other's will, to break down her resistance, to force her to submit to another's desire. It would have been a painful scene for an onlooker to witness; two women sitting opposite each other without moving, joined together by the magnetic attraction of each other's gaze, and almost losing consciousness under the psychical strain. . . . Suddenly someone called me. The infatuation vanished. I got up and left the room.

After this our duels were renewed every day. I realised that this adventuress had purposely forced herself into my home to destroy me and take my place in this world. But I had not sufficient strength to deny myself this struggle. In this rivalry there was a kind of secret intoxication. The very possibility of defeat had hidden in it a sort of sweet seduction. Sometimes I forced myself for whole days to keep away from the pier-glass; I occupied myself with business, with amusements, but in the depths of my soul was always hidden the memory of the rival who in patience and self-reliance awaited my return. I would go back to her and she would step forth in front of me, more triumphantly than ever, piercing me with her victorious gaze and fixing me in my place before her. My heart would stop beating, and I, with a powerless fury, would feel myself under the authority of this gaze.

So the days and weeks went by; our struggle continued, but the preponderance showed itself more and more definitely to be on the side of my rival. And suddenly one day I realised that my will was in subjection to her will, that she was already stronger than I. I was overcome with terror. My first impulse was to flee from my home and go to another town, but I saw at once that this would be useless. I should, all the same, be overcome by the attractive force of this hostile will and be obliged to return to this room, to this mirror. Then there came a second thought—to shatter the mirror, reduce my enemy to nothingness; but to conquer her by brutal strength would mean that I acknowledged her superiority over myself; this would be humiliating. I preferred to remain and continue this struggle to the end, even though I were threatened with defeat.

Soon there could be no doubt that my rival would triumph. At every meeting there was concentrated in her gaze still greater and greater power over me. Little by little I lost the possibility of letting a day pass without once going to my mirror. *She* ordered me to spend several hours daily in front of her. *She* directed my will as a hypnotist directs the will of a sleepwalker. *She* arranged my life, as a mistress arranges the life of a slave. I began to fulfil her demands, I became an automaton to her wordless orders. I knew that deliberately, cautiously, she would lead me by an unavoidable path to destruction, and I already made no resistance. I divined her secret plan—to cast me into the mirror world and to come forth herself into our world—but I had no strength to hinder her. My husband and my relatives seeing me spend whole hours, whole days and nights in front of my mirror, thought me demented and wanted to cure me. But I dared not reveal the truth to them, I was forbidden to tell them all the dreadful truth, all the horror, towards which I was moving.

One of the December days before the holidays turned out to be the day of my destruction. I remember everything clearly, precisely, circumstantially. Nothing in my remembrance is confused. As usual, I went into my boudoir early, at the first beginnings of the winter dawn twilight. I placed a comfortable armchair without a back in front of the mirror, sat down and gave myself up to *her*. Without any delay she appeared in answer to my summons, she too placed an armchair for herself, she too sat down and began to gaze at me. A dark foreboding oppressed my soul, but I was powerless to turn my face away, and I was forced to take to myself the insolent gaze of my rival. The hours went by, the shadows began to fall. Neither of us lighted a lamp. The glass of the mirror glimmered faintly in the darkness. The reflections had become scarcely visible, but the self-reliant eyes gazed with their former strength. I felt neither terror nor ill-will, as on other days, but simply an intolerable anguish and a bitter consciousness that I was in the power of another. Time swam away and on its tide I also swam into infinity, into a black expanse of powerlessness and lack of will.

Suddenly she, that other, the reflected woman, got up from her chair. I trembled all over at this insult. But something invincible, something forcing me from within compelled me also to stand up. The woman in the mirror took a step forward. I did the same. The woman in the mirror stretched forth her arms. I did so too. Looking straight at me with hypnotising and commanding eyes, she moved forward and I advanced to meet her. And it was strange—with all the horror of my position, with all my hate towards my rival, there fluttered somewhere in the depths of my soul a painful consolation, a secret joy—to enter at last into that mysterious world into which I had gazed from my childhood and which up till now had remained inaccessible to me. At moments I hardly knew which of us was drawing the other towards herself, she me or I her, whether she was eager to occupy my place or whether I had devised all this struggle in order to displace her.

But when, moving forward, my hands touched hers on the glass I turned quite pale with repugnance. And *she* took my hand by force and drew me still nearer to herself. My hands were plunged into the mirror as into burning-icy water. The cold of the glass penetrated into my body with a horrible pain, as if all the atoms of my being had changed their mutual relationship. In another moment my face had touched the face of my rival, I saw her eyes right in front of my own, I was transfused into her with a monstrous kiss. Everything vanished from me in a torment of suffering unlike any other—and when I came to my senses after this swoon I still saw in front of me my own boudoir on which I gazed *from out of* the mirror. My rival stood before me and burst into laughter. And I—oh the cruelty of it! I who was dying with humiliation and torture was obliged to laugh too, to repeat all her grimaces in a triumphant joyful laugh. I had not yet succeeded in considering my position when my rival suddenly turned round, walked towards the door, vanished from my sight, and I at once fell into torpor, into non-existence.

Then my life as a reflection began. It was a strange, half-conscious but mysteriously sweet life. There were many of us in this mirror, dark in soul, and slumbering of consciousness. We could not speak to one another, but we felt each other's proximity and loved one another. We could see nothing, we heard nothing clearly, and our existence was like the enfeeblement that comes from being unable to breathe. Only when a being from the world of men approached the mirror, we, suddenly taking up his form, could look forth into the world, could distinguish voices, and breathe a full breath. I think that the life of the dead is like that—a dim consciousness of one's ego, a confused memory of the past and an oppressive desire to be incarnated anew even if only for a moment, to see, to hear, to speak. . . . And each of us cherished and

concealed a secret dream—to free one's self, to find for one's self
a new body, to go out into the world of constancy and steadfast-
ness.

During the first days I felt myself absolutely unhappy in my
new position. I still knew nothing, understood nothing. I took
the form of my rival submissively and unthinkingly when she
came near the mirror and began to jeer at me. And she did this
fairly often. It afforded her great delight to flaunt her vitality before me, her reality. She would sit down and force me also to sit
down, stand up and exult as she saw me stand, wave her arms
about, dance, force me to repeat her movements, and burst out
laughing and continue to laugh so that I should have to laugh too.
She would shriek insulting words in my face and I could make no
answer to them. She would threaten me with her fist and mock at
my forced repetition of the gesture. She would turn her back on
me and I, losing sight, losing features, would become conscious
of the shame of the half-existence left to me. ... And then
suddenly, with one blow she would whirl the mirror round on its
axle and with the oscillation throw me completely into nonentity.

Little by little, however, the insults and humiliations awoke a
consciousness in me. I realised that my rival was now living my
life, wearing my dresses, being considered as my husband's wife,
and occupying my place in the world. Then there grew up in my
soul a feeling of hate and a thirst for vengeance, like two fiery
flowers. I began bitterly to curse myself for having, by my
weakness or my criminal curiosity, allowed her to conquer me. I
arrived at the conviction that this adventuress would never have
triumphed over me if I myself had not aided her in her wiles. And
so, as I became more familiar with some of the conditions of my
new existence, I resolved to continue with her the same fight
which she had carried on with me. If she, a shadow, could occupy
the place of a real woman, was it possible that I, a human being,
and only temporarily a shadow, should not be stronger than a
phantom?

I began from a very long way off. At first I pretended that the
mockery of my rival tormented me quite unbearably. I purposely
afforded her all the satisfaction of victory. I provoked in her the
secret instinct of the executioner throwing himself upon his
helpless victim. She gave herself up to this bait. She was attracted
by this game with me. She put forth the wings of her imagination
and thought out new trials for me. She invited thousands of wiles

to show me over and over again that I was only a reflection, that I
had no life of my own. Sometimes she played on the piano in
front of me, torturing me by the soundlessness of my world.
Sometimes, seated before the mirror she would drink in tiny sips
my favourite liqueurs, compelling me only to pretend that I also
was drinking them. Sometimes, at length, she would bring into
my boudoir people whom I hated, and before my face she would
allow them to kiss her body, letting them think that they were
kissing me. And afterwards when we were alone she would burst
into a malicious and triumphant laugh. But this laugh did not
wound me at all; there was sweetness in its keenness: my expectation of revenge!

Unnoticeably, in the hours of her insults to me, I would
accustom my rival to look me in the eyes and I would gradually
overpower her gaze. Soon at my will I could already force her to
raise and lower her eyelids and make this and that movement of
the face. I had already begun to triumph though I hid my feeling
under a mask of suffering. Strength of soul grew up within me and
I began to dare to lay commands upon my enemy: Today you
shall do so-and-so, to-day you shall go to such-and-such a place,
to-morrow you shall come to me at such a time. And *she* would
fulfil them. I entangled her soul in the nets of my desires woven
together with a strong thread in which I held her soul, and I
secretly rejoiced when I noticed my success. When one day, in the
hour of her laughter, she suddenly caught on my lips a victorious
smile which I was unable to hide, it was already too late. *She*
rushed out of the room in a fury, but as I fell into the sleep of my
nonentity I knew that she would return, knew that she would
submit to me. And a rapture of victory gushed out over my
involuntary lack of strength, piercing with a rainbow shaft of
light the gloom of my seeming death.

She did return! She came up to me in anger and terror, shrieked
to me, threatened me. But I was commanding her to do it. And
she was obliged to submit. Then began the game of a cat with a
mouse. At any time I could have cast her back into the depths of
the glass and come forth myself again into sounding and hard
actuality. But I delayed to do this. It was sweet to me to indulge in
non-existence sometimes. It was sweet to me to intoxicate myself
with the possibility. At last (this is strange, is it not?) there
suddenly was aroused in me a pity for my rival, for my enemy, for
my executioner. Everything in her was something of my own, and

it was dreadful for me to drag her forth from the realities of life and turn her into a phantom. I hesitated and dared not do it, I put if off from day to day, I did not know myself what I wanted and what I dreaded.

And suddenly on a clear spring day men came into the boudoir with planks and axes. There was no life in me, I lay in the voluptuousness of torpor, but without seeing them I knew they were there. The men began to busy themselves near the mirror which was my universe. And one after another the souls who lived in it with me were awakened and took transparent flesh in the form of reflections. A dreadful uneasiness agitated my slumbering soul. With a presentiment of horror, a presentiment even of irretrievable ruin, I gathered together all the might of my will. What efforts it cost me to struggle against the lassitude of half-existence! So living people sometimes struggle with a nightmare, tearing themselves from its suffocating bands towards actuality.

I concentrated all the force of my suggestion into a summons, directed towards her, towards my rival—'Come hither!' I hypnotised her, magnetised her with all the tension of my half-slumbering will. There was little time. The mirror had already begun to swing. They were already preparing to nail it up in a wooden coffin, to take it away: whither I knew not. And with an almost mortal effort I called again and again, 'Come!' And I suddenly began to feel that I was coming to life. *She*, my enemy, opened the door, and came to meet me, pale, half-dead, in answer to my call, with faltering steps as men go to punishment. I fastened my eyes on hers, bound up my gaze with hers, and when I had done this I knew already that I had gained the victory.

I at once compelled her to send the men out of the room. *She* submitted without even making an attempt to oppose me. We were alone together once more. To delay was no longer possible. And I could not bring myself to forgive her craftiness. In her place, in my time, I should have acted otherwise. Now I ordered her, without pity, to come to meet me. A moan of torture opened her lips, her eyes widened as before a phantom, but she came, trembling, falling—she came. I also went forward to meet her, lips curving triumphantly, eyes wide open with joy, swaying in an intoxicating rapture. Again our hands touched each other's, again our lips came near together, and we fell each into the other, burning with the indescribable pain of bodily exchange. In another moment I was already in front of the mirror, my breast filled itself with air, I cried out loudly and victoriously and fell just here, in front of the pier-glass, prone from exhaustion.

My husband and the servants ran towards me. I could only tell them to fulfil my previous orders and take the mirror away, out of the house, at once. That was wisely thought, wasn't it? You see she, that other, might have profited by my weakness in the first minutes of my return to life, and by a desperate assault might have tried to wrest the victory from my hands. Sending the mirror out of the house, I could ensure my own quietude for a long time, as long as I liked, and my rival had earned such a punishment for her cunning. I defeated her with her own tools, with the blade which she herself had raised against me.

After having given this order I lost consciousness. They laid me on my bed. A doctor was called in. I was treated as suffering from a nervous fever. For a long while my relatives had thought me ill, and not normal. In the first outburst of exultation I told them all that had happened to me. My stories only increased their suspicions. They sent me to a home for the mentally afflicted, and I am there now. All my being, I agree, is profoundly shaken. But I do not want to stay here. I am eager to return to the joys of life, to all the countless pleasures which are accessible to a living human being. I have been deprived of them too long.

Besides—shall I say it?—there is one thing which I am bound to do as soon as possible. I ought to have no doubt that I am *this* I. But all the same, whenever I begin to think of her who is imprisoned in my mirror I begin to be seized by a strange hesitation. What if the real I—is there? Then I myself who think this, I who write this, I—am a shadow, I—am a phantom, I—am a reflection. In me are only the poured forth remembrances, thoughts and feelings of that other, the real person. And, in reality, I am thrown into the depths of the mirror in nonentity, I am pining, exhausted, dying. I know, I almost know that this is not true. But in order to disperse the last clouds of doubt, I ought again once more, for the last time, to see that mirror. I must look into it once more to be convinced, that there—is the imposter, my enemy, she who played my part for some months. I shall see this and all the confusion of my soul will pass away, and I shall again be free from care—bright, happy. Where is this mirror? Where shall I find it? I must, I must once more look into its depths! . . .

'Calling Miss Marker'

by

JOY BURNETT

Joy Burnett was born in Brisbane, where her father was Commissioner of Health, and moved to England with her family while still young. An inherited love of the theatre led to her becoming an actress and she started her theatrical career in the chorus of a West End show. As well as working on the stage, Miss Burnett has worked in films and on television.

She has written intermittently for years, with a strong preference for animal stories, and has been published both in Britain and America. Miss Burnett also has a strong penchant for the ghost story and I am proud to have introduced her anthology début in A Wave of Fear. *I am equally proud to be able to introduce this neat tale, especially written for this collection. Miss Burnett says it was a brute to write; I assure you and her it is a delight to read.*

You weren't worried about the first call, were you Miss Marker? You thought it was someone playing a practical joke—a joke in bad taste to wake you at twelve minutes past four in the morning by the ringing of your front door bell. That's what you told the other residents in the dull semi-detached villa situated in a district renowned for its bed-sitters. They laughed when you told them and they teased you, saying it must have been the sausages you had eaten for supper, as they all knew it was almost an impossibility to wake you once you got to sleep. Until then you had felt safe in that grey, indistinguishable house, with its equally indistinguishable occupants; besides there was the cloak of indistinctness you had enveloped yourself in for the past ten years—the personality so quiet with its past safely tucked not only out of sight, but out of mind—or so you thought.

But when the second bell summons came, you began to wonder, didn't you? It came two nights later. Again the persistent ringing, which no one else in the house heard. It finally compelled you to go downstairs, only to find no one there when you opened the front door, and on returning to your room you saw that the time was again 4.12 a.m. on your bedside clock.

The third call came again two nights later and was a repetition of the two previous ones. By now you began to wonder and worry, or was it the beginning of your conscience pricking? You remembered Shakespeare saying 'Conscience doth make cowards of us all.' But you firmly dismissed the suggestion as you lay in bed, listening and waiting. By now the strain was beginning to show on your face, and people commented on it asking, 'Are you feeling all right?' Your answer of 'Perfectly' didn't seem to satisfy them, and they suggested you see a doctor. That was something you definitely shied away from, knowing that fraternity had the ability to dig out one's past. So you continued to lie awake, sweating and with your heart thumping and ears straining until the call came, then ran downstairs to open the front door to the non-existent caller.

But the strain took its toll and when the calls became nightly ones you felt compelled to talk to someone. Why did you choose Martha Kitson, Miss Marker? Did you imagine that with her forthright manner she would allay your fears? But standing before her you didn't find it so easy to talk. You realised you were on thin ice—the past would have to be glossed over should she enquire into causes, so when she asked 'What's the matter?' a jumble of almost incoherent words rushed out. She stopped you talking finally, and told you that you would certainly have to seek medical advice. You saw the look in her eyes—was it suspicion? fear? or the knowledge that your trouble lay deeper than you had acknowledged? Your fervent denial of medical aid appeared to strengthen her suspicion. Careful, Miss Marker, not to overdo it. Actually you were rather clever in overcoming her doubt with that little laugh and straightforward query, 'Do you, too, think I'm mad—I know the others do?' To use a common phrase—it passed the buck to her. Having asked her help, it demanded she make another suggestion, no matter what her private opinion of your trouble might be. But you were in for another shock when she suggested going to the police. 'No! not the police!' The words were wrung from you. Watch it! for the suspicion is back in her eyes. For a few moments all the fears of ten years ago came rushing back. How your heart used to accelerate its beat every time you saw someone or something connected with the law; the dryness of your mouth, and how you used to turn away so that the fear in your eyes wouldn't betray you. But once again you turned the danger away. Perhaps, Miss Marker, you missed your vocation for the stage in that play-acting was your forte. Your derisive question 'What could the police do with an apparently non-existent caller?' unsettled her for the moment; but only for a moment and she went back to your own contention that someone was playing a practical joke. Then you made the excuse that in your disturbed state you would be unable to convince them. So, somehow, it was arranged that she, Martha Kitson, would lodge the complaint saying that the house was nightly disturbed by the ringing of door bells. The police promise was given of keeping a watch on the house.

You really thought your troubles were over, didn't you, because for the next three nights you were not disturbed, and when the police gave their all clear and the prosaic explanation 'that it was probably some crank who got wind we were about and gave up', it brought comfort.

But your peace of mind was short lived, for that very night the bell ringing was resumed, and resumed with double vigour. Twice you had to go downstairs. Nothing—always nothing. When it came again you fought hard against answering. Lying there in the dark you determined not to go, but at the first ring your eyes turned involuntarily to the clock and you saw the illuminated hands stand at 4.12 a.m. Then you remembered the other time it was 4.12 a.m. ten years ago. That night it was wet and cold, but you never noticed the rain, or felt the cold when you went out into the garden carrying that small bundle. Remember how you thought the hole would never be deep enough, and you dug with renewed vigour working in the rain, the wind and the cold? No, it's no use, Miss Marker, burying your head under the pillow, for that memory will always be with you. And now the bell seems to be calling 'Come, Come! Come!!!' It's no use fighting any longer—*you must go*. So with one last agonised moan you get out of bed, open the door, run along the passage and down the stairs.

You never heard the upstairs doors open and human voices demand what all the noise was, for your own shrieks drowned all other noise. Some say there was demoniac laughter intermingled with your cries.

They found you lying by the front door which was open with the rain beating in. Around the entrance there were patches of mud imprinted with what looked like hoof marks—from a cloven hoof. You at last knew your tormentor, Miss Marker. But we will never know whether it was the devil who claimed his own, or your own conscience demanding justice.

A Night of Horror

by

DICK DONOVAN

Dick Donovan was the pseudonym of J. E. Preston Muddock, a writer of detective novels and short stories in the Victorian era. By any standards, Muddock's output was prolific. As Muddock he published over seventy books, starting with A False Heart (1873), and as Donovan, he produced another seventy, all in a space of roughly forty years. His first Donovan book was The Man Hunter (1888) and perhaps his most memorable was Tales of Terror (1899), from which is taken 'A Night of Horror'. Set in a haunted castle in the wild Welsh hills, it is an unadorned traditional ghost story, that has remained out of print for over seventy-five years.

Bleak Hill Castle.

'My dear old Chum,—Before you leave England for the East I claim the redemption of a promise you made to me some time ago that you would give me the pleasure of a week or two of your company. Besides, as you may have already guessed, I have given up the folly of my bachelor days, and have taken unto myself the sweetest woman that ever walked the face of the earth. We have been married just six months, and are as happy as the day is long. And then, this place is entirely after your own heart. It will excite all your artistic faculties, and appeal with irresistible force to your romantic nature. To call the building a castle is somewhat pretentious, but I believe it has been known as the Castle ever since it it was built, more than two hundred years ago. Hester is delighted with it, and if either of us was in the least degree superstitious, we might see or hear ghosts every hour of the day. Of course, as becomes a castle, we have a haunted room, though my own impression is that it is haunted by nothing more fearsome than rats. Anyway, it is such a picturesque, curious sort of chamber that if it hasn't a ghost it ought to have. But I have no doubt, old chap, that you will make one of us, for, as I remember, you have always had a love for the eerie and creepy, and you cannot forget how angry you used to get with me sometimes for chaffing you about your avowed belief in the occult and supernatural, and what you were pleased to term the "inexplicable phenomena of psychomancy". However, it is possible you have got over some of the errors of your youth; but whether or not, come down and rest assured that you will meet with the heartiest of welcomes.

Your old pal,
Dick Dirckman.'

The above letter was from my old friend and college chum, who, having inherited a substantial fortune, and being passionately fond of the country and country pursuits, had thus the means of gratifying his tastes to their fullest bent. Although Dick and I were very differently constituted, we had always been greatly attached to each other. In the best sense of the term he was what is generally called a hard-headed, practical man. He was fond of saying he never believed in anything he couldn't see, and even that which he could see he was not prepared to accept as truth without due investigation. In short, Dick was neither romantic, poetical, nor, I am afraid, artistic, in the literal sense. He preferred facts to fancies, and was possessed of what the world generally called 'an unimpressionable nature'. For nearly four years I had lost sight of my friend, as I had been wandering about Europe as tutor and companion to a delicate young nobleman. His death had set me free; but I had no sooner returned to England than I was offered and accepted a lucrative appointment in India, and there was every probability of my being absent for a number of years.

On returning home I had written to Dick telling him of my appointment, and expressing a fear that unless we could snatch a day or two in town I might not be able to see him, as I had so many things to do. I had not heard of his marriage; his letter gave me the first intimation of that fact, and I confess that when I got his missive I experienced some curiosity to know the kind of lady he had succeeded in captivating. I had always had an idea that Dick was cut out for a bachelor, for there was nothing of the ladies' man about him. And now Dick was actually married, and living in a remote region, where most town-bred people would die of ennui.

I did not hesitate about accepting Dick's cordial invitation. I determined to spare a few days at least of my somewhat limited time, and duly notified Dick to that effect, giving him the date of my departure from London, and the hour at which I should arrive at the station nearest to his residence.

Bleak Hill Castle was situated in one of the most picturesque parts of Wales; consequently, on the day appointed I found myself comfortably ensconced in a smoking carriage of a London and North-Western train. And towards the close of the day—the time of the year was May—I was the sole passenger to alight at the wayside station, where Dick awaited me with a smart dog-cart. His greeting was hearty and robust, and when his man had packed in my traps he gave the handsome little mare that drew the cart the reins, and we spanked along the country roads in rare style.

A drive of eight miles through the bracing Welsh air meant that it was dark when we arrived and I had no opportunity of observing the external characteristics of Bleak Hill Castle; but there was nothing in the interior that suggested bleakness. It was warm, comfortable and well-lit.

Following the maid up a broad flight of stairs, and along a lofty and echoing corridor, I found myself in a large and comfortably-furnished bedroom. A bright wood fire burned upon the hearthstone, for although it was May the temperature was still very low on the Welsh hills. Hastily changing my clothes, I made my way to the dining-room, where Mrs Dirckman emphasised the welcome her husband had already given me. She was an exceedingly pretty and rather delicate-looking little woman, in striking contrast to her great, bluff, burly husband. A few neighbours had been gathered together to meet me, and we sat down, a dozen all told, to a perfect dinner.

It was perhaps natural, when the coffee and cigar stage had arrived, that the conversation should turn upon our host's residence, by way of affording me—a stranger to the district—some information. Of course, the information was conveyed to me in a scrappy way, but I gathered in substance that Bleak Hill Castle had originally belonged to a Welsh family, chiefly distinguished by the extravagance and gambling propensities of its male members. It had gone through some exciting times, and numerous strange and startling stories were told of it. There were stories of wrong, and shame, and death, and more than a suggestion of dark crimes. One of these stories turned upon the mysterious disappearance of the wife and daughter of a young scion of the house, whose career had been somewhat shady. His wife was considerably older than he, and it was generally supposed that he had married her for money. His daughter, a girl of about twelve. was an epileptic patient, while the husband and father was a gloomy, disappointed man. Suddenly the wife and daughter disappeared. At first no surprise was felt; but, then, some curiosity was expressed to know where they had gone to; and curiosity led to wonderment, and wonderment to rumour—for people will gossip, especially in a country district. Mr Greeta Jones, the husband, had to submit to much questioning as to where his wife and child were staying. But being sullen and morose of temperament he contented himself by brusquely saying, 'They had gone to London.' But as no one had seen them go, and no one had heard of their going, the statement was accepted as a perversion of fact. Nevertheless, incredible as it may seem, no one thought it worthwhile to insist upon an investigation, and a few weeks later Mr Greeta Jones himself went away—and to London, as was placed beyond doubt. For a long time Bleak Hill Castle was shut up, and throughout the country side it began to be whispered that sights and sounds had been seen and heard at the castle which were suggestive of things unnatural, and soon it became widely believed that the place was haunted.

On the principle of giving a dog a bad name you have only to couple ghosts with the name of an old country residence like this castle for it to fall into disfavour, and to be generally shunned. As might have been expected in such a region the castle *was* shunned; no tenant could be found for it. It was allowed to go to ruin, and for a long time was the haunt of smugglers. They were cleared out in the process of time, and at last hard-headed, practical Dick Dirckman heard of the place through a London agent, went down to see it, took a fancy to it, bought it for an old song, and soon converted the half-ruined building into a country gentleman's home, and thither he carried his bride.

Such was the history of Bleak Hill Castle as I gathered it in outline during the post-prandial chat on that memorable evening.

On the following day I found the place all that my host had described it in his letter to me. Its situation was beautiful in the extreme; and from its windows there was a magnificent view of landscape and sea. He and I rambled about the house, he evinced a keen delight in showing me every nook and corner, in expatiating on the beauties of the locality generally, and of the advantages of his dwelling-place in particular. Why he reserved taking me to the so-called haunted chamber until the last I never have known; but so it was; and as he threw open the heavy door and ushered me into the apartment, he smiled ironically and remarked:

'Well, old man, this is the ghost's den; and as I consider that a country mansion of this kind should have its haunted room, I have let this place go untouched. But I needn't tell you that I regard the ghost stories as rot.'

I did not reply to my friend at once, for the room absorbed my attention. It was unquestionably the largest of the bedrooms in the Castle, and, while in keeping with the rest of the house, had characteristics of its own. The walls were panelled with dark oak, the floor was polished oak. There was a deep V-shaped bay, formed by an angle of the castle, and in each side of the bay was a diamond-paned window, and under each window an oak seat, which was also a chest with an ancient iron lock. A large wooden bedstead with massive hangings stood in one corner; the rest of the furniture was of a very nondescript character. In a word, the room was picturesque, and to me it at once suggested all sorts of dramatic situations of a weird and eerie character. There was a very large fire-place with a most capacious hearthstone, on which stood a pair of ponderous and rusty steel dogs. Finally, the window commanded superb views, and altogether my fancy was pleased, and my artistic susceptibilities appealed to in an irresistible manner, so that I replied to my friend thus:

'I like this room, Dick. Let me occupy it, will you?'

He laughed.

'Well, upon my word, you are an eccentric fellow to want to give up the comfortable den which I have assigned to you for this mouldy, draughty, dingy, old lumber room. However'—here he shrugged his shoulders—'there is no accounting for tastes, so I'll tell the servants to put the bed in order, light a fire, and cart your traps from the other room.'

I was glad I had carried my point, for I frankly confess to having romantic tendencies. I was fond of old things, old stories and legends, old furniture, and anything that was removed above the dull level of commonplaceness. This room, in a certain sense, was unique, and I was charmed with it.

When pretty little Mrs Dirckman heard of the arrangements she said, with a laugh that did not conceal a certain nervousness, 'I am sorry you are going to sleep in that wretched room. It always makes me shudder, for it seems so uncomfortable. Besides, you know, although Dick laughs at me and calls me a little goose, I am inclined to believe there may be some foundation for the current stories. Anyway, I wouldn't sleep in the room for a crown of gold. I do hope you will be comfortable, and not be frightened to death by gruesome apparitions.'

I hastened to assure my hostess that I should be comfortable enough, while as for apparitions, I was not likely to be frightened by them.

The rest of the day was spent in exploring the country round about, and after dinner, Dick and I played billiards until one o'clock, and then, having drained a final 'peg', I retired to rest. When I reached the haunted chamber I found that much had been done to give an air of cheerfulness and comfort to the place. Some rugs had been laid about the floor, a modern chair or two introduced, a wood fire blazed on the earth. On a little occasional table that stood near the fire was a silver jug, filled with hot water, and an antique decanter containing spirits, together with lemon and sugar, in case I wanted a final brew. I could not but feel grateful for my host and hostess's thoughtfulness, and having donned my dressing-gown and slippers, I drew a chair near the fire, and proceeded to fill my pipe for a few whiffs previous to tumbling into bed. This was a habit of mine that afforded me solace and conduced to restful sleep. So I lit my pipe, and fell to pondering and trying to see if I could draw any suggestions as to my future from the glowing embers. Suddenly a remarkable thing happened. My pipe was drawn gently from my lips and laid upon the table, and at the same moment I heard what seemed to me to be a sigh. For a moment or two I felt confused, and wondered whether I was awake or dreaming. But there was the pipe on the table, and I could have taken the most solemn oath that to the best of my belief it had been placed there by unseen hands.

My feelings, as may be imagined, were peculiar. It was the first time in my life that I had ever been the subject of a phenomenon capable of being attributed to supernatural agency. After a little reflection, and some reasoning with myself, however, I tried to believe that my own senses had made a fool of me, and that in a half-somnolent and dreamy condition I had removed the pipe myself, and placed it on the table. Having come to this conclusion

I divested myself of my clothing, extinguished the two tall candles, and jumped into bed. Although usually a good sleeper, I did not go to sleep at once, but lay thinking of many things. Mingling with my changing thoughts was a low, monotonous undertone—nature's symphony—of booming sea on the distant beach, and a bass piping—rising occasionally to a shrill and weird upper note—of the wind. From its situation the house was exposed to every wind that blew, hence its name 'Bleak Hill Castle'. The booming sea and wind had a lullaby effect, and I fell asleep. How long I slept I do not know, but I awoke suddenly, and with a start, for it seemed as if a stream of ice-cold water was pouring over my face. With an impulse of indefinable alarm I sprang up in bed, and then a strange, awful, ghastly sight met my view.

The sight I gazed upon appalled me. Yet was I fascinated with a horrible fascination, that rendered it impossible for me to turn my eyes away. I seemed bound by some strange weird spell. My limbs appeared to have grown rigid; there was a sense of burning in my eyes; my mouth was parched and dry; my tongue swollen, so it seemed. Of course, these were mere sensations, but they were sensations I never wish to experience again. They were sensations that tested my sanity. And the sight that held me in the thrall was truly calculated to test the nerves of the strongest.

There, in mid-air, between floor and ceiling, surrounded by a trembling, nebulous light, weird beyond the power of any words to describe, was the head and bust of a woman. The face was paralysed into an unutterably awful expression of stony horror; the long black hair was tangled and dishevelled, and the eyes appeared to be bulging from the head. But this was not all. Two ghostly hands were visible. The fingers of one were twined savagely in the black hair, and the other grasped a long-bladed knife, and with it hacked, and gashed, and tore, and stabbed at the bare white throat of the woman, and the blood gushed forth from the jagged wounds, reddening the spectre hand and flowing in one continuous stream to the oak floor, where I heard it drip, drip, drip until my brain seemed as if it would burst, and I felt as if I was going mad. Then I saw with my strained eyes the unmistakable sign of death pass over the woman's face; and next, the devilish hands flung the mangled remnants away, and I *heard* a low chuckle of satisfaction—heard, I say, and swear it, as plainly as I have ever heard anything in this world. The light had faded; the vision of crime and death had gone, and yet the spell held me.

Although the night was cold, I believe I was bathed in perspiration. I think I tried to cry out—nay, I am sure I did—but no sound came from my burning, parched lips; my tongue refused utterance; it clove to the roof of my mouth. Could I have moved so much as a joint of my little finger, I could have broken the spell; at least, such was the idea that occupied my half-stunned brain. It was a nightmare of waking horror, and I shudder now as I recall it all. But the revelation—for revelation it was—had not yet reached its final stage. Out of the darkness was once more evolved a faint, phosphorescent glow, and in the midst of it appeared the dead body of a young girl with her throat all gashed and bleeding, the red blood flowing in a crimson flood over her night-robe, and the cruel, spectral hands, dyed with her blood, appeared again, and grasped her, and lifted her, and bore her along. Then that vision faded, and a third appeared. This time I seemed to be looking into a gloomy, damp, arched cave or cellar, and the horror that froze me was intensified as I saw the hands busy preparing a hole in the wall at one end of the cave; and presently they lifted two bodies—the body of the woman, and the body of the young girl—all gory and besmirched; and the hands crushed them into the hole in the wall, and then proceeded to brick them up.

All these things I saw as I have described them, and this I solemnly swear to be the truth as I hope for mercy at the Supreme Judgment.

It was a vision of crime; a vision of merciless, pitiless, damnable murder. How long it all lasted I don't know. Science has told us that dreams which seem to embrace a long series of years, last but seconds; and in the few moments of consciousness that remain to the drowning man his life's scroll is unrolled before his eyes. This vision of mine, therefore, may only have lasted seconds, but it seemed to me hours, years, nay an eternity. With that final stage in the ghostly drama of blood and death, the spell was broken, and flinging my arms wildly about, I know that I uttered a great cry as I sprang up in bed.

Every detail of the horrific vision I recalled, and yet somehow it seemed to me that I had been the victim of a hideous nightmare. I felt ill; strangely ill. I was wet and clammy with perspiration, and nervous to a degree that I had never before experienced. Nevertheless, I noted everything distinctly. On the hearthstone there was still a mass of glowing red embers. I heard the distant booming of the sea, and round the house the wind moaned with a peculiar, eerie, creepy sound.

Suddenly I sprang from the bed, impelled thereto by an impulse I was bound to obey, and by the same impulse I was drawn towards the door. I laid my hand on the handle. I turned it, opened the door and gazed into the long dark corridor. A sigh fell upon my ears. An unmistakable human sigh, in which was expressed an intensity of suffering and sorrow that thrilled me to the heart. I shrank back, and was about to close the door, when out of the darkness appeared the glowing figure of a woman clad in blood-stained garments and with dishevelled hair. She turned her white corpse-like face towards me, and her eyes pleaded with a pleading that was irresistible, while she pointed the index finger of her left hand downwards, and then beckoned me. Then I followed whither she led. I could no more resist than the un-restrained needle can resist the attracting magnet. Clad only in my night apparel, and with bare feet and legs, I followed the spectre along the corridor, down the broad oak stairs, traversing another passage to the rear of the building until I found myself standing before a heavy barred door. At that moment the spectre vanished, and I retraced my steps like one who walked in a dream. I got back to my bedroom, but how I don't quite know; nor have I any recollection of getting into bed. Hours afterwards I awoke. It was broad daylight. The horror of the night came back to me with overwhelming force, and made me faint and ill. I managed, however, to struggle through with my toilet, and hurried from that haunted room. It was a beautifully fine morning. The sun was shining brightly, and the birds carolled blithely in every tree and bush. I strolled out on to the lawn, and paced up and down. I was strangely agitated, and asked myself over and over again if what I had seen or dreamed about had any significance.

Presently my host came out. He visibly started as he saw me.

'Hullo, old chap. What's the matter with you?' he exclaimed. 'You look jolly queer; as though you had been having a bad night of it.'

'I have had a bad night.'

His manner became more serious and grave.

'What—seen anything?'

'Yes.'

'The deuce! You don't mean it, really!'

'Indeed I do. I have gone through a night of horror such as I could not live through again. But let us have breakfast first, and then I will try and make you understand what I have suffered, and you shall judge for yourself whether any significance is to be attached to my dream, or whatever you like to call it.'

We walked, without speaking, into the breakfast room, where my charming hostess greeted me cordially; but she, like her husband, noticed my changed appearance, and expressed alarm and anxiety. I reassured her by saying I had had a rather restless night, and didn't feel particularly well, but that it was a mere passing ailment. I was unable to partake of much breakfast, and both my good friend and his wife again showed some anxiety, and pressed me to state the cause of my distress. I recounted the experience I had gone through during the night of terror.

So far from my host showing any disposition to ridicule me, as I quite expected he would have done, he became unusually thoughtful, and presently said:

'Either this is a wild phantasy of your own brain, or there is something in it. The door that the ghost of the woman led you to is situated on the top of a flight of stone steps, leading to a vault below the building, which I have never used, and have never even had the curiosity to enter, though I did once go to the bottom of the steps; but the place was so exceedingly suggestive of a tomb that I shut it up, bolted and barred the door, and have never opened it since.'

I answered that the time had come when he must once more descend into that cellar or vault, whatever it was. He asked me if I would accompany him, and, of course, I said I would. So he summoned his head gardener, and after much searching about, the key of the door was found; but even then the door was only opened with difficulty, as lock and key alike were foul with rust.

As we descended the slimy, slippery stone steps, each of us carrying a candle, a rank, mouldy smell greeted us, and a cold noisome atmosphere pervaded the place. The steps led into a huge vault, that apparently extended under the greater part of the building. The roof was arched, and was supported by brick pillars. The floor was the natural earth, and was soft and oozy. The miasma was almost overpowering, notwithstanding ventilating slits in the wall in various places.

We proceeded to explore this vast cellar, and found that there was an air shaft which apparently communicated with the roof of the house; but it was choked with rubbish, old boxes, and the like. The gardener cleared this away, and then, looking up, we could see the blue sky overhead.

Continuing our exploration, we noted in a recess formed by the angle of the walls a quantity of bricks and mortar. Under other circumstances this would not, perhaps, have aroused our curiosity or suspicions. But in this instance it did; and we examined the wall thereabouts with painful interest, until the conviction was forced upon us that a space of over a yard in width, and extending from floor to roof, had recently been filled in. I was drawn towards the new brickwork by some subtle magic, some weird fascination. I examined it with an eager, critical curious interest, and the thoughts that passed through my brain were reflected in the faces of my companions. We looked at each other, and each knew by some unexplainable instinct what was passing in his fellow's mind.

'It seems to me we are face to face with some mystery,' remarked Dick, solemnly. Indeed, throughout all the years I had known him I had never before seen him so serious. Usually his expression was that of good-humoured cynicism, but now he might have been a judge about to pronounce the doom of death on a red-handed sinner.

'Yes,' I answered, 'there is a mystery, unless I have been tricked by my own fancy.'

'Umph! it is strange,' muttered Dick to himself.

'Well, sir,' chimed in the gardener, 'you know there have been some precious queer stories going about for a long time. And before you come and took the place plenty of folks round about used to say they'd seen some uncanny sights. I never had no faith in them stories myself; but, after all, maybe there's truth in 'em.'

Dick picked up half a brick and began to tap the wall where the new work was, and the taps gave forth a hollow sound, quite different from the sound produced when the other parts of the wall were struck.

'I say, old chap,' exclaimed my host, with a sorry attempt at a smile, 'upon my word, I begin to experience a sort of uncanny kind of feeling. I'll be hanged if I am not getting as superstitious as you are.'

'You may call me superstitious if you like, but either I have seen what I have seen, or my senses have played the fool with me. Anyway, let us put it to the test.'

'How?'

'By breaking away some of that new brickwork.'

Dick laughed a laugh that wasn't a laugh, as he asked:

'What do you expect to find?' I hesitated to say, and he added the answer himself—'Mouldering bones, if your ghostly visitor hasn't deceived you.'

'Mouldering bones!' I echoed involuntarily.

'Gardener, have you got a crowbar amongst your tools?' Dick asked.

'Yes, sir.'

'Go up and get it.'

The man obeyed the command.

'This is a strange sort of business altogether,' Dick continued, after glancing round the vast and gloomy cellar. 'But, upon my word, to tell you the truth, I'm half ashamed of myself for yielding to anything like superstition. It strikes me that you'll find you are the victim of a trick of the imagination, and that these bogey fancies of yours have placed us in rather a ridiculous position.'

In answer to this I could not possibly resist reminding Dick that even scientists admitted that there were certain phenomena that could not be accounted for by ordinary laws.

Dick shrugged his shoulders and remarked with assumed indifference:

'Perhaps—perhaps it is so.' He proceeded to fill his pipe with tobacco, and having lit it he smoked with a nervous energy quite unusual with him.

The gardener was only away about ten minutes, but it seemed infinitely longer. He brought both a pickaxe and a crowbar with him, and in obedience to his master's orders he commenced to hack at the wall. A brick was soon dislodged. Then the crowbar was inserted in the hole, and a mass prised out. From the opening came forth a sickening odour, so that we all drew back instinctively, and I am sure we all shuddered. I saw the pipe fall from Dick's lips; but he snatched it up quickly and puffed at it vigorously until a cloud of smoke hung in the fœtid and stagnant air. Then, picking up a candle from the ground, where it had been placed, he approached the hole, holding the candle in such a position that its rays were thrown into the opening. In a few moments he started back with an exclamation:

'My God! the ghost hasn't lied,' he said, and I noticed that his face was sheet white. I peered into the hole and so did the garden-er, and we both drew back with a start, for there in the recess were decayed human remains.

'This awful business must be investigated.' said Dick. 'Come, let us go.'

We needed no second bidding. We were only too glad to quit that place of horror, and get into the fresh air and bright sunlight. We verily felt that we had come up out of a tomb.

Half an hour later Dick and I were driving to the nearest town to lay information of the awful discovery we had made. The subsequent search carried out by the police brought two bodies to light. Critical medical examination left not the shadow of a doubt that they were the remains of a woman and a girl, and each had been brutally murdered. Of course it became necessary to hold an inquest, and the police set to work to collect evidence as to the identity of the bodies hidden in the recess in the wall.

Naturally all the stories which had been current for so many years throughout the country were revived. The chief topic was that of the strange disappearance of the wife and daughter of the last owner of the castle, Greeta Jones. This story had been touched upon the previous night, during the after-dinner chat in my host's smoking room. Jones, as was remembered, had gambled his fortune away, and married a lady much older than himself, who bore him a daughter who was subject to epileptic fits. When this girl was about twelve she and her mother disap-peared from the neighbourhood, and, according to the husband's account, they had gone to London.

Then he left, and people troubled themselves no more about him and his belongings.

A quarter of a century had passed since that period, and Bleak Hill Castle had gone through many vicissitudes until it fell into the hands of Dick Dirckman. The more the history of Greeta Jones was gone into, the more it was clear that the remains which had been bricked up in the cellar were those of his wife and daughter. That the unfortunate girl and woman had been brutally and barbarously murdered was beyond doubt. The question was, who murdered them? After leaving Wales, Greeta Jones—as was brought to light—led a wild life in London. One night, while in a state of intoxication, he was knocked down by a cab, and so seriously injured that he died while being carried to the hospital; and with him his secret, for could there be any reasonable doubt that, even if he was not the actual murderer, he had connived at the crime. But there was reason to believe that he killed his wife and child with his own hand, and that with the aid of a navvy, whose services he bought, he bricked the bodies up in the cellar. It was remembered that a navvy named Howell Williams had been in the habit of going to the castle frequently, and that suddenly he became possessed of what was, for him, a considerable sum of money. For several weeks he drank hard; then, being a single man, he packed up his few belongings and gave out that he was going to California, and all efforts to trace him failed.

So much for this ghastly crime. As to the circumstances that led to its discovery, it was curious that I should have been selected as the medium for bringing it to light. Why it should have been so I cannot and do not pretend to explain. I have recorded facts as they occurred; I leave others to solve the mystery.

It was not a matter for surprise that Mrs Dirckman should have been deeply affected by the terrible discovery, and she declared to her husband that if she were to remain at the castle she would either go mad or die. And so poor Dick, who was devoted to his charming little wife, got out as soon as he could, and once more Bleak Hill Castle fell into neglect and ultimate ruin, until at last it was razed to the ground and modern buildings reared on its site. As for myself, that night of horror I endured under Dick's roof affected me to such an extent that my hair became prematurely grey, and even now, when I think of the agony I endured, I shudder with an indefinable sense of fear.

The Shouting

by

L. T. C. ROLT

When I came to compile this anthology, I wrote and asked the late L. T. C. Rolt (1910–1974) if he had written any further ghost stories, since his excellent volume Sleep No More *(1948). With great courtesy, he offered to write a new story for this collection and the result was 'The Shouting'.*

As it was the first ghost story he had written for over 25 years, I was naturally delighted to receive it and planned to introduce it with great flourish. However, my introduction is of necessity tinged with sadness, for shortly after arranging for the story's inclusion, Mr Rolt died. A bitter irony of fate meant that he would not see publication of his first ghost story in a quarter of a century.

So my publication of this tale is a tribute to one of England's finest ghost-story writers. In Sleep No More, *Rolt has left a slim volume of some of the most original tales in the genre. At the time of writing, plans are afoot to reprint his collection; I can only applaud the good sense of the editor responsible. But it was not only ghost stories that he wrote; his published works included books on engineers and engineering, railways, canals and ballooning. One critic wrote at the time of his death: 'His ambition was to give the history of the Industrial Revolution an imaginative and literary shape and in this he admirably succeeded.'*

L. T. C. Rolt indicated to me that his wife had an experience in Devon, on which he founded this tale. It is an original story and shows that the long pause between writing such tales did not weaken Rolt's ability.

I companioned Edward on many walking tours before I discovered that he had a positive phobia about woods. There was always some very good reason why we should not go through one: the obvious path, though marked on the Ordnance Survey map, might peter out or turn in the wrong direction; if it was hot there would be too many flies in the wood; if it was evening it would be too dark; half the fun of walking was the view and obviously there could be no view in a wood. But at last there came a day when none of these pretexts could avail him, on the contrary it was quite obvious to us, both from the map and from the lie of the land that to avoid going through this particular wood, which was quite a small one incidentally, would involve a needless and lengthy cross country detour including scrambling through many hedges—just the kind of point to point walking that does not appeal to me. On the other hand it was perfectly clear from the stile at the edge of the wood and the path beyond it that there lay a well-used right of way. Yet Edward stopped in his tracks and, knowing there was no valid excuse left to him, said, with an unmistakable fear in his eyes: 'I'd rather not go through that wood if you don't mind.' 'Come on,' I said, 'it's only about a quarter of a mile wide judging from the map and if we leave the path we're in for a hell of a scramble.' Seeing that he still hesitated, I mounted the stile with a 'Well, suit yourself; I know which way I'm going' over my shoulder. I think it was the nearest we ever came to a row in all our time together. What followed was really very odd and cast an entirely new and strange light on my friend. It's odd how long you can know people and yet suddenly discover that you know so little. Edward padded silently behind me, his eyes darting to right and left as though that harmless Herefordshire coppice harboured every species of savage beast, with the odd poisonous snake thrown in for good measure. But it was no laughing matter at the time and I confess that I felt a shade uneasy myself, for it was quite obvious that Edward was terrified almost out of his wits.

I was determined to get to the bottom of this unreasoning terror and that evening in the Scudamore Arms at Combercombe I tackled him about it. 'I'm sorry I persuaded you to walk through that spinney with me. Honestly, if I'd realised that you felt so strongly about. . . .' He cut me short: 'Yes, the truth is that all woods scare me stiff.' '*My mother said I never should play with the gipsies in the wood,*' I quoted at him rather tactlessly. Edward gave me a curiously searching look and 'What made you say that?' he asked sharply. Then he went on 'This has nothing whatever to do with cautionary nursery jingles of that kind. It is due to something that happened to me only ten years ago, just before I met up with you in fact.' And then it all came out.

He was staying in an isolated rented cottage in the bottom of one of those deep and narrow valleys that run down to the Atlantic coast of North Devon and Cornwall. The ridges between them end in formidable bare headlands and vertiginous cliffs that jut out to meet the challenge of Atlantic rollers, but one does not have to go far inland from the coast before their lower slopes are thickly covered with dense woods of scrub oaks, their tops combed by the prevailing south-westerlies that funnel up the valleys till they resemble a smooth green fleece.

Well, Edward said he was lolling in a deck-chair outside his cottage door and enjoying the hot sunshine of late July, when he suddenly heard the patter of feet and the chatter of children approaching down the lane. This surprised him, as there was no village within miles, but when he saw them he thought they must be the children of gipsies who had camped nearby for they were all olive-complexioned with black hair and sloe eyes. They were chattering eagerly together as though anticipating some rare treat, but for the life of him he could not distinguish a word they said. Could they be speaking Romany? he asked himself; surely not. A boy, who looked about fourteen and appeared to be the eldest and the ringleader of the group, was in front and as they passed opposite his cottage gate, Edward got up from his chair, stopped the little party and asked their leader where they were going. Speaking in perfect English the boy replied: 'Oh, we are going up into the woods for the shouting.' The way he said this implied that Edward ought to have known the answer without having to ask. But before he could betray his ignorance by asking what he meant, the boy had broken into a trot and the others, silent now but still radiating a tense expectancy, followed him. Edward watched them cross the little wooden footbridge over the stream and then mount the slope until they disappeared into the wood. Then he went back to his deck-chair pondering on this odd little encounter until he began to doze again.

He was roused by what he described as a most unearthly racket. A shrill eldritch piping and shrieking rising every now and again to a frenzied pitch. So this was 'the shouting'. It struck him as a scarcely human sound, sometimes reminding him of the squealing of slaughtered pigs and sometimes of the strange cries he had once heard coming from a heronry. But what puzzled and disturbed him even more was that this shrill clamour seemed to have an accompanying ground bass, a kind of plain chant that was somehow far more horrible to hear—and at this point Edward became almost alarmingly emphatic—than the shouting itself. There could be no one in that party of children with a voice like that, he speculated; it must be an acoustic trick, something like the sound of the sea beating on the rocks at the end of the valley unnaturally echoed and magnified in that narrow space between the hanging woods. So he rationalised his fear, knowing in his heart that such an explanation could not be true.

It was some time before the children came back, long enough for the sun to have left the floor of the valley although it still shone brilliantly upon the higher slopes above. They walked silently, two by two, over the wooden footbridge and past Edward's gate with never a sideways glance. He might not have been there, leaning over the gate watching them, he said. Soft-footed, they passed him by as though they were entranced, their lips slightly parted, their sloe eyes staring fixedly ahead as though focused upon some remote distance. Young though the children were, Edward admitted he found this strange procession very awe-inspiring.

He had sat on for a while in the deepening shadow before at length curiosity got the better of him, and he set off towards the wood in the direction the children had taken. He had noticed the spot where the children had entered the wood for it was marked by a single ancient and stunted yew tree which contrasted darkly against the green foliage of the oaks and their silvery, lichen-bearded trunks and branches. Once he had climbed the fence and entered the wood he found no path, although the way was still clear to him because the children had beaten down briars, nettles and bracken in their passing. Taller than they, he had to walk bent double to avoid the dense interlacement of branches. It was like walking through some low green tunnel. Suddenly, however, he could stand upright, for he found himself in a small round clearing in the midst of the wood and thought it strange that it was not visible from below considering the steepness of the slope which had left him out of breath.

In the centre of the clearing was a low mound of short green turf, like an island in a pool of bracken. Edward walked on to the top of this central mound and it was at once obvious that it was here that 'the shouting' had taken place. Children were great traditionalists, he reflected, it was doubtless some old country game or ritual handed on by one generation to another. '*My mother said I never should play with the gipsies in the wood*', that silly jingle came into his head unbidden and refused to be banished. Evidently they did not forbid such play in these parts but positively encouraged it, and then he laughed aloud at this feeble joke, and then he started at the most remarkable echo. Of course, woods were famous for this kind of thing, he thought, but then something much more remarkable and alarming happened. The laugh was repeated from a different part of the clearing and this time it was no echo but a sound such as he had never made in his life; a deep, short sound, half bark, half bray, human and yet inhuman. The laugh came again almost the next instant, menacing this time, and from the opposite side of the clearing although he had heard no sound of movement in the wood. At this Edward became terrified. He stood rooted to the spot, peering, now this way, now that, into the darkening wood in an attempt to locate the source of such a dreadful sound. When the laugh came a fourth time, it happened to sound from the precise direction in which he was peering. It may only have been some trick of the failing light he admits apologetically, but an inchoate mass of twigs and oak leaves seemed suddenly to form itself into a gigantic head, a head with an aureole of leafy twigs in place of hair, a beard of grey lichen below a cruelly smiling mouth. There also appeared to be two red eyes, though this may have been the effect of the setting sun shining through chinks in the leafy canopy of the wood. But, on reflection, Edward thought not. It strikes him how as a last desperate attempt on the part of his rational mind to explain in known terms the unknown. For the next instant, sheer panic seized him and he blundered out of the clearing and down through the wood.

Trees, nettles, bracken and briars all seemed to conspire together to prevent his headlong flight. He nearly scalped himself on low branches, nettles stung him, briars whipped at his clothes and flesh, and tough bracken stalks tripped him so that more than once he sprawled headlong. And all the while that awful voice accompanied him, laughing and chuckling over his plight. He thought that if again he should see the face from which it came his reason would snap. Nor could he bear much longer the sound of that voice and, in a vain attempt to drown it, he began to yell at the top of his voice the first ridiculous words that entered into his head 'Mother said I never should play with the gipsies in the wood,' he screamed hysterically.

By the time he finally flung himself over the fence at the edge of the wood his clothes were in tatters and blood was streaming down his forehead and into his eyes from the lacerations on his head. But the horror had left him and, thankfully, he flung himself down on the cool turf now slightly damp with dew. There below him was the dim shape of his cottage beyond the stream and he gazed at it as a traveller from the desert gazes at an oasis.

'And that was that,' concluded my friend, 'Now you know why I dislike—no, dislike is too mild a word—why I *hate* woods.' 'But what about those children?' I queried, 'Did you?...' He answered my question before I had finished it with a shrug of the shoulders. 'No,' he replied, 'There were no gipsies in the district at the time, I made sure of that and I am equally certain they weren't local children either.' After a pause he went on, 'I asked the good lady from Mortford, who came every day on her bike to do the chores for me, whether there was any legend or traditional custom connected with that particular piece of woodland. But all she would say was "I dunno, sir, us do never goo in ther".'

So your guess is as good as mine as to who or what the children were. Personally, now that I have heard Edward's story I am inclined to think they may have been the most frightening thing about the whole strange business.

The Happy Dancers

by

CHARLES BIRKIN

One of the hardest types of story to bring off successfully is the horror tale; not the supernatural tale, but the real horror *tale, dealing solely with the nasty things people do to each other. All too often these days, such tales are mere boring catalogues of the same old 'horrors'—torture, dismemberment, copious blood, acid burns, mutilation, etc.—with ludicrous motivation and abysmal characterisation. At first glance, such a tale would seem the easiest thing in the world to write. The present flood of such stories indicates that far too many writers take only that first glance. Their second glance should be in the direction of Charles Birkin, who is without doubt the greatest living exponent of this particular kind of story. What Charles Birkin's characters do to each other doesn't bear thinking about.*

His first collection The Kiss of Death *was published in 1964, and since then he has proved to be the most consistent writer of quality horror stories in the field today. He first started writing horror tales in the 1930's, when he worked for Philip Allan, an enterprising publisher who specialised in the macabre. 'The Happy Dancers' is one of the stories that Birkin wrote in those days, and has remained out of print for over forty years. It gives me great pleasure to reintroduce a story from the early days of one of our modern masters.*

A beam of pale gold light cut the blue smoke-dimmed atmosphere of the Kasbek, a beam that was focused on the arched door set under the staircase through which the artistes of the cabaret made their entrance. The lights had been lowered, and from time to time a face was thrown into momentary prominence, as its owner drew at a cigar or cigarette. All eyes were turned expectantly towards the spot where Nikakova would appear. There was a rattle of drums; the orchestra struck up a wild tzigane melody, and suddenly Nikakova was before her audience, her gaily coloured skirts whirling around her as she twisted and spun, the vivid ribbons that hung from her tambourine dancing in grotesque rhythm.

Serge sat alone at his table, his eyes following every movement of the dancer before him; and as he watched the professional way in which she captured her audience, and as he joined in the salvo of applause that greeted the end of her performance, he remember-ed his first meeting with her three, no four, years previously.

He had seen her as he was riding through the village at Zaramow—very proud and brave in his new uniform—and on his first leave from the military school in Petrograd. She was barely seventeen, and he some four years her senior. She was dancing then, with an involuntary gaiety, to a group of peasants, and he had been struck by her grace, and amazed that his village could have produced a daughter so delicately beautiful. He was used to the massive and comely buxomness of the country women, but this slender elfin charm, fragile as porcelain. . . .

And silently he had waited, straight-backed on his horse, until she had looked up and caught his intent gaze. And then she had become confused and stopped unhappily, and her audience had looked up and seen the cause of her discomfiture, and an embar-rassed hush had descended abruptly on the laughing group.

He had beckoned to her to come to him, and had asked her name. She told him that she was Louba Kerensky, the daughter of Boris Kerensky, and Serge had frowned with displeasure for her father was a man whose ideas were radical in the extreme—a surly drunken brute, always ready to stir up discontent and trouble. Serge's father, the Grand Duke, had been forced to have him beaten some months before, and had threatened him with Siberia should further correction be necessary, for these were dangerous times.

Serge found it incredible that this frail girl could be his daughter. He smiled down at her. 'You dance divinely—where did you learn?'

Louba smiled. 'Learn? Where should *I* have dancing lessons? I learned from the wind in the trees, and the streams dancing over their pebbled beds, and from the sun dancing on the surface of the lake; and from the butterflies dancing over the coloured flowers, and'—she glanced up at him—'from the laughter dancing in mens' eyes!' And she threw back her head and laughed up at him, vital in her gypsy beauty.

Serge was interested. She was clever, this girl—as well as attractive. He tapped his riding boot with his cane.

'The best of schools, my dear . . . but are all your teachers, then, so gay?'

'No. . . .' she said, and her expression darkened, 'I learned also from the corpses jerking on the gallows, and the flies dancing on the dungheaps, and from Death hovering near starving men during the hard winters of my childhood.'

'A thorough education!' And his laugh was forced.

Serge was intrigued. Well, he was home for six weeks, and a little diversion would help to bring nearer his return to Petrograd and the new friends he had made there.

But when the time had come, he had taken Louba with him—to have her trained as a dancer; and also because he could not give her up.

He noticed with surprise that his cigar had gone out, and as he struck a match he saw Louba threading her way through the tables towards him, eyes bright with the pleasure of success, lips parted in a smile as she received compliments from the officers and their friends seated in parties round the great semi-circle of the dance floor. Teeth flashed white under clipped dark moustaches as heads turned to follow her.

And, as she came, Louba too remembered her first meeting with Serge, how, from the depths that had separated them, she had always admired him, and how she had been determined to make the most of her opportunity; and then how she had come to love him sincerely. When Serge had first taken her, Boris had threatened to kill him, had raved of the injustice of a world where the aristocrats ground down the peasants, bleeding them of their money, battening on the labours, raping their daughters. But the more level-headed of the villagers had restrained him from taking any such action that could only end in failure and disgrace, and which would mean for Boris the salt mines of Siberia.

Louba had never seen her father these last four years, nor had she had any desire to do so; and he, she knew, had no knowledge of where she was, nor of the high position which she had gained for herself by her talent and with her lover's help. Boris, in her childhood, had loved her in a fierce incoherent way, with a passionate, almost frightening, love . . . but she was finished with the peasant life—thank God—with the filth and the squalor and the clumsy-handed inarticulate oafs. She had Serge, admiration, money, comfort and success, and life was indeed good; and when the war was over there would be no more worries.

Louba rested her hand lightly on Serge's shoulder as she sank on to the chair by his side.

'You liked my performance to-night?' she asked.

'Magnificent as always, my darling. And your audience—they loved you.'

'If I danced well it was for you—only for you. You still believe that?' He found her utterly irresistible.

'And when I'm not here?' he asked wryly.

'Your table is always empty,' she said, as if answering a foolish question. 'I will not allow others to occupy it!'

Serge's helpless adoring smile was her answer. He poured her out a glass of champagne.

'You look a little tired, my sweet. Drink this, it will do you good.' There were dark shadows under her eyes.

'You know I never drink. When I dance I cannot drink.'

'I know, Louba. I know well. But you do not dance again tonight. Drink with me—to our future happiness.' His words sounded hollow.

She raised her glass, her exquisite brown eyes smiling up into his, blue and steady, and filled with fatigue.

'To our future happiness!'

But in his heart Serge was ill at ease. Who knew what was going to happen in the future? Even a day from that moment— tomorrow his leave was up, and he went back to the war, which was not going well.

It was the early spring of 1917.

As they were leaving the Club, Louba paused in front of the great golden doorway and gazed up at the sky; she wore an evening coat of white satin with a huge fur collar that emphasised the delicacy of her slender neck, giving her the appearance of an arum lily.

'How lovely the night is—but, Serge, so short ... and tomorrow you return ... to what?'

Her beauty was startling, etched against the background of the night.

Serge beckoned to a commissionaire, and in a few seconds the long low motor car that he had given Louba slid silently to the kerb. He looked at his watch. It was nearly three o'clock. The night air was cool and very sweet.

'Louba, my darling, in five hours I shall be gone.'

Her hand clutched his convulsively. There was silence, each questioning what the future held for them. Then Louba spoke, her voice trying to disguise the fear that filled her mind. She would not talk of the morrow.

'Tretkoff told me that he was going to change the name of the Kasbek to The Happy Dancers.'

'Why?'

'Because it's the one oasis of real gaiety in this war-shadowed city.'

'And when will this momentous change occur?' he asked smiling.

'After he's completed the redecorations. It's to be closed next week for that reason. On your next leave you'll hardly recognise it!'

His next leave . . . when would that be?

The car stopped outside Louba's house. Serge turned to the chauffeur.

'Be here at half-past seven.' The man clicked his heels.

They walked slowly up the steps; and the sky grew lighter as the hours passed, and the faery fingers of the dawn trailed their ragged banners over Petrograd.

Some months later Louba sat in front of the triple mirror on her dressing-table. It would soon be time for her to start for The Happy Dancers, where she was to dance for the last time. She frowned as she rubbed a little rouge into her flawless skin. She was frightened; frightened of Petrograd and the feeling of unrest and hatred that had grown and which now permeated the city.

And her father, Boris, was there, she knew; she had read that he had been one of the agitators who had been arrested that morning and later released. She prayed that he wouldn't discover where she was, but reassured herself that there was little chance of that, for she had changed her name and there was small likelihood of his connecting his daughter Louba with Nikakova, the cabaret dancer. Yes—she was dancing tonight for the last time. She was excited and happy, oh so happy. For Serge. When would he come back? She couldn't tell him in a letter. Serge's child! Her mouth was very tender. She peered once more into her looking-glass, tracing the chiselled lines of her lips with crimson. She could see the room behind her reflected in the mirror, the thick rose carpet, the lights, the broad low bed, and the door. Her eyes widened, her hand was motionless, still clutching her lipstick, for the door was quietly opening. Gently, an inch at a time. But she made no sound. Now she could see a man's arm, and the toe of a highly-polished riding boot. And then he was in the room, and a cry of joy rang out.

'Serge!' He was at her side in three strides and she was in his arms, his mouth pressed on hers, hard and insistent.

'Darling!'

'But why didn't you let me know you were coming?' She pushed him gently away. 'Let me look at you.' She put up her left hand and stroked his hair. 'Serge . . . for how long?' Her voice was high with joy.

'Twenty-four hours. I only knew myself this afternoon. Everything has been so unsettled. Rumours everywhere. And on the way from the station there were angry crowds. Louba, I don't *like* your being here in Petrograd. Tomorrow you must leave. It's not safe, darling. It might even be suicide!'

'I'm all right, my dear. But come, I must go to the Club. I dance there tonight—my swan song!'

And in the warm privacy of the motor car while they made their slow way through the crowd-blocked streets, she told him of their coming child. The journey was slow, and several times their way was blocked. Angry voices shouted at them, and once a stone hit the shining bonnet.

'Serge! My father is here.'

'I know, darling. He's come a long way, hasn't he? In every sense. I saw him in the street on my way to your house. He was addressing a crowd of people outside the Nicholas Theatre. God, how I hate rabble-raising!'

'And he saw you?'

'Yes . . . I don't know . . . what does it matter?' He pressed her hand reassuringly.

'Oh, but it does! What will he do? . . . He means you harm. The city has gone mad. I'm frightened. This is his chance.'

'It's nothing, darling. What *can* he do, here, in Petrograd?'

'But you haven't been here the last few days. There has been rioting, and shops have been looted and smashed. The police seem quite incapable of doing anything to stop it.'

'Or perhaps they don't want to.'

'What do you mean?' Louba whispered, alarmed at last by the hopelessness in her lover's voice.

Serge shrugged his shoulders, and drawing her to him kissed her very gently.

The Happy Dancers was full. But there was a breathless frenzied quality in the gaiety that was new. And two military policemen stood by the gilded doorway. As they went in, one of them saluted and said to Serge:

'I shouldn't go there tonight, there might be trouble.'

Louba overheard his warning and said: 'But we must; I dance here.'

The incident had left a fear in the back of her mind that increased as the evening wore on. Distant shouting was heard, and once the brittle rattle of rifle fire. A sudden silence descended on the diners, but only for a moment. As if to combat this vague menace a hectic babble of talk and merriment broke out. But the laughter was forced, and more drinks were called for, and yet more. Tretkoff spoke to the leader of the orchestra. The music must be louder and with no intervals of silence; there must be no silences.

Boris Kerensky was drunk. His ragged beard was matted with the thick dark beer that, after so many toasts in vodka, had evaded his mouth. He peered at his companions, men and women sunk as low as himself, and all in varying stages of intoxication, both from alcohol and hysteria.

'And you say you know where Serge Poliakoff is?' he repeated, peering into the face of his companion. 'You know where he is . . . tonight?'

'Yes. My brother is the bastard's chauffeur. You'd find him at The Happy Dancers—that's where his tart dances,' replied the man. 'They'll be dancing to a different tune soon,' he went on, 'the bloody swine.' He spat on the floor in his disgust. 'I know what I'm talking about. I was a serf on the estate of that bastard's father.'

Boris got uncertainly to his feet, his brain occupied with one idea. Revenge. Revenge on Serge for stealing Louba—his adorable Louba. It should be easy tonight. His foot slithered in a pool of spittle. He laughed. It had been hard to wait, but now the time had come. He clambered unsteadily on to the rough wooden table and started to harangue the clients of the squalid drinking house, a demagogue, self-worked up into a state of lunacy.

Tretkoff made a sign to the band and walked into the middle of the dancing floor. The babble of talk died down, and an expectant hush fell as they waited for him to speak. Louba had just finished her dance and had rejoined Serge.

'Ladies and gentlemen,' the night club proprietor announced, 'the Club will now be closed for the night. I have received information that it would be wiser for you all to go to your homes. Thank you.'

He turned and walked off the floor. Such an announcement was unheard of—without precedent.

Immediately a stir ruffled the tables. Women struggled into their coats, collected their scattered handbags, shrugging at one another in amazement. Men called loudly for their bills, expostulating with Tretkoff. Serge and Louba watched the confusion, saying nothing.

'Shall we go, darling?' Serge suggested.

'In a few minutes,' she answered. 'I want to have a short talk with Tretkoff and collect my belongings from my dressing-room. Wait until the others have gone. There cannot be cause for such panic.'

In fifteen minutes the restaurant was empty, save for a few sullen and apprehensive waiters whisking away the dirty plates and glasses. Serge saw the little proprietor looking at him and he was pale as a ghost. He raised his hand.

'What's the trouble?' he asked when Tretkoff stood beside him. 'Is it really serious . . . or just a scare?'

'Who knows?' said the portly little man, whose way of life was crashing round his ears. 'The crowds are out of hand and in an ugly mood. There has been skirmishing in many parts of the city. I am now shutting up as quickly as I can. I don't want any trouble here.'

One by one the lights were extinguished, like final farewells to the past.

'You go up, Serge,' Louba said. 'I'll join you in a few minutes. Get the car, my darling.'

Serge walked up the staircase. The club had quite a different atmosphere when it was empty. Depressing and tawdry. The big portals into the street were shut. He rapped on them impatiently with his cane. A small door set at the side was opened by a porter who came out of his alcove on the right. The man smiled charmingly. His demeanour was just the same. 'It is an honour to see Your Highness. I hope that you enjoyed your evening.'

'Mlle Nikakova is coming in a few minutes.'

It was very cold in the open air, and over the roofs Serge saw a red glow, as if a building was ablaze. His car was nowhere to be seen. What the hell could have happened to Vladimir? He heard shouts from an alley near at hand. Worried for her safety he wondered how long Louba would be. The shouting was nearer now; a figure ran into the end of the street where Serge stood, handsome in his uniform, against the painted gold of the wooden door. Three or four men were hard on the heels of the first, and then more and more came until the street was filled. They surged towards him, singing and laughing. Several of the men were waving bottles; others had rifles and swords.

'Hey! There's one of the bloody officers!' a woman shouted. Her cry directed the attention of the whole band to Serge. In a moment he was surrounded by a jeering menacing mob, drunken and bestial, lusting for cruelty and action. Serge looked at them. He must not show his fear. Among the hate-filled faces he saw one he knew. Boris Kerensky. Their eyes met, and Serge read the light of insane rage and triumph in those of his opponent as they recognised one another. He bellowed for silence and started haranguing the crowd, telling of the Grand Duke's treatment of his peasants, of Serge's violation of his daughter, Louba. He called upon them to take the law into their own hands, to make Serge suffer, as he and his had made the people suffer for generations. The attitude of the crowd was threatening, they closed round wolfishly. Then Kerensky stepped forward, his face contorted into a mask of rage, and spat in Serge's face.

For a moment Serge stood still, the next his arm flew out and Boris lay stretched unconscious on the pavement.

Before he could grab his revolver Serge was overwhelmed. As he went down he saw the door open, caught a glimpse of Louba's horrified face, cried 'Go back!' and saw a giant soldier seize her. He struggled towards her through the mass of clawing bodies, but a terrific blow with a rifle butt caught him on the side of the head. He fell as if pole-axed.

A little later he opened his eyes. His head felt as if it were splitting. He groaned ... vague noises sounded in his ears. A brutal kick in the crutch roused him. He was roughly pulled to his feet. Nothing seemed real. He was not fully conscious. Somewhere he heard a woman screaming, then roars of laughter and coarse mocking shouts. He wondered who the woman was and why she was screaming. And then he realised it was Louba. He tried to stagger towards her but was held back by implacable arms. His own were tightly tied behind his back. The stench of the men who were holding him was nauseous and overpowering. The cords hurt—cutting into the flesh of his wrists. What had happened? What was Louba saying? He couldn't hear. . . . Yes, it was clearer now . . .

'. . . You can't do it to me . . . I'm one of you . . . dear Lord . . . I swear it. I swear it on the Holy Virgin. Help . . . help . . .' Her voice rose to a scream. 'Serge . . .' He strained to get to her, his chest heaving with the exertion; but the men who held him were strong. And now they were forcing her against the door—the golden door. God! what were they doing? Those great nails . . . the hammer . . . the ladder . . . where had they got a ladder?

When Boris Kerensky recovered consciousness the street was deserted. He lay huddled in the gutter, his eyes half closed. Dimly he heard shouts, the clatter of horses' hoofs, the rattle of gunfire, cheers and groans. The sky was red with the blaze of burning buildings. He turned his head. To his right stood the golden door of The Happy Dancers, and nailed to it, crucified, hung Serge Poliakoff; his stripped body was white against the gilt, very white, relieved only by the crimson stigmata. He was dead. By his side hung the naked body of a girl, her flesh rent by a vicious sword thrust. As he looked, her eyelids fluttered faintly and she slowly opened her eyes, glazing with the film of death.

And lying in the refuse, a sottish hog, Boris looked once more into the eyes of his daughter, Louba.

The Weed Men

by

WILLIAM HOPE HODGSON

William Hope Hodgson (1875–1918) was the man who influenced Dennis Wheatley and many other macabre authors, who have yet to admit it.

The son of an Essex clergyman, Hodgson left home at an early age and spent eight years at sea. This experience provided him with the background for his most successful tales. He obtained a commission with an artillery regiment on the outbreak of World War I, and was killed while on duty as an observation officer.

He left behind a small but brilliant output of some of the finest macabre tales ever written. Hodgson has been grossly underrated for many years and has only recently been recognised as the master of the genre that he undoubtedly was.

It has long been my ambition to include a story by Hodgson in one of my anthologies. However, this has proved no easy task. His classic volumes of tales, like The Luck of the Strong *(1916) and* Men of the Deep Waters *(1914), have so far proved impossible to get hold of. So I have turned instead to his novels of the uncanny and the supernatural, which were all out of print for many years (two still are). Hodgson regarded his first three—*The Boats of the Glen Carrig *(1907), The House on the Borderland (1908) and The Ghost Pirates (1909)— as a trilogy, which he later followed up with The Night Land (1912).*

'The Weed Men' is an excerpt from The Boats of the Glen Carrig. *The novel, using eighteenth century language, tells of the adventures of a ship's crew after the foundering of their vessel. After eerie happenings—including encounters with living trees and giant crabs— their boat drifts into a continent of seaweed, with an island in the middle. Landing on the island, they find it uninhabited (or so it seems). Just off shore, they discover a ship trapped in the weed with further castaways. The sailors determine to contact those on board. Journeys across the weed are impossible, due to the monstrous creatures living beneath it. A*

plan is evolved to build a huge bow and shoot an arrow, bearing a line, out to the ship. It is then that the sailors encounter the real inhabitants of the island. . . .

   Though only an extract from a novel (which itself deserves reprinting in full) 'The Weed Men' has sufficient pace and terrifying incident to make its inclusion in this book of short stories more than worthwhile.

Now, on the night when I took my watch, I discovered that there was no moon, and, save for such light as the fire threw, the hill top was in darkness. Yet, though I was not much afraid I took all precautions that suggested themselves to me, and built up the fire to a goodly height, after which I took my sword, and made the round of the camp. At the edges of the cliffs which protected us on three sides, I paused, staring down into the darkness, and listening; though this latter was of small use because of the strength of the wind which roared continually in my ears. Yet though I neither saw nor heard anything, I was suddenly gripped by a strange uneasiness, which made me return several times to the edge of the cliffs; but always without seeing or hearing anything to justify my suspicions. And so, presently, being determined to give way to no fancifulness, I avoided the boundary of cliffs, and kept more to that part which commanded the slope, up and down which we made our journeys to and from the beach below.

Then, perhaps half way through my time of watching, there came out of the immensity of weed that lay to leeward, a far distant sound that grew upon my ear, rising and rising into a fearsome screaming and shrieking, and then dying away into the distance in queer sobs, and so at last to a note below that of the wind's. At this, as might be supposed, I was somewhat shaken to hear so dreadful a noise coming out of that desolation, and then, suddenly, the thought came to me that the screaming was from the ship trapped in the weed, and I ran immediately to the edge of the cliff overlooking the weed, and stared into the darkness; but now I perceived, by a light which burned in the hulk, that the screaming had come from some place a great distance to the right of her, and more, as my sense assured me, it could by no means have been possible for those in her to have sent their voices to me against such a breeze as blew at that time.

And so, for a time, I stood nervously pondering and peering away into the blackness of the night; in a little while, I perceived a dull glow upon the horizon, and, presently, there rose into view the upper edge of the moon, and a very welcome sight it was to me; for I had been upon the point of calling the bo'sun to tell him about the sound I had heard; but I had hesitated, being afraid to seem foolish if nothing more should happen. Then, even as I stood watching the moon rise into view there came again the beginning of that screaming, like the sound of a woman sobbing with a giant's voice, and it grew and strengthened until it pierced through the roar of the wind with an amazing clearness, and then slowly, and seeming to echo and echo, it sank away into the distance, and there was again in my ears no sound beyond that of the wind.

At this, having looked fixedly in the direction from which the sound had proceeded, I ran straightway to the tent and roused the bo'sun; for I had no knowledge of what the noise might portend, and this second cry had shaken from me all my bashfulness. Now the bo'sun was upon his feet almost before I had finished shaking him, and catching up his great cutlass which he kept always by his side, he followed me swiftly to the hill top. Here, I explained to him that I had heard a very fearsome sound which had appeared to proceed out of the vastness of the weed-continent, and that, upon a repetition of the noise, I had decided to call him; for it might mean some coming danger. At that, the bo'sun commended me; though chiding me in that I had hesitated to call him at the first occurrence of the crying, and then, following me to the edge of the leeward cliff, he stood there with me, waiting and listening, in case there came again a recurrence of the noise.

For just over an hour we stood there very silent and listening; but there came to us no sound beyond the continuous noise of the wind, and so, by that time, having grown somewhat impatient of waiting, and the moon being well risen, the bo'sun beckoned to me to make the round of the camp with him. Now, just as I turned away, chancing to look downward at the clear water directly below, I was amazed to see an innumerable multitude of great fish were swimming from the weed-continent towards the island. At that, I stepped nearer the edge; for they came so directly towards the island that I expected to see them close in-shore; yet I could not perceive one; for they seemed to vanish at a point some thirty yards distant from the beach, and at that, being amazed both by the numbers of the fish and their strangeness, and the way in which they came on continually, yet never reached the shore, I called to the bo'sun to come and see; for he had gone on a few paces. Upon hearing my call, he came running back; whereat I pointed into the sea below. At that, he stooped forward and peered very intently, and I with him; yet neither one of us could discover the meaning of so curious an exhibition, and so for a while we watched, the bo'sun being as interested as I.

Presently, however, he turned away, saying that we were foolish to stand peering at every curious sight, when we should be looking to the welfare of the camp, and so we began to go the round of the hill top. Now, while we had been watching and listening, we had let the fires die down to a dangerously low level, and consequently, though the moon was rising, there was by no means the same brightness that should have made the camp light. On perceiving this, I went forward to throw some fuel on to the fire, and then, even as I moved, it seemed to me that I saw something stir in the shadow of the tent. And at that, I ran towards the place, uttering a shout, and waving my sword; yet I found nothing, and so, feeling somewhat foolish, I turned to make up the fire, as had been my intention, and whilst I was thus busied, the bo'sun came running over to me to know what I had seen, and in the same instant three of the men ran out of the tent, awakened by my sudden cry. But I had naught to tell them, save that my fancy had played me a trick, and had shown me something where my eyes could find nothing, and at that, two of the men went back to resume their sleep; but the third, the big fellow to whom the bo'sun had given the other cutlass, came with us, bringing his weapon; and, though he kept silent, it seemed to me that he had gathered something of our uneasiness; and for my part I was not sorry to have his company.

Presently, we came to that portion of the hill which overhung the valley, and I went to the edge of the cliff, intending to peer over; for the valley had a very unholy fascination for me. Yet, no sooner had I glanced down than I started, and ran back to the bo'sun and plucked him by the sleeve, and at that, perceiving my agitation, he came with me in silence to see what matter had caused me so much quiet excitement. Now; when he looked over, he also was astounded, and drew back instantly; then, using great caution, he bent forward once more, and stared down, and, at that, the big seaman came up behind, walking upon his toes, and stooped to see what manner of thing we had discovered. Thus we each of us stared down upon a most unearthly sight; for the valley all beneath us was alive with moving creatures, white and unwholesome in the moonlight, and their movements were somewhat like the movements of monstrous slugs; though the things themselves had no resemblance to such in their contours; but reminded me of naked humans, very fleshy and crawling upon their stomachs; yet their movements were surprisingly rapid. And now, looking a little over the bo'sun's shoulder, I discovered that these hideous things were coming up out from the pit-like pool in the bottom of the valley that we had seen the day before, and, suddenly, I remembered the multitudes of strange fish which we had seen swimming towards the island; but, which had all disappeared before reaching the shore, and I had no doubt that they entered the pit through some natural passage known to them beneath the water.

These things below us had each two short and stumpy arms; but the ends appeared divided into hateful and wriggling masses of small tentacles, which slid hither and thither as the creatures moved about the bottom of the valley, and at their hind ends, where they should have grown feet, there seemed other flickering bunches; but it must not be supposed that we saw these things clearly.

Now it is scarcely possible to convey the extraordinary disgust which the sight of these human slugs bred in me; were I success-ful, then others would retch even as I did, the spasm coming on without premonition, and born of very horror. And then, sudden-ly, even as I stared, sick with loathing and apprehension, there came into view, not a fathom below my feet, a face like no other face I had seen, even in a nightmare. And it was *indeed* a face from a *dreadful* nightmare. At that, I could have screamed, had I been in less terror; for the great eyes, as big as crown pieces, the bill like an inverted parrot's, and the slug-like undulating of its white and slimy body, bred in me the dumbness of one mortally stricken. And even as I stayed there, my helpless body bent and rigid, the bo'sun spat a mighty curse in my ear, and, leaning forward, smote at the thing with his cutlass; for in the instant that I had been looking at it, it had advanced upward by so much as a yard. Now, at this action of the bo'sun's, I came suddenly into possession of myself, and thrust downward with so much vigour that I nearly followed the brute's carcass; for I overbalanced, and danced giddily for a moment upon the edge of eternity; and then the bo'sun had me by the waistband and I was back in safety; but in that instant through which I had struggled for my balance, I had discovered that the face of the cliff was nearly hidden by the things which were climbing up towards us, and I turned to the bos'un, crying out to him that there were thousands of them. Yet, he was gone already running towards the fire, and shouting to the men in the tent to haste to our help for their very lives, and then he came racing back with a great armful of the weed, and after him came the big seaman, carrying a burning tuft from the camp fire, and so in a few moments we had a blaze, and the men were bringing more weed; for we had a very good stock upon the hill top; for which the Almighty be thanked.

Now, scarce had we lit one fire, when the bo'sun cried out to the big seaman to make another, further along the edge of the cliff, and, in the same instant, I shouted, and ran over to that part of the hill which lay towards the open sea; for I had seen a number of moving things about the edge of the seaward cliff. Now here there was a deal of shadow; for there were scattered certain large masses of rock about this part of the hill, and these held off both the light of the moon, and that from the fires. Here, I came abruptly upon three great shapes stealthily crawling towards the camp, and, behind these, I saw dimly that there were others. Then, with a loud cry for help, I made at the three, and, as I charged, they rose up on end at me, and I found that they overtopped me, and their vile tentacles were reaching out at me. Then I was smiting, and gasping, sick with the sudden stench of the creatures. And then something clutched at me, something slimy and vile, and great mandibles champed in my face; but I stabbed upward, and the thing fell from me, leaving me dazed and sick, and smiting weakly. Then there came a rush of feet behind, and a sudden blaze, and the bo'sun crying out encouragement, and, directly, he and the big seaman thrust themselves in front of me, hurling from them great masses of burning weed, which they had borne upon a long reed. And immediately the things were gone, slithering hastily down over the cliff edge.

And so, presently, I was more my own man, and made to wipe from my throat the slime left by the clutch of the monster; and afterwards I ran from fire to fire with weed, feeding them, and so a space passed, during which we had safety; for by that time we had fires all about the top of the hill, and the monsters were in mortal dread of fire, else had we been dead, all of us, that night.

Now, a while before the dawn, we discovered, for the second time since we had been upon the island, that our fuel could not last us the night at the rate at which we were compelled to burn it, and so the bo'sun told the men to let out every second fire, and thus we staved off for a while the time when we should have to face a spell of darkness, and the things which, at present, the fires held off from us. And so at last, we came to the end of the weed and the reeds, and the bo'sun called out to us to watch the cliff edges very carefully, and smite on the instant that anything showed; but that, should he call, all were to gather by the central fire for a last stand. And, after that, he cursed the moon which had passed behind a great bank of cloud. And thus matters were, and the gloom deepened as the fires sank lower and lower. Then I heard a man curse, on that part of the hill which lay towards the weed-continent, his cry coming up to me against the wind, and the bo'sun shouted to us all to have a care, and directly afterwards I smote at something that rose silently above the edge of the cliff opposite to where I watched.

Perhaps a minute passed, and then there came shouts from all parts of the hill top, and I knew that the weed men were upon us, and in the same instant there came two above the edge near me, rising with a ghostly quietness, yet moving lithely. Now the first I pierced somewhere in the throat, and it fell backwards; but the second, though I thrust it through, caught my blade with a bunch of its tentacles, and was like to have snatched it from me; but that I kicked it in the face, and at that, being, I believe, more astonished than hurt, it loosed my sword, and immediately fell away out of sight. Now this had taken, in all, no more than some ten seconds; yet already I perceived so many as four others coming into view a little to my right, and at that it seemed to me that our deaths must be very near, for I knew not how we were to cope with the creatures, coming as they were so boldly and with such rapidity. Yet, I hesitated not, but ran at them, and now I thrust not; but cut at their faces, and found this to be very effectual; for in this wise I disposed of three in as many strokes; but the fourth had come right over the cliff edge, and rose up at me upon its hind parts, as had done those others when the bo'sun had suc- coured me. At that, I gave way, having a very lively dread; but, hearing all about me the cries of conflict, and knowing that I could expect no help, I made at the brute: then as it stooped and reached out one of its bunches of tentacles, I sprang back, and slashed at them, and immediately I followed this up by a thrust in the stomach, and at that it collapsed into a writhing white ball, that rolled this way and that, and so, in its agony, coming to the edge of the cliff, it fell over, and I was left, sick and near helpless with the hateful stench of the brutes.

Now by this time all the fires about the edges of the hill were sunken into dull glowing mounds of embers; though that which burnt near to the entrance of the tent was still of a good brightness; yet this helped us but little, for we fought too far beyond the immediate circle of its beams to have benefit of it. And still the moon, at which now I threw a despairing glance, was no more than a ghostly shape behind the great bank of cloud which was passing over it. Then, even as I looked upwards, glancing over my left shoulder, I saw, with a sudden horror, that something had come up behind me, and upon the instant, I caught the reek of the thing, and leapt fearfully to one side, turning as I sprang. Thus was I saved in the very moment of my destruction; for the creature's tentacles smeared the back of my neck as I leapt, and then I had smitten, once and again, and conquered.

Immediately after this, I saw something crossing the dark space that lay between the dull mound of the nearest fire, and that which lay further along the hill top, and so, wasting no moment of time, I ran towards the thing, and cut it twice across the head before ever it could get upon its hind parts, in which position I had learned greatly to dread them. Yet, no sooner had I slain this one, than there came a rush of maybe a dozen upon me; these having climbed silently over the cliff edge in the meanwhile. At this, I dodged, and ran madly towards the glowing mound of the nearest fire, and the brutes followed me almost so quick as I could run; but I came to the fire first, and then, a sudden thought coming to me, I thrust the point of my sword among the embers and threw a great shower of them at the creatures, and at that I had a momentary clear vision of many white hideous faces stretched out towards me, and brown, champing mandibles which had the upper beak shutting into the lower; and the clumped, wriggling tentacles were all a-flutter. Then the gloom came again; but immediately, I threw another and yet another shower of the burning embers towards them, and so, directly, I saw them give back, and then they were gone. At this, all about the edges of the hill top, I saw the fires being scattered in a like manner; for the others had adopted this device to help them in their sore straits.

For a little after this, I had a short breathing space, the brutes seeming to have taken fright; yet I was full of trembling, and I glanced hither and thither, not knowing when one or more of them would come upon me. And ever I glanced towards the moon, and prayed the Almighty that the clouds would pass quickly, else should we all be dead men; and then, as I prayed, there suddenly rose a terrible scream from one of the men, and in the same moment there came something over the edge of the cliff fronting me; but I cleft it before it could rise higher, and in my ears there echoed still the sudden scream which had come from that part of the hill which lay to the left of me: yet I dared not to leave my station; for to have done so would have been to have risked all, and so I stayed, tortured by the strain of ignorance, and my own terror.

Again, I had a little spell in which I was free from molestation; nothing coming into sight so far as I could see to right or left of me; though others were less fortunate, as the curses and sounds of blows told me, and then, abruptly, there came another cry of pain, and I looked up again to the moon, and prayed aloud that it might come out to show some light before we were all destroyed; but it remained hid. Then a sudden thought came into my brain, and I shouted at the top of my voice to the bo'sun to set the great cross-bow upon the central fire; for thus we should have a big blaze—the wood being very nice and dry. Twice I shouted to him, saying:—'Burn the bow! Burn the bow!' And immediately he replied, shouting to all the men to run to him and carry it to the fire; and this we did, and bore it to the centre fire, and then ran back with all speed to our places. Thus, in a minute we had some light, and the light grew as the fire took hold of the great log, the wind fanning it to a blaze. And so I faced outwards, looking to see if any vile faces showed above the edge before me, or to my right or left. Yet, I saw nothing, save, as it seemed to me, once a fluttering tentacle came up, a little to my right; but nothing else for a space.

Perhaps it was near five minutes later, that there came another attack, and, in this, I came near to losing my life, through my folly in venturing too near to the edge of the cliff; for, suddenly, there shot up out from the darkness below, a clump of tentacles, and caught me about the left ankle, and immediately I was pulled to a sitting posture, so that both my feet were over the edge of the precipice, and it was only by the mercy of God that I did not plunge head foremost into the valley. Yet, as it was, I suffered a mighty peril; for the brute that had my foot, put a vast strain upon it, trying to pull me down; but I resisted, using my hands and seat to sustain me, and so, discovering that it could not compass my end in this wise, it slacked somewhat of the stress, and bit at my boot, shearing through the hard leather, and nigh destroying my small toe; but now, being no longer compelled to use both hands to retain my position, I slashed down with a great fury, being maddened by the pain and the mortal fear which the creature had put upon me; yet I was not immediately free of the brute; for it caught my sword-blade; but I snatched it away before it could take a proper hold, cutting its feelers somewhat thereby; though of this I cannot be sure, for they seemed not to grip round the thing, but to *suck* to it; then, in a moment, by a lucky blow, I maimed it, so that it loosed me, and I was able to get back into some condition of security.

And from this onwards, we were free from molestation; though we had no knowledge but that the quietness of the weed men did but portend a fresh attack, and so, at last, it came to the dawn; and in all this time the moon came not to our help, being quite hid by the clouds which now covered the whole arc of the sky, making the dawn of a very desolate aspect.

And so soon as there was a sufficiency of light, we examined the valley; but there were nowhere any of the weed men, no! not even any of their dead; for it seemed that they had carried off all such and their wounded, and so we had no opportunity to make an examination of the monsters by daylight. Yet, though we could not come upon their dead, all about the edges of the cliffs was blood and slime, and from the latter there came ever the hideous stench which marked the brutes; but from this we suffered little, the wind carrying it far away to leeward, and filling our lungs with sweet and wholesome air.

Presently, seeing that the danger was past, the bo'sun called us to the centre fire, on which burnt still the remnants of the great bow, and here we discovered for the first time that one of the men was gone from us. At that, we made search about the hill top, and afterwards in the valley and about the island; but found him not.

Though the bow was destroyed in the fire, the men from the 'Glen Carrig' eventually made contact with the ship and, together with those on board, sailed for home.

Eyes For The Blind

by

FREDERICK COWLES

The early death of Frederick Cowles (1900–1948) cut short a career which had included lecturer, librarian, traveller, antiquarian, bibliophile and prize winning author. Folklore was one of his specialities and his published works on the subject include The Fairy Isle *(1935)* and Romany Wonder Tales *(1935).*

Another of his specialities was ghost stories and here he has been surprisingly neglected by anthologists for over thirty years. His two collections of ghost stories The Horror of Abbot's Grange *(1936) and* The Night Wind Howls *(1938) contain some very good tales, whose neglect is completely unwarranted. I have taken 'Eyes For The Blind' from his first collection. He touches here on a uniquely horrible subject that will strike a chilling chord with everyone.*

The situation in the story between Doctor Taylor and Father Placid is taken from life. Frederick Cowles was very friendly with an old Benedictine monk and they used to discuss hauntings and ghosts. They once went to a reputed haunted house where footsteps were heard on a staircase—where nobody could be seen! In his travels around the country Cowles used to pick up stories of hauntings and would often visit supposed haunted houses. It is such a background of research and knowledge that gave his stories their authentic ring. Like so many writers, he was a great admirer of M. R. James. However, while this story gives a brief nod in the direction of James, it has its own brand of terror.

'What I can never understand about your Church,' said Doctor Taylor, 'is the manner in which it so uncompromisingly condemns spiritualism. I will grant you that there is a lot of quackery about the average spiritualistic séance, but I do think that some of the results prove that there is something in the serious study of the subject.'

'Then you would have the Church risk immortal souls for the sake of the grain of truth there may be in what, you yourself admit, is a tissue of trickery?' replied the Bishop.

'Not at all,' answered the doctor. 'What I object to is a wholesale condemnation of the researches of many people who are inspired by the highest motives. You cannot say there is nothing in spiritualism when it has been definitely proved that some kind of manifestations have been witnessed in circumstances that preclude trickery.'

'The Church does not deny such manifestations, but she does declare that the spirits of the just are in the hands of God and cannot be raised at the whim of any neurotic medium at a séance. Those who have studied the subject (and there are many who have) agree that certain evil spirits can assume appearances to suit their purpose when souls are to be ensnared. For example: a man who hears his dead mother speaking to him at a séance is really being deceived by an evil spirit who is able to imitate the mother's voice.'

'A very thin argument, my lord, if I may say so. What about ghosts that haunt old castles or ruined abbeys?'

'I have never seen any,' smiled the Bishop, 'and if there are such things I should think they are really thought forms associated with the place. But the haunting of such houses is something apart from spiritualism. In that case the things are actually there and are seen, or are said to be seen, without the assistance of mediumistic agency. In spiritualism the ghosts are raised through a medium—there must be a human agent in the matter. The raising of spirits in this way is such a severe strain upon the medium that many of these people have been known to go mad.'

'I will not deny that, but what drives them mad? Has it ever been proved that the evil spirits, which you say appear at séances, have actually taken possession of the faculties of a medium?'

'I think I can answer that question, my lord, if you will give me permission,' interpolated Father Placid. 'Perhaps the doctor may be interested in the tale of Sydney Jackson.'

'Of course,' answered the Bishop. 'I had forgotten that case and, as you had the handling of it, you should certainly know all the facts.'

The little Benedictine lit his pipe and puffed away at it for a few moments. Then he began his story.

'It was nearly twenty years ago that Sydney Jackson first came to see me. He was then a boy of nineteen and wished to be received into the Church. He struck me as being the ideal type of convert—serious and keen to know all the facts before he made his final decision. I remember that I was particularly impressed by his frank blue eyes, and his delicate, artistic hands.

'I instructed him for over three months and then he suddenly stopped coming to me. Naturally I wrote to inquire what had happened, and he replied saying he had decided against joining the Church as he had been convinced of the truth of spiritualism.

'I discovered that he had been brought into contact with Austin Lloyd, who, you may remember, was a famous medium just before the War. Lloyd had persuaded the youth that he possessed mediumistic powers, and the next thing I heard of Sydney was that he was giving séances in Mayfair. I wrote and warned him of the dangers he was courting, but received no reply to my letter. Then war was declared and he joined the forces. Lloyd was killed at Mons, but Sydney came safely through and was the head of some spiritualistic church in London in 1919.

'In 1921 I was appointed chaplain to the prison at ——. The Governor was a Catholic and he and I became very friendly. One day he called me into his office and said, "Father, we have a very curious case coming in tomorrow. Have you ever heard of John Dangerfield?"

'I shuddered. Who had not heard of John Dangerfield? This monster had been convicted of the most vile crimes. His mania was to attack unsuspecting persons, often children, and gouge out their eyes. He had blinded five people in this manner, three of his victims being little children. He was also suspected of attacking quite a number of others. He had been proved guilty of these revolting crimes, but sentence had been suspended as there were doubts regarding his sanity.

' "I see you know of him," went on the Governor. "Well, he is coming here tomorrow, and the doctor is going to have a lively time trying to discover whether he is sane or not. According to the report it seems to be a case of dual identity. At times the man is a low, gross villain answering to the name of Dangerfield. At others he is a very bewildered gentleman who claims to be Sydney Jackson."

'I must have given a start of surprise, which the Governor noticed, and I had to tell him that I had once known a Sidney Jackson.

' "Perhaps it is the same man," he said. "Many people have come forward to swear that he is Jackson, a well-known spiritualistic medium, and not Dangerfield at all. Yet, when the witnesses declare him to be Jackson, he vows that he is Dangerfield. Clearly the man is insane and I don't know why he should be sent here at all."

'The Governor willingly gave me permission to see the prisoner as soon as he arrived, and the following afternoon one of the warders conducted me to Dangerfield's cell.

'One glance was enough. It was Sydney Jackson, but the eyes and hands seemed to be those of another man. Instead of the well-remembered blue eyes and thin delicate hands, this man's eyes were greenish-brown in colour and his hands were coarse and ugly. Yet he was certainly Sydney Jackson.

' "Do you remember me, Sydney Jackson?" I asked.

'He jumped to his feet with an oath, and, mouthing many foul curses and blasphemies, declared that his name was John Dangerfield. Undoubtedly he was quite mad, and the warder led me quickly out of the cell. We looked back through the grille. The man was still shouting curses, and those cruel hands were clawing the air as if the fingers were itching to tear something to pieces.

'The next morning I heard that he had actually attacked one of the warders and endeavoured to push his fingers into the poor chap's eyes. Within two days he was removed to one of the criminal lunatic asylums.

'The case rather preyed upon my nerves and I could not dismiss it from my mind. With my superior's permission I travelled up to London and visited the spiritualistic church where Sydney Jackson had officiated. The man in charge was suspicious of me at first, but when I told him the reason for my coming he was more communicative. He told me that Jackson had been approached, some twelve months before that date, by the owner of some property in Scotland, who had invited him to conduct a séance in a haunted castle. Jackson had gone to Scotland, and it was after his return that the change in him had become evident. My informant gave me the name of the place in Scotland and I went north on the following day.

'Ecclefain is off the beaten track and I had to hire a car to take me there from Fort William. I found a tiny village with a grim old castle on the moors above. I was told that the castle was deserted but the laird lived in a house about a mile from the village.

'He turned out to be a dour old fellow and not at all friendly. I asked him if he had been Sydney Jackson's host about a year ago. He admitted that he had, and I could see that he was mortally afraid of something.

' "Would you like to tell me about it?" I asked. "Jackson is now in a criminal lunatic asylum, and declares that he is really John Dangerfield."

' "John Dangerfield," he exclaimed. "Oh, God! Has it come to that?"

' " Now tell me the meaning of it all," I suggested.

' "It was no fault of mine," the man groaned. "I would never have asked him if I had even guessed at the consequences. I only wanted a chance to rid the old castle of its ghost. Three generations ago my family had to abandon it, and it's a poor thing when the laird of Ecclefain has to live in a pigsty like this whilst his own house is given over to a ghost."

'I agreed that it was, and he went on to tell me the story of the haunting and the attempted séance. I cannot imitate his broad Scots dialect so shall have to tell the tale in plain English.

'It seems that about 1694 the district around Ecclefain had been terrorized by a wizard. This man had practised black magic in an attempt to discover hidden treasure, and human eyes had figured largely in his experiments. To obtain these he had gouged the eyes out of little children, and had even gone to graveyards and taken the eyes from newly-buried corpses. At last the district had risen against him and he had been haled before the laird. With primitive justice the laird had directed that the wizard's eyes be burned out of their sockets, and the man then thrown from the top of the castle tower. This sentence had been carried out to the letter. The name of the wizard, as you may have guessed, was John Dangerfield.

'From that day the castle was haunted by the ghost of a man without eyes—a ghost that endeavoured to scratch the eyes out of any human being who crossed its path. Things were brought to a head when the infant son of the reigning laird, some time in the eighteenth century, had been found dead with his eyes torn from their sockets. From that day the castle had been abandoned.

'By chance the present laird had heard of Sydney Jackson, and in a rash moment had invited him to Scotland hoping that, in some way, he could discover how to lay the ghost. Jackson had decided to spend a night in the haunted castle. He left Ecclefain the next morning without saying a word to anyone.

'I returned to my monastery convinced that, instead of laying the ghost of John Dangerfield, Sydney Jackson had become possessed by the evil spirit of the wizard. For over two months I grappled with the problem, and then, one morning, there came a telephone call from my friend the Prison Governor asking if I could go over to the —— Criminal Lunatic Asylum at once, and see the man who called himself John Dangerfield.

'The asylum is about fourteen miles from the abbey, but I soon covered the distance on my motor-bike. A doctor was there to meet me and he told me all the facts of the case. After two months of continual madness Jackson had suddenly become quiet, and had answered to his own name. That very morning he had asked the authorities to get into touch with me and to say it was a matter of life and death.

'The doctor took me along to the cell where Jackson was confined. The blaspheming wretch I had interviewed two months before had changed into a cultured gentleman. Blue eyes looked into mine, and the hands were the delicate, white hands I used to admire so long ago.

'He greeted me eagerly. "Father," he exclaimed, "it is good of you to have come. Please keep him away from me. If he comes back I shall be doomed for ever. If only I had taken your advice and had nothing to do with spiritualism!"

'We talked for some time, and it was obvious that he knew little of what had happened whilst he had acted as John Dangerfield. He expressed his desire to be received into the Church and I agreed to perform the ceremony that evening and to bring him the Blessed Sacrament in the morning.

'He hated my leaving him, but I had to return to the monastery for the necessary things. I was only away for a few hours and fortunately he was still the same when I got back. I gave him a short instruction, went through the order of reception, administered conditional Baptism, and heard his confession. Dusk had already fallen by then and only a dim light filtered in from the corridor. Suddenly, as he was kneeling before me, I noticed a shadow on the wall. It was the silhouette of a bearded man, and he seemed to be creeping nearer and nearer to Jackson. The poor fellow noticed the shadow almost as soon as I did.

' "Save me from him, Father," he screamed. "He will not let me go."

'Even as I looked it seemed that a second pair of hands were forming over Jackson's. I lifted the crucifix and cried out, "In the Name of the Father and of the Son and of the Holy Ghost, I bid you return to the place from whence you have come." As I uttered the words I was hurled across the cell by a powerful hand, and I distinctly saw two green eyes look balefully into mine. But I had won. Jackson was sobbing gently, but he was still Jackson, and the confession was finished without further incident.

'In the morning I rode over with the Blessed Sacrament and was relieved to hear that Jackson had passed a quiet night. He knelt reverently to receive the Host, but, just as I was about to place it on his tongue, a hand gripped my wrist and held it back. I managed to make the sign of the Cross with the Holy Sacrament and, as I did so, my wrist was set free from the grip and a most unholy howl echoed through the cell. But I, through the grace of God, had won. I knew it with absolute certainty and I also knew that the foul thing from the grave could never approach Sydney Jackson again.

'And what happened to Jackson after he had been restored to his normal self?' asked the doctor.

'The asylum authorities kept a very careful eye upon him and, after three years, he was released. He is now a lay-brother in a community of enclosed monks in the Austrian Tyrol.'

'An astounding story,' exclaimed the doctor, 'and it only goes to prove the existence of such things as disembodied spirits.'

'Ah, yes!' said the Bishop quietly, 'but I think you will agree that it also proves the wisdom of the Church in refusing to allow her children to dabble in the thing called spiritualism.'

'I think it does,' the doctor agreed.

Mr Ash's Studio

by

H. R. WAKEFIELD

H. R. Wakefield (1889–1964) needs no introduction to ghost story enthusiasts. His classic tales have made him known to macabre readers the world over, in large part due to the efforts of the late August Derleth, who dutifully published Wakefield stories when the rest of the world seemed to have forgotten him. Wakefield published six collections in Britain and another in America, as well as novels and studies in criminology.

Wakefield was on occasion capable of surprising changes in style. His experiences in Europe in World War I gave him the background for 'Day-Dream in Macedon', one of his best and most under-rated tales. Publishing experience helped him with tales like 'The Last To Leave' and 'And He Shall Sing'. And in 'Corporal Humpit of the 4th Musketeers' he had some surprisingly ironic comments to make on war.

But it was his tales of terror that made his name and of these 'Mr Ash's Studio' is one of the best, yet least known. It was included in a compendium volume of his tales, Ghost Stories *published in 1932 and is a nice tale of witchcraft.*

It was the return of the road-breaking battalion with their accursed compressed-air drills which made Mr Horrocks's greying hairs bristle with determination. He could oathfully endure the foul orchestra of horns and gears, the cacophony of canned dance music; even the piano pounding of the infernal brat in the flat below. But at the first renewal of that quivering, booming patter from East Street he knew something must be done if he was to finish his novel. 'Why not take a studio while you're looking for another flat?' said a friend in the club. He picked up a copy of the *Connoisseur*. 'Here you are. "Within ten minutes' walk of Knightsbridge Tube Station, roomy, out-door studio. Very quiet. Easy terms.'' Why not have a look at that? There are heaps of others vacant if it doesn't suit you.'

Very occasionally, about twice a year, Mr Horrocks acted with extreme decision. Within ten minutes he was on his way to the agents. He was a small, sturdy, thrusting little person of forty-six. He had a long head, rather flat along the top, the hair at the sides brushed forward which gave him a slightly old-fashioned appearance. His eyes were very quick and dark, mouth small and mobile, chin pointed but emphatic. He made a rather contradictory impression on the discerning beholder, alert but contemplative, irascible but benign. He regarded censors, kill-joys, puritans and that sort with an unbridled loathing in theory—but if he came in actual contact with one of them he was—in practice —courteous, understanding, reasonable, inquisitive; the true novelist's mind being inevitably timeserving.

'Anyone in Rooper's Court will direct you,' said the agent, handing him a key. 'Ask for Mr Ash's studio.'

'Thank you,' replied Mr Horrocks and trotted off. Keeping a wary eye open, he eventually discovered Rooper's Court, which began in a narrow arched passage-way off the Brompton Road and developed into what had been known in his youth as a 'Mews'. Now it was a series of lock-up garages and an occasional small private house—re-built coachmen's quarters. There were many chauffeurs sluicing and attending to their charges. Mr Horrocks, looking round for a guide, caught sight of a tall young man standing at the door of a charming little yellow house with gay blue window boxes. Mr Horrocks went up to him and put his question.

'Certainly,' he replied in a pleasant, genial way. 'Come with me.' He conducted Mr Horrocks to an opening on the right-hand side round a corner where was a small square railed-in grass space. At the far end was a rather high hut with a corrugated iron roof, over which leaned a plane tree with many drooping branches.

'That's the studio,' said the tall young man, 'the door is up the other end.'

'Thanks very much,' said Mr Horrocks. 'It looks nice and quiet.'

The young man seemed to be considering something. 'Are you a painter?' he asked presently.

'No,' replied Mr Horrocks. 'I try to write, my name is Samuel Horrocks; but I don't suppose you've ever heard of it.'

'Of course I have. And may I say I greatly admire your stories of the supernatural. May I ask how you were put on to this studio?'

'Oh, I just happened to see it advertised.'

The young man remained thoughtful for a moment. Then he appeared to make up his mind. 'Well,' he said, 'I hope you'll find it all right for your purposes. My name is Landen and I live in that little yellow house. If I can be of any service to you, let me know.' Mr Horrocks thanked him and they said good-bye.

'Very courteous young fellow,' thought Mr Horrocks as he stepped forward; 'looks highly intelligent, too, but I wonder what service he thought he could render me?' Ah, there was the door. He pushed the key in the lock. He had to use some force to open the door as it was jammed from damp, he supposed, at the bottom and sides. He found himself in a room surprisingly more spacious than its exterior suggested. There appeared to be two rooms, as a matter of fact, for there was another door at the far end. The place was lit by three high windows. It smelled rather fusty and there were patches of damp on the distempered walls. Ah, there was an easel with a picture on it and a couple of rather dilapidated chairs. He'd see what was behind the other door. It *was* another room, quite a small one, full of odds and ends, packing cases, an oil stove, a kettle and so on. What a peculiar smell! What was that red stain on the small packing case? He bent down. Good heavens it was alive, a cluster of moths. How very curious! Beautiful colour. They must be feeding on something. He put out his hand to disturb them when suddenly they all sprang up at his face. Little brutes! He lashed out at them and beat a hasty retreat, shutting the door behind him. Venomous little beasts! Well, what about this studio? He wasn't greatly taken with it, but it was most certainly quiet. Mr Horrocks was a shop-assistant's glad-dream, for he almost invariably took the first thing offered him and hurried out of the shop. The last thing he wanted was to go hunting about, fussing with agents and keys, and asking his way and that sort of thing. He wanted a place to work in and he wanted it at once. This would surely do. Not in the winter, perhaps, but with the summer coming on—Why not in the winter? Mr Horrocks vaguely considered this proviso. Too damp, perhaps, and also—well there was something rather—rather sombre about it. It was the contrast, no doubt, between its aloofness, quietness and isolation and the raging stress and promiscuous din only a hundred yards away. Something like that.

Oh yes, it would do. He'd get a desk in and a stove for the damp, and just exploit that aloofness and quiet. That was settled. He strolled over to the easel. Portrait of a woman. Good-looking girl—in a way very beautiful, and yet there was something about her expression—something enigmatic. Wonder who this fellow Ash was. Ah, there were his palette and brushes on the floor behind the easel. Curious smudged, rainbow thing, a palette. It was rather humiliating, but he hadn't really the smallest knowledge of the way a painter went to work. However, he'd never pretended otherwise. How loud his footsteps sounded on the wood floor! Showed how quiet it was. Before leaving he peeped through the door into the small room. Yes, there they were back again, forming a sort of pattern—wonderful patch of colour, dark ruby. Little brutes seemed to be staring at him. He laughed out loud. What an echo! He must get some lunch. He'd take the studio that afternoon for a month. That was settled and a great relief. As he caught hold of the door on getting outside, it seemed to swing hard at him of its own momentum and it slammed harshly, thrusting him back. He was a little ruffled. Not exactly a hospitable atmosphere about that place, he thought.

The tall young man was still standing outside the yellow house as he repassed up the court. 'Well?' he asked.

'I've decided to take it,' said Mr Horrocks. 'It's not, perhaps, a very cheerful spot, but its quietness decided me.'

The young man nodded. 'Are you taking it for long?'

'No, just by the month.'

'I see. Well, good luck with the book—I hope you'll give us some more ghost stories soon.'

'It's rather difficult to get plots for them,' replied Mr Horrocks, 'but I'll do my best. Good-morning.'

Three days later he revisited the studio, which now housed a desk, a couple of comfortable chairs and his portable typewriter. It was a brilliantly fine May morning and the place seemed a bit more genial, but not really very much, he considered. However, now for work. He was about a third of the way through his novel and irritatingly uncertain exactly how to develop it. Also he had promised his agent to have a ghost story ready fairly soon for the Christmas number of a magazine which paid very well. But at the moment he hadn't an idea in his head. For the time being he would concentrate on the novel. He sat down at his desk and began to cogitate. His weakness, he knew it well, was a tendency to flippancy. The more he saw and read of the world and its denizens the harder he found it to take them with the proper seriousness. As far as the tale of humanity was concerned he was inclined to laugh at the wrong places, a serious flaw in a novelist! His characters would adopt an unbecoming impishness at critical moments and mock their creator's efforts to control them. It was probably due to the fact that their creator had never succeeded in measuring humanity flatteringly in accordance with the Cosmic Scale. He was, therefore, delighted to find that the atmosphere of Mr Ash's studio was an excellent corrective to this levity. He wrote a whole chapter by lunch time, a very critical chapter, and he knew that it was good. The motley streak was rigidly eliminated from it. With an aching arm but satisfied soul he got up at half past one, yawned, stretched himself and found himself regarding the picture on the easel. Seen by this stronger light it appeared a very vivid piece of work. It almost seemed as if it had been more worked on than when he'd seen it before. Certainly her face was a puzzle. He went up to it and covered first her eyes, then her mouth and chin with his hand in an attempt to discover where the secret of that oddness lay. As a result he decided it was immanent and not to be traced. He'd have a look and see what those little red devils were doing. There they were bunched on the packing case making that same pattern, motionless and intent. Funny pattern, almost like a human face. Vague memories of 'bughunting' at school came back to him. He was very certain that nothing resembling them had ever found its way into his killing bottle. Singular markings on their heads. He bent down, and at once the swarm rose together and flew savagely into his face. He struck out at them. How extraordinary, it seemed impossible to touch one! Artful little dodgers. What a filthy smell they made, nauseating and corrupt. He'd leave them alone in future.

He spent the afternoon at Kew Gardens, in his opinion the most delectable place in the world on a fine spring day. As he strolled about the lawns and threw crumbs to the birds, he sought some inspiration for that infernal ghost story. A reviewer had once credited him with the possession of a 'malignant imagination' for such fiction. At the moment he had a malignant lack of it. All the same the atmosphere of that studio ought to be kinetic. Presently he felt like a rest and sat down on a seat by the rhododendrons. Drowsily he began to daydream. A succession of images elusively patrolled his brain. A girl's head on an easel—a dark stain on a packing case. He found himself examining the studio almost inch by inch, for his visualising power was very highly developed. He scrutinised the girl's face closely and then was jerked back into full consciousness, for it had seemed to him that a brush had fallen on the face and slightly emphasised the line from her left nostril to upper lip. Amusing illusion! Might be an idea for a story there; whole thing taking place in narrator's subconscious. Damned difficult. Well he must be getting home, those —— road-breakers would have knocked off by the time he reached there.

From then on he went to the studio four days a week, always in the morning, sometimes in the afternoon. He invariably approached it with oddly mixed emotions. Never had he known any place more stimulating to his imagination, yet he never felt at home there. The moment he unlocked the door he felt a sense of obscure excitement, which, in fact, began to come over him as soon as he passed into Rooper's Court, and intensified itself until he was actually inside and face to face with the girl on the easel. And as he wrote he often paused and looked up at her. Each time he came to the studio she seemed subtly and indefinably to have changed, developed, become at once more 'realised' yet harder to 'nail down' and analyse. He imagined that was what was meant by learning to 'see' a painting; that like a poem or a piece of music it only revealed its inner, profounder meaning to those who lavished as much care on deciphering it as the artist had in inscribing it. She was very useful, too, for she seemed to have become identified in a way with the chief female character in his novel—'heroine' would have been a somewhat satirical term for that dark-hearted vampire. And how excellently and reassuringly the book was going! For once his publisher's plaintive and oft-repeated blurbed insistence that 'Samuel Horrocks's latest work is also his greatest', showed every evidence of being justified. Certainly it revealed an almost ruthless lack of flippancy. As it moved to its inevitable climax, the shadows darkened and gathered round it. That meant drastically revising the first third of it, a laborious necessity but unescapable.

He left the little room and the moths alone. Their business was none of his, he felt, and somehow they were peculiar to the place. He gathered that Mr Ash, whoever he might be, had felt a keen interest in them, for he discovered a little sketch-book, presumably his, on one of the window ledges. This contained

dozens of preliminary studies for the girl's head, each one decor-
atively framed in moth-clusters. One of them gave him rather a
dubious reaction, for the girl's head was flung hard back from her
shoulders, and there was poured over her face a stream of dark red;
delicately though unmistakably articulated into the couched shape
of moths. What the artist was thinking about when he put his
pencil to work on so morbid a conception Mr Horrocks was at a
loss to understand; yet it fascinated him, and he several times
examined it in a hurried, shamefaced way. All the same, if it hadn't
been someone else's property he was almost certain he would
have torn it into very small pieces.

He spent, perhaps, twenty hours a week in the studio, yet in a
sense he was there for much longer. That was due to his recently
developed tendency to day-dream, reinforced by his abnormal
power of visualisation. This tendency was by no means welcome,
in fact it was decidedly exasperating, for his subconscious, the
breeding-ground, he supposed, of these day-dreams, appeared to
be quite determined that he should be compelled to take an
urgent interest in what occurred at the studio when its tenant
wasn't there. Of course *nothing* went on, and yet the fact remained
that he might be taking a walk or trying to read when all of a
sudden he would find himself, as it were, just inside the studio and
regarding its interior. His view of it was hazy and it appeared
much diminished but it was quite recognisable. He couldn't see
his desk or chairs, but there was the girl's head on the easel, and
there the windows and the door into the little room. And he was
forced to admit there was frequently something else, *someone*, to
be more precise, and that he—yes, it was a man—was moving
about. A tall man with an odd walk, as if he limped. But however
hard he concentrated he could never quite get this person into
focus. The effort to do so often made him sweat and his heart
race, but he simply couldn't get a proper look at this person's
face. Surely he was tall and dark. Who could he be? While he was
still in this fussed state and before he pulled himself together and
called himself a fool, he often felt a violent, crazy impulse to dash
off to Rooper's Court to make quite certain whether there was or
was not someone prowling about the studio. More than once he
could only just rally enough strength of mind to resist this
insensate craving. He reassured himself that this eccentric pre-
occupation with a dingy hut was a symptom of over-work, not
exactly that, perhaps, but excessive absorption in his novel. But

how blessed that all those wavering uncertain currents had coalesced so perfectly into a steady stream. He had to thank the dingy hut for that, and he could see the end in sight.

He met Landen when he was leaving the studio late one afternoon and accepted his invitation to come in for a glass of sherry. The little yellow house was as charming inside as out, fitted and furnished with a nice careless discretion.

'So you really find the place a congenial workshop?' his host enquired on hearing of the progress the book was making.

'Well, it depends on what you mean by that,' replied Mr Horrocks. 'I've certainly written forty thousand words there and, as golfers say, I "don't want them back," but congenial—well, I mustn't be ungrateful—but it's not an adjective I feel appropriate to the place.'

Landen was silent for a moment. 'No,' he said presently, 'I think I understand what you mean.'

'You've been inside it?'

'Oh, yes,' said Landen.

'It's got an atmosphere of its own. Almost, one might say, a personality. There are places like that, I think,'

'Are you clairvoyant in that way? I mean have you had actual experiences of a psychic sort?'

'As a matter of fact, I have,' replied Mr Horrocks, 'quite a number. But as I've found that these experiences were not shared by others, I've kept quiet about them.'

'That is my case also,' said Landen, 'And I've learnt to keep my mouth shut, when to open it results in being regarded as a self-assertive liar. It must be a great relief to you to get them out of your system in the form of fiction. Are you writing a story now?'

Mr Horrocks shrugged his shoulders. 'I'm not sure,' he said, 'but I'm inclined to think there *is* one forming itself in my harassed old pate. But I mustn't hurry it or keep pulling it up to have a look, like an impatient fisherman. If it's hooking something I shall feel that unmistakable "bite" when the time comes.'

'That's rather a revealing metaphor,' said Landen. 'I can't write fiction—"think of stories"—myself, I'm an architect, but I understand just what you mean. By the way, I always remember that story of yours, *At the Going Down of The Sun*; I believe the Ray theory of psychic phenomena you hinted at there is the most probable.'

'It was the undoubted evidence for phantoms of the living which gave me the idea,' replied Mr Horrocks, somewhat gratified.

'Yes, quite,' said Landen. 'By the way, you don't work at night in the studio, do you?'

'I haven't so far.'

'Well, I shouldn't. There are some tough characters about this neighbourhood at night. If they saw a light they might pay you a somewhat unceremonious visit.'

'I should, of course, lock the door,' said Mr Horrocks.

'Yes, naturally, but all the same, I shouldn't run any risk.'

At length the day came when Mr Horrocks typed the word FINIS and the date below it, May 29th, and knew that the preceding ninety thousand words represented the best work he'd done in his life; so good and yet so alien to his customary manner both in atmosphere and style that he hardly recognised it as his. Almost, he modestly said to himself, as if he'd been a tiny bit inspired. Tomorrow he'd hand it to his publisher and go straight off to Cornwall for a long rest. And then he'd start hunting for a tolerably quiet flat. So it was good-bye to the studio. Would he be sorry to bid it farewell? Once again he failed to give a decided answer to that question. It had been a most excellent tonic and stimulant to his imagination, yet he *was* a little afraid of it. Yes, better to say the word, there was something about it which ruffled his nerves and no doubt caused that ridiculous yet oppressive day-dreaming. He'd have a last leisurely stroll round it; and a last look at the girl. It really was a most baffling illusion for he could have sworn that the expression on her face had drastically changed. She was still exquisitely beautiful and she'd always looked like one to be wary of, but now she wore an air of mocking, heartless frigidity, a most lovely, perilous vampire, a devil. He had a sudden desire to crash his fist into her face. And then he laughed at himself and said out loud, 'Well, my most adorable but evil one, I shan't see you again. Give my love to Mr Ash and —' He stopped abruptly. He had spoken in a light, bantering tone, but the echo of his words came back to him in a most mournful yet somehow mocking way. He felt a sudden gust of uneasiness and depression and impulsively turned the canvas round. On the back of it he casually noticed some carefully drawn but undecipherable hieroglyphics. And now for a last look at the little red beasts. Yes, there they were, glowing, motionless and obscene, like a stain of blood with a hundred eyes. Supposing he picked up that piece of planking and crashed it down on them. The little devils seemed to read his thoughts, for they sprang up at him and drove him from the room. How they stank! Well, that was that. As he opened the door to leave he took a last look back and then the door swung hard at him—'Runk!'—and slammed to. As he strolled towards his club for lunch his mind turned to the subject of that infernal ghost story he'd got to write. It was beginning to get urgent. Obscurely he felt that the studio was the only possible place in which to conceive of it and write it. Perhaps he'd given it up too soon. What a curse it was! Just as he'd finished a most delicate and exhausting piece of work, he'd got to tackle another. Well he would have *one* day off, he told himself irritably, If his imagination wouldn't let him rest, he'd drown it. The bank rate had been lowered that morning and his business friends at the club, who'd been feeling the over-draft severely, were in the mood for some alcoholic enthusiasm and celebration. Mr Horrocks was reasonably abstemious, but for once he found their spiritual state catching and comforting. Consequently, after a large and cheerful lunch, sherry, hock and a double port, he was more than prepared for a restorative snooze in his favourite chair in the chess-room. It was sweet and dreamless, so he was all the more annoyed, when on awaking he found himself staring, not at the trees in St James's Park, but straight down the length of the studio. And there was that—no he *wouldn't* look. He got up brusquely and went to the bar. He completely mistrusted the *fata Morgana* amenities of alcohol, but his nerves were jangled and something must be done. He did it with discretion. The result was quite unexpected and bizarre, for he began to experience an exalted resolve to visit the studio again that night, and then and there conceive of that accursed short story. He was sure of it. He'd have a good dinner, just enough to keep his optimism untarnished but leave his head fairly clear, and *he'd get that story*. It sounded ludicrous, but he'd had such irrational surges of certainty before and they'd always been justified. He *would* go.

Successfully maintaining his resolution and good hope, he hailed a taxi at ten-thirty and twenty minutes later was at Rooper's Court, feeling rather excited and venturous. Yet the enterprise began to reveal itself rather more starkly in the court than it had in the club smoking-room. It was a boisterous night, the wind veering to the west and stiffening sharply. The weather was breaking, and with much low cloud it was very dark. Rooper's Court appeared desolate and uninviting. Lander seemed to be in, as there was a light in his sitting-room. This reminded Mr Horrocks of his advice about not visiting the studio after dark. Oh well, he could take care of himself. As he turned the corner he took an electric torch from his pocket. That tree made it damned dark. What a wind! Curious sound the branches made on the roof; like stealthy footsteps. Ah, there was the keyhole. Door had stuck as usual. He put his shoulder to it, whereupon it yielded so suddenly that he staggered forward and dropped the torch. Then the door swung back and crashed. Now where was that cursed torch? His hands swept the floor. Ah, there it was. Click, Click. Blast the thing, it wouldn't work now! Yes, just a faint glow. He'd wait a moment till his eyes got used to it. Rather a fool to have come. What was he really doing in this rather dreadful place? How those branches lashed the roof. Yes really rather a dreadful place. What would those moths be doing? Probably just making that pattern and listening to him, their foul little eyes staring and intent. He moved forward cautiously. He could just see his way now. What a daunting suggestion of menace seemed hovering in the place. Well, that was an absurd exaggeration. After all, that was the atmosphere he'd come to absorb. Hullo! what was that? It almost seemed as if the room had become smaller, as if the walls had come crouching in towards him. Ah there was the easel! But he'd turned the girl's face round! Who could have—Good God, the moths were on it! He stood motionless and rigid, his heart beating wildly, for wasn't her head flung back from the shoulders and weren't they crawling, crawling—! And weren't those walls closing in on him, and who was that standing and watching him from the small door? For a moment he felt he could never move again; then he wrenched himself free and began to run for the door. He dropped the torch and with trembling hands groped his way along a wall. Where was the door! Was that it? No! Yes! Yes! As he flung it open it seemed as though a myriad little wings came beating round his eyes. He tore down the path, the door crashing to behind him. As he reached the corner someone approached him. He flinched back. Then a voice said, 'It's all right. This is Landen. You're perfectly safe. Come with me—'

'But how did you know?' cried Mr Horrocks hysterically.

'I heard you shouting,' he replied quietly, 'and guessed the rest.'

Mr Horrocks walked panting by his side to his house and into the sitting-room. There was a tantalus and glasses on the table. 'Sit down,' said Landen, 'and make yourself comfortable while I mix you a drink.'

'It's very good of you,' said Mr Horrocks. 'I'm afraid I quite lost my head but I had rather a shock. I see now I should have taken your advice, but I didn't realise—'

'Perhaps I should have been more explicit,' replied Landen, handing him a glass, 'but as you found the place congenial for your writing I didn't want to prejudice you against it, but it is, of course, well, shall we say highly *impregnated*. You've gone into such matters far more than I, but as you have stated, they remain without convincing explanation.'

'Absolutely so,' replied Mr Horrocks, raising his glass with a still unsteady hand. 'Any tentative suggestions I have made were simply guesswork. There is no theory ever advanced which begins to cover the ground. It was horrible, horrible!'

'I'll give you such facts as I know about that studio,' said Landen, sitting down and lighting a cigarette. 'It was built by a person named Raphael Ash four years ago. His father was a Highland Scot in business at Teheran. There he married a Persian woman of high degree. Their son was brought up in Persia and eventually sent to Oxford. A friend of mine was up at New College with him. He was a very enigmatic character. Outwardly imperturbable and bland, yet keeping himself aloof from college life and somehow forbidding. He was extremely unpopular for some reason, I believe, not unconnected with a certain doubt as to how he spent his plentiful leisure time. The occupants of the other rooms in his corridor thought at times they saw and heard somewhat dubious things. So four enterprising and intoxicated sportsmen broke into his rooms one night. They got rather badly frightened, but would say nothing of their experiences. By a coincidence they all died within a year or so. Ash came under the notice of the college authorities and was sent down by them after a couple of terms; for reasons best known to themselves. Whereupon he built this studio and began to paint. He also fell in love. I may say he inherited a great deal of money. The lady concerned seemed for a time to reciprocate his feelings and she certainly made his money fly. However, someone else desired her and he was just as rich and socially far more eligible. I knew this lady and you have seen a brilliantly clever likeness of her, but no portrait could do her justice. She was exquisitely lovely, an accomplished actress and an utterly amoral, soul-less rogue. Well, she married the other man and went to live with him at his place in Surrey. A few weeks later she met her death. She was seen one afternoon by a gamekeeper running through a wood near the house. He stated at the inquest that she was beating out at something with her hands. He imagined she was being attacked by a swarm of bees and ran after her; but before he could reach her she had fallen over the edge of a quarry. She was dying when he got to her, but still beating out with her hands as if to keep something from her face. Shortly after Ash was shot dead in the small room in the studio—'

'Good God!' exclaimed Mr Horrocks. 'Was it suicide?'

'That was the verdict,' replied Landen slowly. 'The evidence was slightly conflicting. One witness stated that he had heard voices coming from the studio that afternoon, and the medical evidence was slightly indefinite. However, the coroner was satisfied. Well, that's all I know about Mr Ash and his studio—or almost. When I came to live here I discovered it had a certain reputation amongst the frequenters of the court. I wondered why, got the key and went there late one winter evening. And then I no longer wondered. It has had one temporary tenant beside you since Ash died. He gave it up after a few days. I believe it is to be pulled down soon. And now you must have another little drink and I'll join you.'

'Well, just a very small one. There is one other thing; those moths—'

'You will not find their like in the Natural History Museum,' replied Landen. 'Perhaps you might search the world over and never do so; for I once described them to a distinguished Orientalist and he told me that he had never met anyone who had encountered such an insect, but that he'd received obscure hints concerning such creatures, though there was a very general reluctance to refer to them. Once or twice he had succeeded in overcoming this reluctance. He gathered that they were known as "The Servants of Eblis"—in a rough translation. Personally he didn't believe in their existence and was greatly puzzled as to how I'd heard of them. I will tell you something; you and one other are the only persons I've known who could see them.'

'Who could see them?' echoed Mr Horrocks, astonished.

'Yes, I have made some experiments. You and I, in that respect at least are privileged people.'

'And that other?' asked Mr Horrocks, after a pause.

'She is dead,' replied Landen quietly. Mr Horrocks was silent for a while. Presently he said, 'Was Ash very dark and did he limp slightly?'

'Yes,' replied Landen.

Montage of Death

by

ROBERT HAINING

I am very pleased to be able to present a new name in the field of the macabre—Robert Haining. If the surname sounds familiar, it is because his brother Peter is Britain's most prolific anthologist of tales of terror.

Robert Haining (1947—) has followed a different career from that of his brother. After studying at university in England, he went to America in 1970 to do postgraduate study at Northwestern University, Chicago. He regards his interest in horror stories as a reaction to the well-ordered world of the scientist. One of his chief interests is the cinema, which he regards as the best vehicle for horror fantasy. However, his first effort in the field of terror is this admirable short story here published for the first time anywhere.

Robert Haining lists among his favourite authors Edgar Allan Poe and H. P. Lovecraft. Poe can probably be found in 'Montage of Death' if you look hard enough, along with many other authors. What can also be found in this story is a broad streak of originality and a flair for writing horror fiction that bodes well for the future. I am convinced that, by publishing 'Montage of Death', I will be the first of many editors to use a story by Robert Haining.

'It's not that I don't believe in what you call horror, it's just that I don't believe in your interpretation.' My companion sat back in his chair, gazing intently at me, urging me to ask the obvious.

'And what is your interpretation?' I asked.

'I don't believe in these ghost things you talk about—ghouls and the like. Real horror, unimaginable fear, is born in the mind. We are no more than highly complex and highly sensitive computers, because we are no more than our mind—our brain. Upset our brains and our world collapses though outwardly we appear quite normal. Real horror comes to the mentally disturbed—the normal events we sense in the course of a day are to them deformed and distorted. They struggle to rationalise, but this only confuses them more. They become lost in a web of part reality, part unreality. Their judgement becomes shattered as the most ordinary events, like a half-lit room, or a knock on the door take on ghastly significance. They are totally unsure.'

He paused briefly. 'Let me give you an example. Five days ago a struggling young artist hanged himself in a small flat in the East End of London. He was only twenty-five and, from what we can gather, had some talent but less luck. But it was the manner of this death that drew the attention of the police, for not only had he hanged himself, but as he dangled from the rope he had stabbed himself six times with a knife. A blunt, bread knife. The immediate questions were why had he killed himself, and why in so gruesome a manner? I want to read you a letter that he wrote presumably only hours before he took his life. Perhaps it will explain to you why I take the view I do.'

'My name is Gerald Miller. I am an artist. Do not pity me, for death comes as a release to the tormented mind. Even as I write I crave death, but write I must if I am not to be thought of as a coward. I once saw a film where they shot people out of kindness and mercy to relieve the agony after a nuclear explosion. I know that there is a mental agony that is as great. I feel it now, but no one would kill me. They would put me in an asylum but that is no good. My mind is in the deepest hell, for it no longer tells me what I see or feel. Everything changes, nothing is the same for any length of time—perhaps I shall not finish this before my mind is transformed again. We are our minds—they are us. We are not separate from them, our identity is in them. If our mind falters we have no hope.

'I once conceived an idea—perhaps I was mad when I first conceived it, but it seemed real. I would make a statue in wax, and if my own genius was not enough as it seemed not to be, I would purchase waxwork figures that I thought to have some good quality—like a well-shaped hand, or a distinguished head, or a well-modelled leg, and cut that portion off to melt down to use in my statue. I hoped that by doing this I would somehow be inspired by the same muse that inspired that first artist. You think it is silly? I may have been mad to think of it. To say now that I think it was worthwhile may mean that I am still mad. Still I wished to try. Why not? I had no other talent.

'There is not much to tell. I spent weeks searching for such figures. I tried every back street shop I could find. Often I could not buy because it was too expensive. Rarely did I find the genius I sought. But after three months I had acquired twelve waxwork figures all of which possessed some characteristic I admired. Perhaps it was only a flicker—perhaps it wasn't there. But I saw touches of genius in their work which only I had recognised, and would put them together, mould them afresh into a great work of art.'

My companion stopped reading.

'Do you think he was mad then?'

'The idea is rather far fetched, but it was not dissimilar to what all good artists should do—study the work of others better than themselves. But actually to use their material?'

'Yes, that struck me too. Why did he have to use their material? He seemed to be destroying their genius.'

'Read on,' I said.

'So I began to work. Cutting up the figures was harder than I'd thought. In fact it proved incredibly difficult, and sometimes I would have to saw to get through. I spent hours in that dimly lit room downstairs, cutting the limbs and heads and torsos off my favourite waxworks. I worked all night on some occasions. Cutting! Cutting! Cutting!

'It was whilst I was cutting the fifth waxwork that I noticed blood on my hand. I first thought I had cut my hand and not felt it. I wiped it off and continued, surprised, though, to find no cut on my hand. Then more blood. Oh God! I can see it still. My hands were covered in blood, the knife too—and the waxwork. It gushed as if an artery had been cut. I was covered in blood. And all the while I stared at its face. And suddenly all around me, the waxworks I had cut were bleeding too. I leapt up and threw down the knife and rushed from the room. Waxworks bleeding—it couldn't be true. Waxworks can't bleed. I ran upstairs and washed my hands, took off my clothes and burned them. I stood shivering in the middle of the room.

'I cannot remember all that happened that night. I lay on the bed thinking about the waxworks, the blood and the fact they were downstairs. Was it blood or had I suffered an hallucination? Was it a trick of the light? Or was it a trick of a tired mind? I did not ask if it was the trick of a mind slowly going mad. I wandered all next day in the parks of London. I did not know where I went. Somehow I had to face that room again, to see if it was real blood I saw. But whichever it was, I would be left confused and frightened. And so it was not till five days after that terrible night that I ventured back into the room.

'I pushed open the door and let it swing back on its hinges. A scene of utter confusion lay before me. Chairs and tables were lying on the floor—I thought then that I had pushed them over when I had fled. On the floor, too, lay the pieces of waxwork and the knife I had thrown down. But there was no blood. Even now I don't know if I was relieved or not. I was relieved that the horrific was not true, but frightened that what had happened once, might happen again.

'So I continued working. I had to otherwise all my money spent would have been utterly wasted. I worked shorter hours than I had done before that terrible night. I was petrified in case it should happen again. At night I lay on my bed, thinking about it. Was it real? Was it an hallucination? Eventually I began to convince myself that it was all a dream. After all wasn't that the only rational explanation?

'By the middle of March I had composed myself sufficiently to be able to work longer hours, but it meant that I often went for walks in the evening. On one such walk something else happened to break through my blissful disregard. I can remember now, as I turned for home, walking past a graveyard. Through the trees I saw a man shovelling earth into a grave. God knows why, but I opened the graveyard gate and walked in. As I approached he must have heard my footsteps on the gravel for he stopped. He withdrew his spade from the mound of dirt and turned round very slowly. He smiled and said in a quiet voice. "Good evening. What brings you out at such a late hour?" I said nothing but walked towards the grave. I can remember hearing him say, "A man shouldn't look on death." And he kept repeating it. But his voice faded and I moved closer to the edge of the grave and looked in. There was no coffin, only a face appearing through the dirt that had been replaced. I stared at it. Oh God! I fell back and was violently sick on the ground. That face was the face of the waxwork figure that had first bled. And suddenly everything was no more and I was walking along the banks of the Thames near the mud flats. The moon was high and I was alone. I shivered and fell on the mud and looking towards the half moon prayed to God to end this misery.

'I think it must have been two days before I eventually returned home. I can remember staring up at the front door, not sure whether it was my house and even if it was, whether I should go in. But I went in. The waxworks! I moved to the door and threw it open. Lying there were the fragments of the twelve dismembered waxworks. I leant against the door, breathing heavily and my heart pounding, but inwardly relieved. All was normal. Nowhere could I find the head that had startled me earlier, and once again I began to imagine it was all a nightmare. I did not wish to believe it was anything else.

'As the days passed the work proceeded well. The moulds were made and the figure began to take shape. I threw the remnants of the twelve figures somewhere. It is funny but I can't remember where. It only goes to show what I had always thought. . . .'

'He goes off on a long ranting piece about his insanity,' said my companion. 'It is almost illegible and of not much interest. He degrades himself to the limit. Calls himself every obscenity under the sun. It demonstrates the absolute despair he was in and the utter contempt he had for himself.' He continued with the letter.

'But I must return to the narrative, for I have not much time. Nor is there much more to tell. I think if another such incident as I had had with the waxworks, or at the graveyard (which I might add I have never seen since), had occurred again, I would have given up the scheme. But there was not much more to do. I must press on.

'The events of the past two days are painful to me, but I must relate them. They have confirmed my belief either in my personal insanity or a hostile world that is utterly incomprehensible to me. Either way there is no hope for me. It was again, early evening when I came to put the finishing touches to my work. A touch of paint, that was all. Already I had begun to feel the object was a monstrosity rather than a work of art. My idea had failed, but perhaps I had learnt from my mistake. Still it was almost done. I was thirsty so I left the room to make some tea. As I wound my way back through the unending corridors of the house from the kitchen to the workroom, I became uneasy. I began to shiver and so I buttoned my coat. Turning the handle of the workroom door, I noticed a draught coming from underneath it. I paused only briefly. Inside the candle had gone out and as I began to relight it a strange smell overwhelmed me. Like the smell of rotting meat and damp. In the flickering half light of that room was the most incredible creature I have ever seen. It had a human form—but yet was not human. It leered at me—its head slumped forward and a thin smile on its lips—the face I had seen in the grave, the face of the waxwork that had bled. My waxwork had been changed into a savage beast—a creature so horrific I could bear the sight no more. I ran from the room. Either I am mad, or . . .'

'That is the end of the letter. After writing it, as you know, he hanged himself.'

'What do you think he saw?' I asked 'Had his waxwork been changed or was he going mad?'

'I cannot judge,' my companion replied, 'let it suffice to say at this point that when he went downstairs and opened the door he saw the most hideous and monstrous waxwork; but it was undeniably human, it merely lacked artistic merit. It seemed then that the man suffered a terrible hallucination. The slightly eccentric mind had been pushed beyond the limit in a room of flickering candles and the realisation of his own lack of talent.'

'So there is no horror except in the mind.'

'But that is not the end of the story. True, I, too, was content with that explanation except for one small fact. There was no handle on the outside of the door. Do you remember that when he first returned to the room where he had the experience of the waxworks bleeding, he pushed open the door, but when he returned on the last occasion before he saw this "creature" he had to turn a handle? It seemed a small point, and true enough, there was no catch on the door of the place where he discovered the waxwork model. I went to the kitchen through the "maze of corridors" he talked about. But it was no maze—a long passage, but no maze.'

I must have looked particularly eager at this point for he said firmly: 'nor did we discover any secret passages. Only a door to a coal cellar. When we first opened it we were met by utter darkness. We got a lamp and staggered in and immediately were hit by the foulest smell. Our artist described it as the smell of rotting meat and damp. It was that indeed, and bitterly cold. As our lamps played along the walls and floors of the coal cellar, we were met by the most hideous scene of devastation. Dismembered corpses lay across the floor. Blood covered the floor and in one corner, supported by props, was the most hideous and gruesome creature I have ever seen. It was indeed a partly human form but its head was lolled forward and, but for its supports, it would have collapsed to the floor and broken up into the fragments of human body of which it was constructed. A veritable Frankenstein's monster—but utterly dead. The most crude stitching held it together. Around it lay the corpses that had gone together to make up this hideous replica of a human form.'

'Surely he could not have killed these people himself?'

'No, indeed. They were identified and shown to come from various graveyards where they had been lain to rest inside the last three months. His only crime was grave robbing.'

'How can you explain it? A dual personality? A most hideous one. It would be nice to say that while he constructed his waxwork masterpiece, his "other half" robbed graves and took a most hideous vengeance on these corpses who stood for all those critics who had mocked him. Who knows why it happened? The "why?" is not important. That he had two halves to his life and never the twain did meet is obvious. When they did meet they sparked off the insanity that lay in his brain. As reality and reality mixed they created for him an unreality that he could not bear—yet all the time it was real. But both forms of reality were bearable while they did not meet. It is interesting that before the corpses could be re-interred in their graves, from each had to be removed the dismembered remains of a waxwork figure.'

Pallinghurst Barrow

by

GRANT ALLEN

'I shall be amply content to pick up the crumbs that fall from the table of the Hardys, the Kiplings, the Merediths, and the Wellses.' This was how Grant Allen (1848–1899) introduced a collected volume of his stories, published shortly before his early death. It would be nice to relate that history and the reading public allowed Allen to pick up these crumbs; such is not the case. Almost as soon as he died, Allen followed the familiar path to obscurity. I was fortunate in being able to include one of his forgotten tales in my last anthology; I am equally fortunate in being able to present another.

Canadian-born Grant Allen graduated from Oxford and went on to teach, write novels, philosophise, and produce a long string of scientific papers and articles. It was his decision to present a particular scientific argument in a fictional form that led to his being asked for more stories, and paved the way to his eventual publication of several volumes of short stories.

'Pallinghurst Barrow', originally published in the Illustrated London News, *was included in his 1893 collection,* Ivan Greet's Masterpiece, *and has the same theme as the story by Eleanor Scott which follows it—the haunting of a prehistoric burial mound. On the strength of this tale alone, Allen could well have been justified in adding the names of F. Marion Crawford, Robert W. Chambers and Julian Hawthorne to that list of his contemporaries from whose table he hoped to 'pick up the crumbs'.*

I.

Rudolph Reeve sat by himself on the Old Long Barrow on Pallinghurst Common. It was a September evening, and the sun was setting. The west was all aglow with a mysterious red light, very strange and lurid—a light that reflected itself in glowing purple on the dark brown heather and the dying bracken. Rudolph Reeve was a journalist and a man of science; but he had a poet's soul. He sat there long, watching the livid hues that incarnadined the sky—redder and fiercer than anything he ever remembered to have seen since the famous year of the Krakatoa sunsets—though he knew it was getting late, and he ought to have gone back long since to the manor-house to dress for dinner. Mrs Bouverie-Barton, his hostess, was always such a stickler for punctuality and dispatch. But, in spite of Mrs Bouverie-Barton, Rudolph Reeve sat on. There was something about that sunset and the lights on the bracken—something weird and unearthly—that positively fascinated him.

The view over the common, which stands high and exposed, a veritable waste of heath and gorse, is strikingly wide and expansive. Pallinghurst Ring, or the 'Old Long Barrow', a well-known landmark, familiar by that name from time immemorial to all the country-side, crowns its actual summit, and commands from its top the surrounding hills far into the shadowy heart of Hampshire. On its terraced slope Rudolph sat and gazed out, in the exquisite flush of the dying reflections from the dying sun upon the dying heather. He sat and wondered to himself why death is always so much more beautiful, so much more poetical, so much calmer than life.

He was just going to rise, however, dreading the lasting wrath of Mrs Bouverie-Barton, when of a sudden a very weird yet definite feeling caused him for one moment to pause and hesitate. Why he felt it he knew not; but even as he sat there on the grassy tumulus, covered close with short sward of subterranean clover, he was aware, through no external sense, but by pure internal consciousness, of something living and moving within the barrow. He shut his eyes and listened. No; fancy, pure fancy! Not a sound broke the stillness of early evening, save the drone of insects—those dying insects, now beginning to fail fast before the first chill breath of approaching autumn. Rudolph opened his eyes again and looked down on the ground. In the little hollow by his feet innumerable plants of sundew spread their murderous rosettes of sticky red leaves, all bedewed with viscid gum, to catch and roll round the struggling flies that wrenched their tiny limbs in vain efforts to free themselves. But that was all. Nothing else was astir. In spite of sight and sound, however, he was still deeply thrilled by this strange consciousness as of something in the barrow underneath; something living and moving —or was it moving and dead? Something crawling and creeping as the long arms of the sundews crawled and crept around the helpless flies, whose juices they sucked out. A weird and awful feeling, yet strangely fascinating! He hated the vulgar necessity for going back to dinner. Why do people dine at all? So material! so commonplace! And the universe all teeming with strange secrets to unfold! He knew not why, but a fierce desire possessed his soul to stop and give way to this overpowering sense of the mysterious and the marvellous in the dark depths of the barrow.

With an effort he roused himself, and put on his hat, for his forehead was burning. The sun had now long set, and Mrs Bouverie-Barton dined at 7.30 punctually. He must rise and go home. Something unknown pulled him down to detain him. Once more he paused and hesitated. He was not a superstitious man, yet it seemed to him as if many strange shapes stood by unseen, and watched with great eagerness to see whether he would rise and go away, or yield to the temptation of stopping and indulging his curious fancy. Strange!—he saw and heard absolutely nothing; yet he dimly realized that unseen figures were watching him close with bated breath, and anxiously observing his every movement, as if intent to know whether he would rise and move on, or remain to investigate this causeless sensation.

For a minute or two he stood irresolute; and all the time he so stood the unseen bystanders held their breath and looked on in an agony of expectation. He could feel their outstretched necks; he could picture their strained attention. At last he broke away. 'This is nonsense,' he said aloud to himself, and turned slowly homeward. As he did so, a deep sigh, as of suspense relieved, but relieved in the wrong direction, seemed to rise—unheard, impalpable, spiritual—from the invisible crowd that gathered around him immaterial. Clutched hands seemed to stretch after him and try to pull him back. An unreal throng of angry and disappointed creatures seemed to follow him over the moor, uttering speechless imprecations on his head, in some unknown tongue—ineffable, inaudible. This horrid sense of being followed by unearthly foes took absolute possession of Rudolph's mind. It might have been merely the lurid redness of the afterglow, or the loneliness of the moor, or the necessity of being back not one minute late for Mrs Bouverie-Barton's dinner-hour; but, at any rate, he lost all self-control for the moment, and ran—ran wildly, at the very top of his speed, all the way from the barrow to the door of the manor-house garden. There he stopped and looked round with a painful sense of his own stupid cowardice. This was positively childish: he had seen nothing, heard nothing, had nothing definite to frighten him; yet he had run from his own mental shadow, like the veriest schoolgirl, and was trembling still from the profundity of his sense that somebody unseen was pursuing and following him. 'What a precious fool I am,' he said to himself, half angrily, 'to be so terrified at nothing! I'll go back there by-and-by, just to recover my self-respect, and to show myself, at least, I'm not really frightened.'

But even as he said it he was internally aware that his baffled foes, standing grinning their disappointment with gnashed teeth at the garden gate, gave a chuckle of surprise, delight, and satisfaction at his altered intention.

II.

There's nothing like light for dispelling superstitious terrors. Pallinghurst Manor-house was fortunately supplied with electric light; for Mrs Bouverie-Barton was nothing if not intensely modern. Long before Rudolph had finished dressing for dinner, he was smiling once more to himself at his foolish conduct. Never in his life before—at least, since he was twenty—had he done such a thing; and he knew why he'd done it now. It was a nervous breakdown. He had been overworking and Sir Arthur Boyd, the famous specialist on diseases of the nervous system, had recommended him 'a week or two's rest and change in the country'. That was why he had accepted Mrs Bouverie-Barton's invitation to form part of her autumn party at Pallinghurst Manor; and that was also doubtless why he had been so absurdly frightened at nothing at all just now on the common.

He went down to dinner, however, in very good spirits. His hostess was kind; she permitted him to take in that pretty American. Conversation with the soup turned at once on the sunset. 'You were on the barrow about seven, Mr Reeve,' Mrs Bouverie-Barton observed severely, when he spoke of the afterglow. 'You watched that sunset close. How fast you must have walked home! I was almost half afraid you were going to be late for dinner.'

Rudolph coloured slightly. 'Oh dear no, Mrs Bouverie-Barton,' he answered gravely. 'I may be foolish, but not, I hope, criminal. I know better than to do anything so weak and wicked as that at Pallinghurst Manor. I *do* walk rather fast, and the sunset—well, the sunset was just too lovely.'

'Elegant,' the pretty American interposed.

'It always is, this night every year,' little Joyce said quietly, with the air of one who retails a well-known scientific fact. 'It's the night, you know, when the light burns bright on the Old Long Barrow.'

Joyce was Mrs Bouverie-Barton's only child—a frail and pretty little creature, just twelve years old, very light and fairylike, but with a strange cowed look which, nevertheless, somehow curiously became her.

'What nonsense you talk, my child!' her mother exclaimed, darting a look at Joyce which made her relapse forthwith into instant silence. 'I'm ashamed of her, Mr Reeve; they pick up such nonsense as this from their nurses.'

But the child's words, though lightly whispered, had caught the quick ear of Archie Cameron, the distinguished electrician. He made a spring upon them at once; for the merest suspicion of the supernatural was to Cameron irresistible. 'What's that, Joyce?' he cried, leaning forward across the table. 'No, Mrs Bouverie-Barton, I really *must* hear it. What day is this today, and what's that you just said about the sunset and the light on the Old Long Barrow?'

Joyce glanced pleadingly at her mother, and then again at Cameron. A very faint nod gave her grudging leave to proceed with her tale, under maternal disapproval. Joyce hesitated and began. 'Well, this is the night, you know,' she said, 'when the sun turns, or stands still, or crosses the tropic, or goes back again, or something.'

Mrs Bouverie-Barton gave a dry little cough. 'The autumnal equinox,' she interposed severely, 'at which, of course, the sun does nothing of the sort you suppose. We shall have to have your astronomy looked after, Joyce; such ignorance is exhaustive. But go on with your myth, please, and get it over quickly.'

'The autumnal equinox; that's just it,' Joyce went on, unabashed. 'I remember that's the word, for old Rachel, the gipsy, told me so. Well, on this day every year, a sort of glow comes up on the moor; I know it does, for I've seen it myself; and the rhyme about it goes—

"Every year on Michael's night
Pallinghurst Barrow burneth bright."

Only the gipsy told me it was Baal's night before it was St Michael's; and it was somebody else's night, whose name I forget, before it was Baal's. And the somebody was a god to whom you must never sacrifice anything with iron, but always with flint or with a stone hatchet.'

Cameron leaned back in his chair and surveyed the child critically. 'Now, this is interesting.' he said; 'profoundly interesting. For here we get, what is always so much wanted, first-hand evidence. And you're quite sure, Joyce, you've really seen it?'

'Oh! Mr Cameron, how can you!' Mrs Bouverie-Barton cried, 'I take the greatest trouble to keep all such rubbish out of Joyce's way; and then you men of science come down here and talk like this to her, and undo all the good I've taken months in doing.'

'Well, whether Joyce has ever seen it or not,' Rudolph Reeve said gravely, 'I can answer for it myself that I saw a very curious light on the Long Barrow to-night; and, furthermore, I felt a most peculiar sensation.'

'What was that?' Cameron asked, bending over towards him eagerly.

'Why, as I was sitting on the barrow,' Rudolph began, 'just after sunset, I was dimly conscious of something stirring inside, not visible or audible, but——'

'Oh, I know, I know!' Joyce put in, leaning forward with her eyes staring curiously; 'a sort of a feeling that there was somebody somewhere, very faint and dim, though you couldn't see or hear them; they tried to pull you down, clutching at you like this: and when you ran away, frightened, they seemed to follow you and jeer at you. Great gibbering creatures! Oh, I know what all that is! I've been there, and felt it.'

'Joyce!' Mrs Bouverie-Barton put in, with a warning frown, 'what nonsense you talk! You're really too ridiculous. How can you suppose Mr Reeve ran away—a man of science like him—from an imaginary terror?'

'Well, I won't quite say I ran away,' Rudolph answered, somewhat sheepishly. 'We never do admit these things, I suppose, after twenty. But I certainly did hurry home at the very top of my speed—not to be late for dinner, you know, Mrs Bouverie-Barton; and I *will* admit, Joyce, between you and me only, I was conscious all the way of something very much like your grinning followers behind me.'

Mrs Bouverie-Barton darted him another look of intense displeasure. 'I think,' she said, in a chilly voice, 'at a table like this and with such thinkers around, we might surely find something rather better to discuss than such worn out superstitions. Professor Spence, did you light upon any fresh palæoliths in the gravel-pit this morning?'

III.

Later, in the drawing-room, a small group collected by the corner bay, remotest from Mrs Bouverie-Barton's own presidential chair, to hear Rudolph and Joyce compare experiences of the light above the barrow. When the two dreamers of dreams and seers of visions had finished, Mrs Bruce, the esoteric Buddhist, opened the flood-gates of her torrent speech with triumphant vehemence. 'This is just what I should have expected,' she said, looking round for a sceptic, that she might turn and rend him. 'Novalis was right. Children are early men. They are freshest from the truth. They come straight to us from the Infinite. Little souls just let loose from the free expanse of God's sky see more than we adults do—at least, except a few of us. We ourselves, what are we but accumulated layers of phantasmata? Spirit-light rarely breaks in upon our grimed charnel of flesh. The dust of years overlies us. But the child, bursting new upon the dim world of Karma, trails clouds of glory from the beatific vision. So Wordsworth held; so the Masters of Tibet taught us, long ages before Wordsworth.'

'It's curious,' Professor Spence put in, with a scientific smile, restrained at the corners, 'that all this should have happened to Joyce and to our friend Reeve at a long barrow. It has been shown conclusively that long barrows, which are the graves of the small, squat people who preceded the inroad of Aryan invaders, are the real originals of all the fairy hills and subterranean palaces of popular legend. You know the old story of how Childe Roland to the dark tower came, of course. Well, that dark tower was nothing more or less than a long barrow; perhaps Pallinghurst Barrow itself, perhaps some other; and Childe Roland went into it to rescue his sister, Burd Ellen, who had been stolen by the fairy king, after the fashion of his kind, for a human sacrifice. The Picts were a deeply religious people, who believed in human sacrifice. They felt they derived from it high spiritual benefit. And the queerest part of it all is that in order to see the fairies you must go round the barrow *widdershins*—that is the opposite way from the way of the sun—on this very night of all the year, Michaelmas Eve, which was the accepted old date of the autumnal equinox.'

'All long barrows have a chamber of great stones in the centre, I believe,' Cameron suggested tentatively.

'Yes, all or nearly all; megalithic, you know; unwrought; and that chamber's the subterranean palace, lit up with the fairy light that's so constantly found in old stories of the dead, and which Joyce and you, alone among the moderns, have been permitted to see, Reeve.'

'It's a very odd fact,' Dr Porter, the materialist, interposed musingly, 'that the only ghosts people ever see are the ghosts of a generation very very close to them. One hears of lots of ghosts in eighteenth-century costumes. because everybody has a clear idea of wigs and small-clothes from pictures and fancy dresses. One hears of far fewer in Elizabethan dress, because the class most given to beholding ghosts are seldom acquainted with ruffs and farthingales; and one meets with none at all in Anglo-Saxon or Ancient British or Roman costumes, because those are only known to a comparatively small class of learned people; and ghosts, as a rule, avoid the learned—except you, Mrs Bruce—as they would avoid prussic acid. Millions of ghosts of remote antiquity must swarm about the world, though, after a hundred years or thereabouts they retire into obscurity and cease to annoy people with their nasty cold shivers. But the queer thing about these long-barrow ghosts is that they must be the spirits of men and women who died thousands and thousands of years ago, which is exceptional longevity for a spiritual being; don't you think so, Cameron?'

'Europe must be chock-full of them!' the pretty American assented, smiling; 'though America hasn't had time, so far, to collect any considerable population of spirits.'

But Mrs Bruce was up in arms at once against such covert levity, and took the field in full force for her beloved spectres. 'No, no,' she said, 'Dr Porter, there you mistake your subject. Man is the focus of the glass of his own senses. There are other landscapes in the fifth and sixth dimensions of space than the one presented to him. As Carlyle said, each eye sees in all things just what each eye brings with it the power of seeing. And this is true spiritually as well as physically. To Newton and Newton's dog Diamond what a different universe! One saw the great vision of universal gravitation, the other saw—a little mouse under a chair. Nursery rhymes summarise for us the gain of centuries. Nothing was ever destroyed, nothing was ever changed, and nothing new is ever created. All the spirits of all that is, or was, or ever will be people the universe everywhere, unseen, around us; and each of us sees of them those only he himself is adapted to seeing. The rustic or the clown meets no ghosts of any sort save the ghosts of the persons he knows about otherwise; if a man like yourself saw a ghost at all—which isn't likely for you starve your spiritual side by blindly shutting your eyes to one whole aspect of nature— you'd be just as likely to see the ghost of a Stone Age chief as the ghost of a Georgian or Elizabethan.'

'Did I catch the word "ghost"?' Mrs Bouverie-Barton put in, coming up unexpectedly with her angry glower. 'Joyce, my child, go to bed. This is no talk for you. And don't go chilling yourself by standing at the window in your nightdress, looking out on the common to search for the light on the Old Long Barrow, which is all pure moonshine. You nearly caught your death of cold last year with that nonsense. It's always so. These superstitions never do any good to any one.'

And, indeed, Rudolph felt a faint glow of shame himself at having discussed such themes in the hearing of that nervous and high-strung little creature.

IV.

In the course of the evening, Rudolph's head began to ache, as it often did. He knew that headache well; it was the worst neuralgic kind—the wet-towel variety—the sort that keeps you tossing the whole night long without hope of respite. About eleven o'clock, when the men went into the smoking-room, the pain became unendurable. He called Dr Porter aside. 'Can't you give me anything to relieve it?' he asked piteously, after describing his symptoms.

'Oh, certainly,' the doctor answered, with brisk medical confidence. 'I'll bring you up a draught that will put that all right in less than half an hour. What Mrs Bruce calls Soma—the fine old crusted remedy of our Aryan ancestor; there's nothing like it for cases of nervous inanition.'

Rudolph went up to his room, and the doctor followed him a few minutes later with a very small phial of a very thick green viscid liquid. He poured ten drops carefully into a measured medicine-glass, and filled it up with water. It amalgamated badly. 'Drink that off,' he said. Rudolph drank it.

'I'll leave you the bottle,' the doctor went on, laying it down on the dressing-table, 'only use it with caution, Ten drops in two hours if the pain continues. Not more than ten, recollect. It's a powerful narcotic—I dare say you know its name: it's Cannabis Indica.'

Rudolph thanked him inarticulately, and flung himself on the bed without undressing. He had brought up a book with him—that delicious volume, Joseph Jacobs's *English Fairy Tales*—and he tried in some vague way to read the story of Childe Roland, to which Professor Spence had directed his attention. But his head ached so much he could hardly read it; he only gathered with difficulty that Childe Roland had been instructed by witch or warlock to come to a green hill surrounded with terrace-rings—like Pallinghurst Barrow—to walk round it thrice, *widdershins*, saying each time—

> 'Open door! open door!
> And let me come in,'

and when the door opened to enter unabashed the fairy king's palace. And the third time the door did open, and Childe Roland entered a court, all lighted with a fairy light or gloaming; and then he went through a long passage, till he came at last to two wide stone doors; and beyond them lay a hall—stately, glorious, magnificent—where Burd Ellen sat combing her golden hair with a comb of amber. And the moment she saw her brother, up she stood, and she said—

> 'Woe worth the day, ye luckless fool,
> Or ever that ye were born;
> For come the King of Elfland in
> Your fortune is forlorn.'

When Rudolph had read this far his head ached so much he could read no further; so he laid down the book, and reflected once more in some half-conscious mood on Mrs. Bruce's theory that each man could see only the ghosts he expected. That seemed reasonable enough, for according to our faith is it unto us always. If so, then these ancient and savage ghosts of the dim old Stone Age, before bronze or iron, must still haunt the grassy barrows under the waving pines, where legend declared they were long since buried; and the mystic light over Pallinghurst moor must be the local evidence and symbol of their presence.

How long he lay there he hardly quite knew; but the clock

struck twice, and his head was aching so fiercely now that he helped himself plentifully to a second dose of the thick green mixture. His hand shook too much to be puritanical to a drop or two. For a while it relieved him; then the pain grew worse again. Dreamily he moved over to the big north oriel to cool his brow with the fresh night air. The window stood open. As he gazed out a curious sight met his eye. At another oriel in the wing, which ran in an L-shaped bend from the part of the house where he had been put, he saw a child's white face gaze appealingly across to him. It was Joyce, in her white nightdress, peering with all her might, in spite of her mother's prohibition, at the mystic common. For a second she started. Her eyes met his. Slowly she raised one pale forefinger and pointed. Her lips opened to frame an inaudible word; but he read it by sight. 'Look!' she said simply. Rudolph looked where she pointed.

A faint blue light hung lambent over the Old Long Barrow. It was ghostly and vague. It seemed to rouse and call him.

He glanced towards Joyce. She waved her hand to the barrow. Her lips said, 'Go.' Rudolph was now in that strange semi-mesmeric state of self-induced hypnotism when a command, of whatever sort or by whomsoever given, seems to compel obedience. Trembling he rose, and taking his candle descended the stair noiselessly. Then, walking on tiptoe across the tile-paved hall, he reached his hat from the rack, and opening the front door stole out into the garden.

The Soma had steadied his nerves and supplied him with false courage; but even in spite of it he felt a weird and creepy sense of mystery and the supernatural. Indeed, he would have turned back even now, had he not chanced to look up and see Joyce's pale face still pressed close against the window and Joyce's white hand still motioning him mutely onward. He looked once more in the direction where she pointed. The spectral light now burnt clearer and bluer, and more unearthly than ever, and the illimitable moor seemed haunted from end to end by innumerable invisible and uncanny creatures.

Rudolph groped his way on. His goal was the barrow. As he went, speechless voices seemed to whisper unknown tongues encouragingly in his ear; horrible shapes of elder creeds appeared to crowd round him and tempt him with beckoning fingers to follow them. Alone, erect, across the darkling waste, stumbling now and again over roots of gorse and heather, but steadied, as it seemed, by invisible hands, he staggered slowly forward, till at last, with aching head and trembling feet, he stood beside the immemorial grave of the savage chieftain. Away over in the east the white moon was just rising.

After a moment's pause, he began to walk round the tumulus. But something clogged and impeded him. His feet wouldn't obey his will; they seemed to move of themselves in the opposite direction. Then all at once he remembered he had been trying to go the way of the sun, instead of *widdershins*. Steadying himself, and opening his eyes, he walked in the converse sense. All at once his feet moved easily, and the invisible attendants chuckled to themselves so loud that he could almost hear them. After the third round his lips parted, and he murmured the mystic words: 'Open door! Open door! Let me come in.' Then his head throbbed worse than ever with exertion and giddiness, and for two or three minutes he was unconscious of anything.

When he opened his eyes again a very different sight displayed itself before him. Instantly he was aware that the age had gone back upon its steps ten thousand years, as the sun went back upon the dial of Ahaz; he stood face to face with a remote antiquity. Planes of existence faded; new sights floated over him; new worlds were penetrated; new ideas, yet very old, undulated centrically towards him from the universal flat of time and space and matter and motion. He was projected into another sphere and saw by fresh senses. Everything was changed, and he himself changed with it.

The blue light over the barrow now shone clear as day, though infinitely more mysterious. A passage lay open through the grassy slope into a rude stone corridor. Though his curiosity by this time was thoroughly aroused, Rudolph shrank with a terrible shrinking from his own impulse to enter this grim black hole, which led at once, by an oblique descent, into the bowels of the earth. But he couldn't help himself. For, O God! looking round him, he saw, to his infinite terror, alarm, and awe, a ghostly throng of naked and hideous savages. They were spirits, yet savages. Eagerly they jostled and hustled him, and crowded round him in wild groups, exactly as they had done to the spiritual sense a little earlier in the evening, when he couldn't see them. But now he saw them clearly with the outer eye; saw them as grinning and hateful barbarian shadows, neither black nor white, but tawny-skinned and low-browed; their tangled hair falling unkempt in matted locks about their receding foreheads; their jaws large and fierce; their eyebrows shaggy and protruding like a gorilla's; their loins just girt with a few scraps of torn skin; their whole mien inexpressibly repulsive and bloodthirsty.

They were savages, yet they were ghosts. The two most terrible and dreaded foes of civilized experience seemed combined at once in them. Rudolph Reeve crouched powerless in their intangible hands; for they seized him roughly with incorporeal fingers, and pushed him bodily into the presence of their sleeping chieftain. As they did so they raised loud peals of discordant laughter. It was hollow; but it was piercing. In that hateful sound the triumphant whoop of the Red Indian and the weird mockery of the ghost were strangely mingled into some appalling harmony.

Rudolph allowed them to push him in; they were too many to resist; and the Soma had sucked all strength out of his muscles. The women were the worst: ghastly hags of old, witches with pendant breasts and bloodshot eyes, they whirled round him in triumph, and shouted aloud in a tongue he had never before heard, though he understood it instinctively, 'A victim! A victim! We hold him! We have him!'

Even in the agonized horror of that awful moment Rudolph knew why he understood those words, unheard till then. They were the first language of our race—the natural and instinctive mother-tongue of humanity.

They hauled him forward by main force to the central chamber, with hands and arms and ghostly shreds of buffalo-hide. Their wrists compelled him as the magnet compels the iron bar. He entered the palace. A dim phosphorescent light, like the light of a churchyard or of decaying paganism, seemed to illumine it faintly. Things loomed dark before him; but his eyes almost instantly adapted themselves to the gloom, as the eyes of the dead on the first night in the grave adapt themselves by inner force to the strangeness of their surroundings. The royal hall was built up of cyclopean stones, each as big as the head of some colossal Sesostris. They were of ice-worn granite and a dusky grey sandstone, rudely piled on one another, and carved in relief with representations of serpents, concentric lines interlacing zigzags, and the mystic swastika. But all these things Rudolph only saw vaguely, if he saw them at all; his attention was too much concentrated on devouring fear and the horror of his situation.

In the very centre a skeleton sat crouching on the floor in some loose, huddled fashion. Its legs were doubled up, its hands clasped round its knees, its grinning teeth had long been blackened by time or by the indurated blood of human victims. The ghosts approached it with strange reverence, in impish postures.

'See! We bring you a slave, great King!' they cried in the same barbaric tongue—all clicks and gutturals. 'For this is the holy night of your father, the Sun, when he turns him about on his yearly course through the stars and goes south to leave us. We bring you a slave to renew your youth. Rise! Drink his hot blood! Rise! Kill and eat him!'

The grinning skeleton turned its head and regarded Rudolph from its eyeless orbs with a vacant glance of hungry satisfaction. The sight of human meat seemed to create a soul beneath the ribs of death in some incredible fashion. Even as Rudolph, held fast by the immaterial hands of his ghastly captors, looked and trembled for his fate, too terrified to cry out or even to move and struggle, he beheld the hideous thing rise and assume a shadowy shape, all pallid blue light, like the shapes of his jailers. Bit by bit, as he gazed, the skeleton seemed to disappear, or rather to fade into some unsubstantial form, which was nevertheless more human, more corporeal, more horrible than the dry bones it had come from. Naked and yellow like the rest, it wore round its dim waist just an apron of dry grass, or, what seemed to be such, while over its shoulders hung the ghost of a bearskin mantle. As it rose, the other spectres knocked their foreheads low on the ground before it, and grovelled with their long locks in the ageless dust, and uttered elfin cries of inarticulate homage.

The great chief turned, grinning, to one of his spectral henchmen. 'Give a knife!' he said curtly, for all that these strange shades uttered was snapped out in short, sharp sentences, and in a monosyllabic tongue, like the bark of jackals or the laugh of the striped hyena among the graves at midnight.

The attendant, bowing low once more, handed his liege a flint flake, very keen-edged, but jagged, a rude and horrible instrument of barbaric manufacture. But what terrified Rudolph most was the fact that this flake was no ghostly weapon, no immaterial shard, but a fragment of real stone, capable of inflicting a deadly gash or long torn wound. Hundreds of such fragments, indeed, lay loose on the concreted floor of the chamber, some of them roughly chipped, others ground and polished. Rudolph had seen such things in museums many times before; with a sudden rush of horror, he recognized now for the first time in his life for what purpose the savages of that far-off day had buried them with their dead in the chambered barrows.

With a violent effort he wetted his parched lips with his tongue, and cried out thrice in his agony the one word 'Mercy!'

At that sound the savage king burst into a loud and fiendish laugh. It was a hideous laugh, halfway between a wild beast's and a murderous maniac's: it echoed through the long hall like the laughter of devils. 'What does he say?' the king cried, in the same transparently natural words, whose import Rudolph could understand at once. 'How like birds they talk, these white-faced men, whom we get for our only victims since the years grew foolish! "Mu-mu-mu-moo!" they say; "Mu-mu-mu-moo!" more like frogs than men and women!'

Then it came over Rudolph instinctively, through the maze of his terror, that he could understand the lower tongue of these elfin visions because he and his ancestors had once passed through it; but they could not understand his, because it was too high and too deep for them.

He had little time for thought, however. Fear bounded his horizon. The ghosts crowded round him, gibbering louder than before. With wild cries and heathen screams they began to dance about their victim. Two advanced with measured steps and tied his hands and feet with a ghostly cord. It cut into the flesh like the stab of a great sorrow. They bound him to a stake which Rudolph felt conscious was no earthly and material wood, but a piece of intangible shadow; yet he could no more escape from it than from the iron chain of an earthly prison. On each side of the stake two savage hags, long-haired ill-favoured, inexpressibly cruel-looking, set two small plants of Enchanter's Nightshade. Then a fierce orgiastic shout went up to the low roof from all the assembled people. Rushing forward together, they covered his body with what seemed to be oil and butter; they hung grave-flowers round his neck; they quarrelled among themselves with clamorous cries for hairs and rags torn from his head and clothing. The women, in particular, whirled round him with frantic Bacchanalian gestures, crying aloud as they circled, 'O great chief! O my king! we offer you this victim; we offer you new blood to prolong your life. Give us in return sound sleep, dry graves, sweet dreams, fair seasons!'

They cut themselves with flint knives. Ghostly ichor streamed copious.

The king meanwhile kept close guard over his victim, whom he

watched with hungry eyes of hideous cannibal longing. Then, at a
given signal, the crowd of ghosts stood suddenly still. There was
an awesome pause. The men gathered outside, the women
crouched low in a ring close up to him. Dimly at that moment
Rudolph noticed almost without noticing it that each of them
had a wound on the side of his own skull; and he understood
why: they had themselves been sacrified in the dim long ago to
bear their king company to the world of spirits. Even as that
thought struck him, the men and women with a loud whoop
raised hands aloft in unison. Each grasped a sharp flake, which
they brandished savagely. The king gave the signal by rushing at
him with a jagged and saw-like knife. It descended on Rudolph's
head. At the same moment, the others rushed forward, crying
aloud in their own tongue, 'Carve the flesh from his bones! Slay
him! hack him to pieces!'

Rudolph bent his head to avoid the blows. He cowered in
abject terror. Oh! what fear would any Christian ghost have
inspired by the side of these incorporeal pagan savages! Ah!
mercy! mercy! They would tear him limb from limb! They would
rend him in pieces!

At that instant he raised his eyes, and, as by a miracle of fate,
saw another shadowy form floating vague before him. It was the
form of a man in sixteenth-century costume, very dim and uncertain. It might have been a ghost—it might have been a vision—
but it raised its shadowy hand and pointed towards the door.
Rudolph saw it was unguarded. The savages were now upon him,
their ghostly breath blew chill on his cheek. 'Show them iron!'
cried the shadow in an English voice. Rudolph struck out with
both elbows and made a fierce effort for freedom. It was with
difficulty he roused himself, but at last he succeeded. He drew his
pocket-knife and opened it. At sight of the cold steel, which no
ghost or troll or imp can endure to behold, the savages fell back,
muttering. But only for a moment. Next instant with a howl of
vengeance even louder than before, they crowded round him and
tried to intercept him. He shook them off with wild energy, though
they jostled and hustled him, and struck him again and again
with the sharp flint edges. Blood was flowing freely now from
his hands and arms—red blood of this world; but still he fought
his way out by main force with his sharp steel blade towards the
door and the moonlight. The nearer he got to the exit, the thicker
and closer the ghosts pressed around, as if conscious that their

power was bounded by their own threshold. They avoided the knife, meanwhile, with superstitious terror. Rudolph elbowed them fiercely aside, and lunging at them now and again, made his way to the door. With one supreme effort he tore himself madly out, and stood once more on the open heath, shivering like a greyhound. The ghosts thronged grinning by the open vestibule, their fierce teeth, like wild beasts', confessing their impotent anger. But Rudolph started to run, wearied as he was, and ran a few hundred yards before he fell and fainted. He dropped on a clump of white heather by a sandy ridge, and lay there unconscious till the morning.

V.

When the people from the Manor-house picked him up next day, he was hot and cold, terribly pale from fear, and mumbling incoherently. Dr Porter had him put to bed without a moment's delay. 'Poor fellow!' he said, leaning over him, 'he's had a very narrow escape indeed of a bad brain fever. I oughtn't to have prescribed Cannabis in his excited condition; or, at any rate, if I did, I ought, at least, to have watched its effect more closely. He must be kept very quiet now, and on no account whatever, nurse, must either Mrs Bruce or Mrs Bouverie-Barton be allowed to come near him.'

But late in the afternoon Rudolph sent for Joyce.

The child came creeping in with an ashen face. 'Well?' she murmured, soft and low, taking her seat by the bedside; 'so the King of the Barrow very nearly had you!'

'Yes,' Rudolph answered, relieved to find there was somebody to whom he could talk freely of his terrible adventure. 'He nearly had me. But how did you come to know it?'

'About two by the clock,' the child replied, with white lips of terror, 'I saw the fires on the moor burn brighter and bluer: and then I remembered the words of a terrible old rhyme the gipsy woman taught me—

> ' "Pallinghurst Barrow—Pallinghurst Barrow!
> Every year one heart thou'lt harrow!
> Pallinghurst Ring—Pallinghurst Ring!
> A bloody man is thy ghostly king.
> Men's bones he breaks, and sucks their marrow,
> In Pallinghurst Ring on Pallinghurst Barrow;"

and just as I thought it, I saw the lights burn terribly bright and
clear for a second, and I shuddered for horror. Then they died
down low at once, and there was moaning on the moor, cries of
despair, as from a great crowd cheated, and at that I knew that
you were not to be the Ghost-king's victim.'

Randalls Round

by

ELEANOR SCOTT

Every May Day the villagers of Padstow in Cornwall, dance in the streets to a hypnotically monotonous tune. They are led in the dance by the Hobby Horse, a man dressed in an outlandish costume, whose object is to catch the girls under the swaying skirt of the Horse. Bear this in mind when you read the following story, for it makes the events in Randalls all the more horribly credible. As with Grant Allen's story, the action centres round a prehistoric tumulus.

'Randalls Round' is the title story of Eleanor Scott's single collection of ghostly tales, published in 1929 and since then completely forgotten. It is a pity, for the collection is one of the best ever written between the wars.

'Of course, I don't pretend to be aesthetic and all that,' said Heyling in that voice of half contemptuous indifference that often marks the rivalry between Science and Art, 'but I must say that this folk-song and dance business strikes me as pretty complete rot. I dare say there may be some arguments in favour of it for exercise and that, but I'm dashed if I can see why a chap need leap about in fancy braces because he wants to train down his fat.'

He lit a cigarette disdainfully.

'All revivals are a bit artificial, I expect,' said Mortlake in his quiet, pleasant voice, 'but it's not a question of exercise only in this case, you know. People who know say that it's the remains of a religious cult—sacrificial rites and that. There certainly are some very odd things done in out-of-the-way places.'

'How d'you mean?' asked Heyling, unconvinced. 'You can't really think that there's any kind of heathen cult still practised in this country?'

'Well,' said Mortlake, 'there's not much left now. More in

Wales, I think, and France, than here. But I believe that if we could find a place where people had never lost the cult, we might run into some queer things. There are a few places like that,' he went on, 'places where they're said to perform their own rite occasionally. I mean to look it up some time. By the way,' he added, suddenly sitting upright, 'didn't you say you were going to a village called Randalls for the week-end?'

'Yes—little place in the Cotswolds somewhere. Boney gave me an address.'

'Going to work, or for an easy?'

'Not to work. Boney's afraid of my precious health. He thinks I'm overworking my delicate constitution.'

'Well, if you've the chance, I wish you'd take a look at the records in the old Guildhall there and see if you can find any references to folk customs. Randalls is believed to be one of the places where there is a genuine survival. They have a game, I think, or a dance, called Randalls Round. I'd very much like to know if there are any written records—anything definite. Not if you're bored, you know, or don't want to. Just if you're at a loose end.'

'Right, I will,' said Heyling; and there the talk ended.

It is unusual for Oxford undergraduates to take a long week-end off in the Michaelmas term with the permission of the college authorities; but Heyling, from whom his tutor expected great things, had certainly been reading too hard. The weather that autumn was unusually close and clammy, even for Oxford; and Heyling was getting into such a state of nerves that he was delighted to take the chance of getting away from Oxford for the week-end.

The weather, as he cycled out along the Woodstock Road was moist and warm; but as the miles slipped by and the ground rose, he became aware of the softness of the air, the pleasant lines of the bare, sloping fields, the quiet of the low, rolling clouds. Already he felt calmer, more at ease.

The lift of the ground became more definite, and the character of the country changed. It became more open, bleaker; it had something of the quality of moorland, and the little scattered stone houses had that air of being one with the earth that is the right of moorland houses.

Randalls was, as Heyling's tutor had told him, quite a small place though it had once boasted a market. Round a little square space, grass-grown now, where once droves of patient cattle and flocks of shaggy Cotswold sheep had stood to be sold, were grouped houses, mostly of the seventeenth or early eighteenth century, made of the beautiful mellow stone of the Cotswolds; and Heyling noticed among these one building of exceptional beauty, earlier in date than the others, long and low, with a deep, square porch and mullioned windows.

'That's the Guildhall Mortlake spoke of, I expect,' he said to himself as he made his way to the Flaming Hand Inn, where his quarters were booked. 'Quite a good place to look up town records. Queer how that sort of vague rot gets hold of quite sensible men.'

Heyling received a hearty welcome at the inn. Visitors were not very frequent at that time of year, for Randalls is rather far from the good hunting country. Even a chance week-ender was something of an event. Heyling was given a quite exceptionally nice room (or, rather, pair of rooms—for two communicated with one another) on the ground floor. The front one, looking out on to the old square, was furnished as a sitting-room; the other gave on to the inn yard, a pleasant cobbled place surrounded by a moss-grown wall and barns with beautiful lichened roofs. Heyling began to feel quite cheerful and vigorous as he lit his pipe and prepared to spend a lazy evening.

As he was settling down in his chair with one of the inn's scanty supply of very dull novels, he was mildly surprised to hear children's voices chanting outside. He reflected that Guy Fawkes' Day was not due yet, and that in any case the tune they sang was not the formless huddle usually produced on that august occasion. This was a real melody—rather an odd, plaintive air, ending with an abrupt drop that pleased his ear. Little as he knew of folk-lore, and much as he despised it, Heyling could not but recognise that this was a genuine folk air, and a very attractive one.

The children did not appear to be begging; their song finished, they simply went away; but Heyling was surprised when some minutes later he heard the same air played again, this time on a flute or flageolet. There came also the sound of many feet in the market square. It was evident that the whole population had turned out to see some sight. Mildly interested, Heyling rose and lounged across to the bay window of his room.

The tiny square was thronged with villagers, all gazing at an

empty space left in the centre. At one end of this space stood a
man playing on a long and curiously sweet pipe: he played the
same haunting plaintive melody again and again. In the very
centre stood a pole, as a maypole stands in some villages; but
instead of garlands and ribbons, this pole had flung over it the
shaggy hide of some creature like an ox. Heyling could just see the
blunt heavy head with its short thick horns. Then, without a word
or a signal, men came out from among the watchers and began a
curious dance.

Heyling had seen folk-dancing done in Oxford, and he recognised some of the features of the dance; but it struck him as being
a graver, more barbaric affair than the performances he had seen
before. It was almost solemn.

As he watched, the dancers began a figure that he recognised.
They took hands in a ring, facing outwards; then, with their
hands lifted, they began to move slowly round, counter-clockwise.
Memory stirred faintly, and two things came drifting into Heyling's mind: one, the sound of Mortlake's voice as the two men
had stood watching a performance of the Headington Mummers
—'That's the Back Ring. It's supposed to be symbolic of death—a
survival of a time when a dead victim lay in the middle and the
dancers turned away from him.' The other memory was dimmer,
for he could not remember who had told him that to move in a
circle counter-clockwise was unlucky. It must have been a Scot,
though, for he remembered the word *widdershins*.

These faint stirrings of memory were snapped off by a sudden
movement in the dance going on outside. Two new figures
advanced—one a man, whose head was covered by a mask made
in the rough likeness of a bull; the other shrouded from head to
foot in a white sheet, so that even the sex was indistinguishable.
Without a sound these two came into the space left in the centre
of the dance. The bull-headed man placed the second figure with
its back to the pole where hung the hide. The dancers moved
more and more slowly. Evidently some crisis of the dance was
coming.

Suddenly the bull-headed man jerked the pole, so that the
shaggy hide fell outspread on the shrouded figure standing before
it. It gave a horrid impression—as if the creature hanging limp on
the pole had suddenly come to life, and with one swift, terrible
movement had engulfed and devoured the helpless victim standing passively before it.

Heyling felt quite shocked—startled, as if he ought to do something. He even threw the window open, as though he meant to spring out and stop the horrid rite. Then he drew back, laughing a little at his own folly. The dance had come to an end: the bull-headed man had lifted the hide from the shrouded figure and thrown it carelessly over his shoulder. The flute-player had stopped his melody, and the crowd was melting away.

'What a queer performance!' said Heyling to himself. 'I see now what old Mortlake means. It does look like a survival of some sort. Where's that book of his.'

He rummaged in his rucksack and produced a book that Mortlake had lent him—one volume of a very famous book on folklore. There were many accounts of village games and 'feasts', all traced in a sober and scholarly fashion to some barbaric, primitive rite. He was interested to see how often mention was made of animal masks, or of the hides or tails of animals being worn by performers in these odd revels. There was nothing fantastic or strained in these accounts—nothing of the romantic type that Heyling scornfully dubbed 'æsthetic'. They were as careful and well authenticated as the facts in a scientific treatise. Randalls was mentioned, and the dance described—rather scantily, Heyling thought, until, reading on, he found that the author acknowledged that he had not himself seen it, but was indebted to a friend for the account of it. But Heyling found something that interested him.

'The origin of this dance,' he read, 'is almost certainly sacrificial. Near Randalls is one of those "banks" or mounds, surrounded by a thicket, which the villagers refuse to approach. These mounds are not uncommon in the Cotswolds, though few seem to be regarded with quite as much awe as Randalls Bank, which the country people avoid scrupulously. The bank is oval in shape, and is almost certainly formed by a long barrow of the Paleolithic age. This theory is borne out by the fact that at one time the curious Randalls Round was danced about the mound, the "victim" being led into the fringe of the thicket that surrounds it.' (A footnote added, 'Whether this is still the case I cannot be certain.') 'Permission to open the tumulus has always been most firmly refused.'

'That's amusing,' thought Heyling, as he laid down the book and felt for a match. 'Jove, what a lark it would be to get into that barrow!' he went on, drawing at his pipe. 'Wonder if I could get leave? The villagers seem to have changed their ways a bit—they do their show in the village now. They mayn't be so set on their blessed mound as they used to be. Where exactly is the place?'

He drew out an ordnance map, and soon found it—a field about a mile and a half north-west of the village, with the word 'Tumulus' in Gothic characters.

'I'll have a look at that to-morrow,' Heyling told himself, folding up the map. 'I must find out who owns the field, and get leave to investigate a bit. The landlord would know who the owner is, I expect.'

Unfortunately for Heyling's plans, the next day dawned wet, although occasional gleams gave hope that the weather would clear later. His interest had not faded during the night, and he determined that as soon as the weather was a little better he would cycle out to Randalls Bank and have a look at it. Meanwhile it might not be a bad plan to see whether the Guildhall held any records that might throw a light on his search, as Mortlake had suggested. He accordingly hunted out a worthy who was, among many other offices, Town Clerk, and was led by him to the fifteenth-century building he had noticed on his way to the Flaming Hand.

It was very cool and dark inside the old Guildhall. The atmosphere of the place pleased Heyling; he liked the simple groining of the roof and the worn stone stair that led up to the Record Room. This was a low, pleasant place, with deep windows and a singularly beautiful ceiling; Heyling noticed that it also served the purpose of a small reference library.

While the Town Clerk pottered with keys in the locks of chests and presses, Heyling idly examined the titles of the books ranged decorously on the shelves about the room. His eye was caught by the title, *Prehistoric Remains in the Cotswolds*. He took the volume down. There was an opening chapter dealing with prehistoric remains in general, and, glancing through it, he saw mentions of long and round barrows. He kept the book in his hand for closer inspection. He really knew precious little about barrows, and it would be just as well to find out a little before beginning his exploration. In fact, when the Town Clerk left him alone in the Record Room, that book was the first thing he studied.

It was a mere text-book, after all, but to Heyling's ignorance it revealed a few facts of interest. Long barrows, he gathered, were older than round, and more uncommon, and were often objects of superstitious awe among the country folk of the district,

who generally opposed any effort to explore them, but the whole
chapter was very brief and skimpy, and Heyling had soon
exhausted its interest.

The town records, however, were more amusing, for he very
soon found references to his particular field. There was a lawsuit
in the early seventeenth century, which concerned it, and the
interest to Heyling was redoubled by the vagueness of certain
evidence. A certain Beale brought charges of witchcraft against
'divers Persouns of y Towne'. He had reason for alarm, for
apparently his son, 'a young and comely Lad of twenty years' had
completely disappeared: 'wherefore ye sd. Jno. Beale didd openlie
declare and state that ye sd. Son Frauncis hadd been led away by
Warlockes in y Daunce (for his Ring, ye wh. he hadd long
worne, was found in ye Fielde wh. ye wot of) and hadd by them
beene done to Deathe in yr Abhominable Practicinges.' The case
seemed to have been hushed up, although several people cited by
'ye sd. Jno. Beale' admitted having been in the company of the
missing youth on the night of his disappearance—which, Heyling
was interested to notice, was that very day, 31st October.

Another document, of a later date, recorded the attempted sale
of the 'field wh. ye wot of'—(no name was ever given to the
place)—and the refusal of the purchaser to fulfil his contract
owing to 'ye ill Repute of ye Place, the wh. was unknowen to
Himm when he didd entre into his Bargayn'.

The only other documents of interest to Heyling were some of
the seventeenth century, wherein the authorities of the Common-
wealth inveighed against 'ye Lewd Games and Dauncyng, ye wh.
are Service to Sathanas and a moste strong Abhominatioun to
ye Lorde'. These spoke openly of devil worship and 'loathlie
Ceremonie at ye Banke in ye Fielde'. It seemed that more than
one person had stood trial for conducting these ceremonies, and
against one case (dated 7th November, 1659) was written,
'Convicti et combusti'.

'Good Lord—burnt!' exclaimed Heyling aloud. 'What an
appalling business! I suppose the poor beggars were only doing
much the same thing as those chaps I saw yesterday.'

He sat lost in thought for some time. He thought how that odd
tune and dance had gone on in this remote village for centuries;
had there been more to it once, he wondered? Did that queer
business with the hide mean—well, some real devilry? Pictures
floated into his mind—odd, squat little men, broad of shoulder

and long of arm, naked and hairy, dancing in solemn, ghastly worship, dim ages ago. . . . This business was getting a stronger hold of him than he would have thought possible.

'Strikes me that if there is anything of the old devilry left, it'll be in that field,' he concluded at last. 'The dance they do now is all open and above board; but if they still avoid the field, as that book of Mortlake's seems to think, that might be a clue. I'll find out.'

He rose and went down to inform the Town Clerk that his researches were over, and then went back to the inn in a comfortable frame of mind. Certainly his week-end was bringing him distraction from his work; no thought of it had entered his head since he first heard the children singing outside the inn.

The landlord of the Flaming Hand was a solid man who gave the impression of honesty and sense. Heyling felt that he could depend upon him for a reasonable account of 'the fielde which ye wot of'. He accordingly tackled him after lunch, and was at once amused, surprised and annoyed to find that the man hedged as soon as he was questioned on the subject. He quite definitely opposed any idea of exploration.

'I'm not like some of 'em, sir,' he said. 'I wouldn't go for to say that it'd do any 'arm for you to take a turn in the field while it was light, like. But it ain't 'ealthy after dark, sir, that field aren't. Nor it ain't no sense to go a-diggin' and a-delvin' in that there bank. I've lived in this 'ere place a matter of forty year, man and boy, and I know what I'm a-sayin' of.'

'But why isn't it healthy? Is it marshy?'

'No, sir, it ain't not to say marshy.'

'Don't the farmers ever cultivate it?'

'Well, sir, all I can say is I been in this place forty year, man and boy, and it ain't never been dug nor ploughed nor sown nor reaped in my mem'ry. Nor yet in my father's, nor in my grandfather's. Crops wouldn't do, sir, not in that field.'

'Well, I want to go and examine the mound. Who's the owner? —I ought to get his leave, I suppose.'

'You won't do that, sir.'

'Why not?'

' 'Cause I'm the owner, sir, and I won't 'ave any one, not the King 'isself, nor yet the King's son, a-diggin' in that bank. Not for a waggon-load of gold, I won't.'

Heyling saw it was useless.

'Oh, all right! If you feel like that about it!' he said carelessly.

The stubborn, half-frightened look left the host's eyes.

'Thank you, sir,' he said, quite gratefully.

But he had not really gained the victory. Heyling was as obstinate as he, and he had determined that before he left Randalls he would have investigated that barrow. If he could not get permission, he would go without. He decided that as soon as darkness fell he would go out on the quiet and explore in earnest. He would borrow a spade from the open cart-shed of the inn—a spade and a pick, if he could find one. He began to feel some of the enthusiasm of the explorer.

He decided that he would spend part of the afternoon in examining the outside of the mound. It was not more than a ten minutes ride to the field, which lay on the road. It was as the landlord had said, uncultivated. Almost in the middle of it rose a mass of stunted trees and bushes, a thick mass of intertwining boughs that would certainly take some strength to penetrate. Was it really a tomb, Heyling wondered? And he thought with some awe of the strange prehistoric being who might lie there, his rude jewels and arms about him.

He returned to the inn, his interest keener than ever. He would most certainly get into that barrow as soon as it was dark enough to try. He felt restless now, as one always does when one is looking forward with some excitement to an event a few hours distant. He fidgeted about the room, one eye constantly on his watch.

He wanted to get to the field as soon as possible after dark, for his casual inspection of the afternoon had shown him that the task of pushing through the bushes, tangled and interwoven as they were, would be no light one; and then there was the opening of the tumulus to be done—that soil, untouched by spade or plough for centuries, to be broken by the pick until an entrance was forced into the chamber within. He ought to be off as soon as he could safely secure the tools he wanted to borrow.

But fate was against him. There seemed to be a constant flow of visitors to the Flaming Hand that evening—not ordinary labourers dropping in for a drink, but private visitors to the landlord, who went through to his parlour behind the bar and left by the yard at the side of the inn. It really did seem like some silly mystery story, thought Heyling impatiently; the affair in the market-place, the landlord's odd manner over the question of the field, and now this hushed coming and going from the landlord's room!

He went to his bedroom window and looked out into the yard. He wanted to make quite sure that the pick and spade were still in the open cart-shed. To his relief they were; but as he looked he got yet another shock. A man slipped out from the door of the inn kitchen and slipped across the yard into the lane that lay behind the inn. Another followed him, and a little later another; and all three had black faces. Their hands showed light, and their necks; but their faces were covered with soot, so that the features were quite indistinguishable.

'This is too mad!' exclaimed Heyling half aloud. 'Jove, I didn't expect to run into this sort of farce when I came here. Wonder if *all* old Cross's mysterious visitors have had black faces? Anyway, I wish they'd buck up and clear out. I may not have another chance to go to that mound if I don't get off soon.'

The queer happenings at the inn now appeared to him solely as obstacles to his own movements. If their import came into his mind at all, it was to make him wonder whether there were any play like a mummers' show which the village kept up; of games, perhaps, like those played in Scotland at Hallowe'en. . . . By Jove! That probably was the explanation. It *was* All Hallows' Eve! Why couldn't they buck up and get on with it, anyhow?

His patience was not to be tried much longer. Soon after nine the noises ceased; but to make doubly sure, Heyling did not leave his room till ten had struck from Randalls church.

He got cautiously out of his bedroom window and landed softly on the cobbles of the yard. The tools still leaned against the wall of the open shed—trusting man, Mr Cross, of the Flaming Hand! The shed where his cycle stood was locked, though, and he swore softly at the loss of time this would mean in getting to the field. It would take him twenty-five minutes to walk.

As a matter of fact, it did not take him quite so long, for impatience gave him speed. The country looked very beautiful under the slow-rising hunter's moon. The long bare lines of the fields swept up to the ridges, black against the dark serene blue of the night sky. The air was cool and clean, with the smell of frost in it. Heyling, hurrying along the rough white road, was dimly conscious of the purity and peace of the night.

At last the field came in sight, empty and still in the cold moonlight. Only the mound, black as a tomb, broke the flood of light. The gate was wide open, and even in his haste this struck Heyling as odd.

'I could have sworn I shut that gate,' he said to himself. 'I remember thinking I must, in case any one spotted I'd been in. It just shows that people don't avoid the place as much as old Cross would like me to believe.'

He decided to attack the barrow on the side away from the road, lest any belated labourer should pass by. He walked round the mound, looking for a thin spot in its defence of thorn and hazel bushes; nut there was none. The scrub formed a thick belt all round the barrow, and was so high that he could not see the top of the mound at all. The confounded stuff might grow half-way up the tumulus for all he could see.

He abandoned any idea of finding an easy spot to begin operations. It was obviously just a question of breaking through. Then, just as he was about to take this heroic course, he stopped short, listening. It sounded to him as if some creature were moving within the bushes—something heavy and bulky, breaking the smaller branches of the undergrowth.

'Must be a fox, I suppose,' he thought, 'but he must be a monster. It sounds more like a cow, though of course it can't be. Well here goes.'

He turned his back to the belt of thick undergrowth, ducked his head forward, and was just about to force his way backwards through the bushes when again he stopped to listen. This time it was a very different sound that arrested him—it was the distant playing of a pipe. He recognised it—the plaintive melody of Randalls Round.

He paused, listening. Yes—feet were coming up the road—many feet, pattering unevenly. There *was* some village game afoot, then!

The words of Mortlake's book came back to his mind. The author had said that at one time the barrow was the centre of the dance. Was it possible that it was so still—that there was a second form, less decorous perhaps, which took place at night?

Anyhow, he mustn't be seen, that was certain. Lucky the mound was between him and the road. He stole cautiously towards the hedge on the far side of the field. Thank goodness it was a hedge and not one of those low stone walls that surround most fields in the Cotswolds.

As he took cautious cover he couldn't help feeling a very complete fool. Was it really necessary to take this precaution. And then he remembered the look of stubborn determination on the land-

lord's face. Yes, if he were to investigate the barrow he must keep
dark. Besides, there might be something to see in this business—
something to delight old Mortlake's heart.

The tune came nearer, and the sound of footsteps was muffled.
They were in the grassy field, then. Heyling cautiously raised his
head from the ditch where he lay; but the mound blocked his
view as yet. What luck that he'd happened to go to Randalls just
at that time—Hallowe'en! He remembered the documents in the
Guildhall, and Jno. Beale's indictment of the men who, he averred,
had made away with his son at Hallowe'en. Heyling's blood
tingled with excitement.

The playing came closer, and now Heyling could see the figures
of men moving into the circle they formed for Randalls Round.
Again he was struck by the queer barbaric look of the thing and by
the gravity of their movements; and then his heart gave a sudden
heavy thump. The dancers had all the blackened mask-like faces
of the men he had seen leaving the inn. How odd! thought
Heyling. They perform quite openly in the village square, and
then steal away at night, disguising their faces. . . .

The dance was extraordinarily impressive, seen in that empty
field under the quiet moon. There was no sound but the whispering of their feet on the long dry grass and the melancholy music
of the pipe. Then, quite suddenly, Heyling heard again the
cracking, rustling sound from the dense bushes about the mound.
It was exactly like the stirring of some big clumsy animal. The
dancers heard it too; there came a sort of shuddering gasp;
Heyling saw one man glance at his neighbour, and his eyes shone
light and terrified in his blackened face.

The melody came slower, and with a kind of horror Heyling
knew that the crisis of the dance was near. Slowly the dancers
formed the ring, their faces turned away from the mound; then
from outside the circle came a shrouded figure led by a man
wearing a mask like a bull's head. The veiled form was led into
the ring. The pipe mourned on.

Again, shattering the quiet, came a snapping, crashing noise
from the inmost recesses of the bushes about the barrow. There
was some big animal in there, crashing his way out. . . .

Then he saw it, bulky and black in the pure white light—some
horrible primitive creature, with heavy lowered head. The
dancers circled slowly; the air of the flute grew faint.

Heyling felt cold and sick. This was loathsome, devilish. . . . He buried his head in his arms and tried to drown the sound of that mourning melody.

Sounds came through the muffling hands over his ears—a crunching, tearing sound, and then a horrible noise like an animal lapping. Sweat broke out on Heyling's back. It sounded like bones. . . . He could not think, or move, or pray. . . . The haunting music still crooned on. . . .

The crashing, snapping noise again as the branches broke. *It*, whatever it was, was going back into its lair. The tune grew fainter and fainter. Steps sounded again on the road—slow steps, with no life in them. The horrible rite was over.

Very cautiously Heyling got to his feet. His knees trembled, and his breath came short and rough. He felt sick with horror and with personal fear as he skirted the mound. His fascinated eyes saw the break in the hazels and thorns; then they fell upon a dark mark on the ground—dark and wet, soaking into the dry grass. A white rag, dappled with dark stains, lay near. . . .

Heyling could bear no more. He gave a strangled cry as he rushed, blindly stumbling, falling sometimes, out of the field and down the road.

The Skeleton at the Feast/Medusan Madness

by

E. H. VISIAK

Ignored through life
It seems, said I,
That even death
Has passed me by.

To celebrate his *93rd birthday, E. H. Visiak (1878–1972) wrote this
sadly apt epigram. It sums up the life of the man called 'the world's
greatest authority on Milton'.*

*Edward Harold Physick adopted the name Visiak in 1910; it is an
old variation of his real name. He was born into a family which was
already distinguished in the field of sculpture. As a young man, he was
employed by the Indo-European Telegraph Company from 1897 to
1914. After this, he took up teaching for some time but eventually
devoted himself entirely to scholarship and writing. Visiak died in
Hove in August 1972, after a long illness, and I do not think that,
even now, his rare talents have been fully recognised.*

*In the field of research into the works of Milton, Visiak was un-
rivalled. His works* Milton Agonistes *(1923) and* The Portent of
Milton *(1958) were very well received, and the Nonesuch* Milton
*(1938), which Visiak edited, has been used as a universal authority
ever since.*

It was poetry that first made Visiak's name famous, with his book
Buccaneer Ballads *(1910), which he later followed up with* Flints
and Flashes *(1911) and* The Phantom Ship *(1912). His anti-war
sentiments were expressed in grim poetical form in* The Battle Fiends
(1916).

*As a macabre writer, Visiak has found a little wider reputation,
for his classic novel* Medusa *(1929) was reprinted twice in his life-
time, in 1946 and 1963. In it, he uses the style of Robert Louis
Stevenson (one of his literary heroes) to tell the strange tale of a*

voyage into unknown waters. It is a book replete with chillingly original spectral images and events, one of the few novels of the twentieth century that can honestly be called unique. The Medusa theme obviously fascinated Visiak, for he used it again in this rare short story. Set in an ostensibly normal mental home, it gradually progresses from light to dark, and needs at least two readings to be appreciated properly.

Before reading the short story, however, I invite you to sample E. H. Visiak's poetical style. 'The Skeleton at the Feast' comes from The Phantom Ship. *It is undoubtedly one of the shortest and most horrifying pieces ever written in this country.*

Though Visiak's output was very small, he can truly be regarded as one of the most outstanding writers in the field of the macabre of the last hundred years. I hope that after reading these two pieces, you will agree with me.

The Skeleton at the Feast

Dance in the wind, poor skeleton!
You that was my deary one,
You they hanged for stealing sheep.
Dance and dangle, laugh and leap!
Tomorrow night at Squire's ball,
I am to serve a sheep in hall:
My Lady's wedding, Lord love her!
Wait until they lift the cover!

Medusan Madness

The dreariness of the place was beyond expression. It had once been an ornate mid-Victorian mansion; and externally nothing had been altered. There were even peacocks there. As I sat on the balustraded terrace, with its grey, corroded Cupids, a peacock screeched, now and then, from somewhere in the grounds. The extensive lawns seemed to hold something dismally unnatural in their bleak, bright greenness, appearing queerly dull in the distance, on the fringe of a grey-dark plantation. The month was October and the time late afternoon; but nothing could have dispersed, or modified, the blight in that atmosphere—not the most genial summer sun.

A few of the inmates were moving here and there about the sidepaths. I especially noticed a very tall old lady, with silvery white hair, who walked with a stick, but extraordinarily upright.

'What beautiful hair that woman has!' I said to my poor friend.

'Yes, and she's got a beautiful mind, too,' he answered in his slow, gentle voice. 'I couldn't possibly endure this if it weren't for her.'

'Why is . . .'

'Why is she here? She wouldn't mind your asking that, and I'm sure that I don't. She is here because she is sane.'

'I see,' I said.

'*What* do you see?'

'A rather pretty young woman bringing our tea,' I answered, laughing; but suddenly arrested by the look in his eyes.

It gave me the impression of a pang.

'Pretty!' he groaned, 'Oh, my God!'

He sat silent, with an appearance of intense stillness, as if he were frozen. He seemed to be staring at something that he saw in the air; but the expression in his eyes was so terrible that I could not look at them. In the meantime, the maid set down the tea-things, glanced at him, and at me—rather peculiarly, I thought—and went her way.

'I'm awfully sorry, Evans,' I said as he seemed to be recovering. 'I really don't know what I said to . . . to distress you so much.'

'Of course you don't,' he answered in a feeble, strained voice; 'and I dare say this will resolve any doubts that may have come to you as to whether I really am insane. You don't know my secret, and I cannot tell it to you. I couldn't tell it to anyone—except to that woman,' he added, pointing to the tall lady in the grounds.

He drank some tea, and continued moodily:

'Schopenhauer was wrong in ascribing reality to the will. It is futile to attribute reality to an aspect. Besides, if you must single out in that way, the completely enlightened will would cease to function. What you call the conscience would cease also.'

'You mean that there would no longer be any *desire*——?'

'Desire would be swallowed up. There would be no more sea . . .'

He looked at me strangely, and continued:

'You have perception; but have you understanding? Are you . . . I wonder.'

The troubled look returned to his eyes, growing into an expression of settled pain. It is distressing to see suffering which one cannot by any means alleviate. In the faded light, the vast lawn and the shrubberies beyond appeared to extend in interminable gloom. The grounds seemed now deserted, and the peacock had ceased to give, at intervals, its peculiarly disagreeable and desolate cry. Only the tall woman continued to stalk in the side-path, looking queer and ghostly in the distance, with her silvery hair; and I had a fancy that she possessed the scene, in some way, like an embodiment of its mid-Victorian past. I felt wretchedly depressed, and eager, even anxious, to be gone.

But the diversion of talking with me was clearly of some service to my friend; so that I determined to prolong my visit, and also to repeat it very soon.

He was looking fixedly in the direction of the woman.

'She is going to come in,' he said presently. 'If she turns across the lawn, I'll tell you my story. It will be a signal.'

'Telepathy,' I said.

'Yes. More than that. Another man might have taken it that I was in love with her,' he added.

'Very likely he would,' I answered. 'But why do you laugh like that?'

'Why? Oh, you'll soon understand. She's turning.'

Suddenly I felt terrified. I did not want to hear his story. I dreaded it. I had divined it, somehow. I do not mean specifically, but essentially and *atmospherically*.

'Are you . . . are you,' I asked, 'quite sure that you want to tell me, Evans? Wouldn't it . . . distress you too much?'

'I *must* tell you.'

'It was off Japan,' he went on in a rather disjointed way—'five days after leaving Osaka, where I had put in on a voyage to San Francisco. Ah, it's a long time since I smoked . . .'

I had taken out my pipe and pouch.

'Why did you give it up?' I asked, grasping at the chance of a diversion.

'It gave me up, like other forms of illusion—all except . . .'

' "The believing that we do something when we do nothing," ' I quoted hurriedly. 'It's not so simple as that, is it?'

'I had a steam-yacht,' he went on—he did not seem to have heard my question—'She was one of the fine Nineties yachts, built to sail as well as steam. It was near sunset; very calm—yes, very. Breathless—that is the very word. I remember thinking queerly, it's holding its breath. Of course, I wasn't clear what I meant; but I really did feel something. There really was some extraordinary tension—possession; and the sky! It was such an extraordinary, such an indescribable colour. It was intense, intense dark, dark, dark blue! But this did not diminish the light—the light that was so brilliant for me to see. . . . Oh, God! . . .'

'Evans,' I cried as I evaded his look, 'do *not* go on! You're in agony. You can't stand it, Evans!'

'No. I shall be better. She is coming.'

He pointed to the tall woman, who was approaching the foot of the terrace across the lawn.

'Diomedea,' he shouted suddenly, 'what is the word?'

She answered with a strange gesture, letting fall her stick, clasping her hands, slowly unfolding them, spreading them out with the palms falling away downward. It was a gesture that expressed absolute emptiness, absolute abandonment. It perfectly expressed this, with the rhythmic beauty of unanswerable, irresistible eloquence.

She reversed the movement. I can only describe the effect as magical. I felt that, into an immeasurable vacuity, there was pouring a welling, solvent tide.

'You can go on now,' I said, feeling the words flow from me like a sigh.

I had not observed the woman particularly. She impressed me as being impersonal in some way. I could see her, of course, despite the dim light; and my impression is that she had a strangely classical Greek cast of face and extraordinarily bright, light blue eyes. But it is quite impossible to explain why, or how, I am unable to describe her at all clearly. She seemed *interior* to us; though that is too crudely definite a word to convey my meaning.

As to that amazing, wonderful language of her hands, it cannot be described as ceremonial, or symbolic—a ritual sign-language, in any way. It was too immediate, too essential in fact, to be styled language. The expression was identical with the idea; the form—which was also the substance—with the rhythm. Perhaps, in effecting this inner—and also outer—visualization, she became, or gave the effect of becoming, impersonal, and accordingly obscure.

She was gone. I did not see her go. My consciousness, as far as I can express the experience, was submerged in a kind of vast ocean. I think Evans was proceeding with his story, emphasizing insistently the peculiar dark blue, or blue dark, colour of the sky all above and around his yacht. But, for me, there was only the vague, neutral element of what, I suppose, was a subconscious, or partially subconscious, state.

Presently, however, I saw what he had seen—the skies duskily glowing in their deep, dark blueness, the sea almost black. The whole scene was overpoweringly impressive, sultry, intimidating. The virtually flat immobility of the waters seemed an impossible phenomenon.

Doubtless, it was impossible to normal visualization. It is conceivable, however, that the normal pitch of the senses can be altered. Supposing, as Plato imagined, that the atmosphere in which we breathe and move might appear to an inhabitant of the upper, or ethereal element to have the comparative density of water: then, the sea would appear to such an observer, analogously, as solid. Scientifically, in fact, the ground is not so stable as it appears. It has its waves, which, like the colours above and below our range of vision, we are not able to perceive.

Now, I had emerged out of the subconscious state, as I have told—but how, or where?

There was something upon that sea. A figure was appearing. I was seized with indescribable sensations; emotions: fear, wonder, amazement, expectancy, strangeness—all-uniting, all-modifying strangeness!

Evans continued, telling his story, divulging his secret; which henceforth was also to be my secret—incommunicably so: even though in trying to describe what I saw and felt, I strain the ineptitude of words into nonsense.

But while I vainly tug at the sense and superficial letter of expression, I cannot but wonder whether, if power were given me I could transmute, transfuse, the pining torment by the force of some liberating symbol. What superlative, irresistible genius might not be operated by the sting and flame of such cratered condensation! A thin steam of vague, insignificant analogies is, at least, some alleviation.

The appearance was monstrously beautiful—the figure, or creature, that suddenly became visible on that sea—so concretely visible—against those dark, violet dark, glowing, deep skies. It was as the incarnate bloom of which they were the umbrageous foil. It sweetly, faintly, delicately embodied the moon-like magic which is reflected in the soft splendour of the pearl. It was the essential, stark-naked, overpowering manifestation in form and voluptuous, smooth feminine feature of the grace that falls away continually in the brimmed contours of the waves.

Thus I saw it—and thus might see it still, unharmed, unhaunted in this horror of desolation, in this yearning, irremediable torment of desire; this racking hell! But it stirred; it moved; it turned upon me its penetrative, dream-like glance.

I did not leave this house. Diomedea helps us. She is coming now.

Out of the Sea

by

A. C. BENSON

This is perhaps the most interesting and unusual tale in this collection, not only for its content but because of the circumstances surrounding the author A. C. Benson (1862–1925). His life was subject to two influences—one good, one bad—which did much to shape his character and ultimately his writing.

The first and good influence came about through his 'fan mail'. Benson's many books of essays had earned him a huge reading audience, many of whom wrote to him with their problems. He always felt obliged to answer these letters and it was not unusual for him to write more than twenty letters a day, all personally composed for each particular correspondent. One of his many admirers was an American woman, rich in her own right, who had married a wealthy European. She and Benson struck up a real friendship by post, and when, in 1915, Benson became Master of Magdalene College, Cambridge, he wrote and told her of his plans for the College. She offered to help him financially. On the strict understanding that his role in the matter would only be that of a trustee of a fund, Benson agreed. She made over to him more than £45,000 in the next few months, and more was to follow. With it, Benson was able to help transform Magdalene into one of the foremost Colleges of the University.

Incredibly, Benson and his benefactress never met. In the same manner as Madame von Meck and Tchaikovsky, they continued a warm friendship solely through their letters.

The other, and totally opposite, influence was the recurring fits of depression that Benson suffered from all his life. These fits often spanned years and were greatly exacerbated by the knowledge that his sister Margaret had died in the grip of homicidal mania after just the same fits of depression. The fear, though it was unjustified, that he might follow the same path haunted Benson till his death. It is extremely relevant to point out that all Benson's best stories of the macabre—and

*there are many—take place in isolated communities, cut off by geography
or choice, from the rest of the world. Some even occur in a timeless, semi-
medieval setting, where the 'reality' against which one has to judge
Benson's supernatural manifestations, is itself strangely unreal. Benson
obviously knew only too well that shadow world of depression where an
almost perceptible veil drops between the individual and his surroundings
and used this knowledge to intensify the images of his stories.*

*The ghost in 'Out of the Sea' is so unusual that it makes the inclusion
of this rare gem all the more worthwhile. The story comes from his
second collection of uncanny tales The Isles of Sunset (1905) and
creates a superb atmosphere of doom and foreboding. Remember when
you read it that more of the author than is common went into the making
of the tale.*

It was about ten o'clock on a November morning in the little
village of Blea-on-the-Sands. The hamlet was made up of some
thirty houses, which clustered together on a low rising ground.
The place was very poor, but some old merchant of bygone days
had built in a pious mood a large church, which was now too
great for the needs of the place; the nave had been unroofed in a
heavy gale, and there was no money to repair it, so that it had
fallen to decay, and the tower was joined to the choir by roofless
walls. This was a sore trial to the old priest, Father Thomas, who
had grown grey there; but he had no art in gathering money,
which he asked for in a shamefaced way; and the vicarage was a
poor one, hardly enough for the old man's needs. So the church
lay desolate.

The village stood on what must once have been an island; the
little river Reddy, which runs down to the sea, there forking into
two channels on the landward side; towards the sea the ground
was bare, full of sand-hills covered with a short grass. Towards
the land was a small wood of gnarled trees, the boughs of which
were all brushed smooth by the gales; looking landward there
was the green flat, in which the river ran, rising into low hills;
hardly a house was visible save one or two lonely farms; two or
three church towers rose above the hills at a long distance away.
Indeed Blea was much cut off from the world; there was a bridge
over the stream on the west side, but over the other channel was
no bridge, so that to fare eastward it was requisite to go in a boat.
To seaward there were wide sands, when the tide was out; when
it was in, it came up nearly to the end of the village street. The

people were mostly fishermen, but there were a few farmers and labourers; the boats of the fishermen lay to the east side of the village, near the river channel which gave some draught of water; and the channel was marked out by big black stakes and posts that straggled out over the sands, like awkward leaning figures, to the sea's brim.

Father Thomas lived in a small and ancient brick house near the church, with a little garden attached. He was a kindly man, much worn by age and weather, with a wise heart, and he loved the quiet life with his small flock. This morning he had come out of his house to look abroad, before he settled down to writing his sermon. He looked out to sea, and saw with a shadow of sadness the black outline of a wreck that had come ashore a week before, and over which the white waves were now breaking. The wind blew steadily from the north-east, and had a bitter poisonous chill in it, which it doubtless drew from the fields of the upper ice. The day was dark and overhung, not with cloud, but with a kind of dreary vapour that shut out the sun. Father Thomas shuddered at the wind, and drew his patched cloak round him. As he did so, he saw three figures come up to the vicarage gate. It was not a common thing for him to have visitors in the morning, and he saw with surprise that they were old Master John Grimston, the richest man in the place, half farmer and half fisherman, a dark surly old man; his wife, Bridget, a timid and frightened woman, who found life with her harsh husband a difficult business, in spite of their wealth, which, for a place like Blea, was great; and their son Henry, a silly shambling man of forty, who was his father's butt. The three walked silently and heavily, as though they came on a sad errand.

Father Thomas went briskly down to meet them, and greeted them with his accustomed cheerfulness. 'And what may I do for you?' he said. Old Master Grimston made a sort of gesture with his head as though his wife should speak; and she said in a low and somewhat husky voice, with a rapid utterance, 'There is a matter, Father, we would ask you about—are you at leisure?' Father Thomas said, 'Ay, I am ashamed to be not more busy! Let us go in the house.' They did so; and even in the little distance to the door, the Father thought that his visitors behaved very strangely. They peered round from left to right, and once or twice Master Grimston looked sharply behind them, as though they were followed. They said nothing but 'Ay' and 'No' to the

Father's talk, and bore themselves like people with a terrible fear. Father Thomas made up his mind that it was some question of money, for nothing else was wont to move Master Grimston's mind. So he led them into his parlour and gave them seats, and then there was a silence, while the two men continued to look furtively about them, and the wife sat with her eyes upon the priest's face. Father Thomas knew not what to make of this, till Master Grimston said harshly, 'Come wife, tell the tale and make an end; we must not take up the Father's time.'

'I hardly know how to say it, Father,' said Bridget, 'but a strange and evil thing has befallen us; there is something come to our house, and we know not what it is—but it brings fear with it.' A sudden paleness came over her face, and she stopped, and the three exchanged a glance in which terror was visibly written. Master Grimston looked over his shoulder swiftly, and made as though to speak, yet only swallowed in his throat; but Henry said suddenly, in a loud and woeful voice: 'It is an evil beast out of the sea.' And then there followed a dreadful silence, while Father Thomas felt a sudden dread leap up in his heart, at the contagion of fear that he saw written on the faces round him. But he said with all the cheerfulness he could muster, 'Come, friends, let us not begin to talk of sea-beasts; we must have the whole tale. Mistress Grimston, I must hear the story—be content—nothing can touch us here.' The three seemed to draw a faint comfort from his words, and Bridget began:

'It was the day of the wreck, Father. John was up early before the dawn; he walked out to the sands, and Henry with him—and they were the first to see the wreck—was not that it?' At these words the father and son seemed to exchange a very swift and secret look, and both grew pale. 'John told me there was a wreck ashore, and they went presently and roused the rest of the village; and all that day they were out, saving what could be saved. Two sailors were found, both dead and pitifully battered by the sea, and they were buried, as you know, Father, in the churchyard next day; John came back about dusk and Henry with him, and we sat down to our supper. John was telling me about the wreck, as we sat beside the fire, when Henry, who was sitting apart, rose up and cried out suddenly, "What is that?"'

She paused for a moment, and Henry, who sat with face blanched, staring at his mother, said, 'Ay, I did—it ran past me suddenly.' 'Yes, but what was it?' said Father Thomas trying to smile; 'a dog or cat, perhaps?' 'It was a beast,' said Henry slowly, in a trembling voice—'a beast about the size of a goat. I never saw the like—yet I did not see it clear; I but felt the air blow, and caught a whiff of it—it was salt like the sea, but with a kind of dead smell behind.' 'Was that all you saw?' said Father Thomas; 'Perhaps you were tired and faint, and the air swam round you suddenly—I have known the like myself when weary.' 'Nay, nay,' said Henry, 'this was not like that—it was a beast, sure enough.' 'Ay, and we have seen it since,' said Bridget. 'At least I have not seen it clearly yet, but I have smelt its odour, and it turns me sick —but John and Henry have seen it often—sometimes it lies and seems to sleep, but it watches us; and then again it is merry, and will leap in a corner—and John saw it skip upon the sands near the wreck—did you not, John?' At these words the two men again exchanged a glance, and then old Master Grimston, with a dreadful look in his face, in which great anger seemed to strive with fear, said 'Nay, silly woman, it was not near the wreck, it was out to the east.' 'It matters little,' said Father Thomas, who saw well enough this was no light matter. 'I never heard the like of it. I will myself come down to your house with a holy book, and see if the thing will meet me. I know not what this is,' he went on, 'whether it is a vain terror that hath hold of you; but there are spirits of evil in the world, and the sea, too, doubtless hath its monsters; and it may be that one has wandered out of the waves, like a dog strayed from his home. I dare not say, till I have met it face to face. But God gives no power to such things to hurt those who have a fair conscience.'—And here he stopped and looked at the three; Bridget sat regarding him with hope in her face; but the other two sat looking at the ground; and the priest divined in some secret way that all was not well with them. 'But I will come at once,' he said, rising, 'and I will see if I can cast out or bind the thing, whatever it be—for I am in this place as a soldier of the Lord, to fight with the works of darkness.' He took a clasped book from a table, and lifted up his hat, saying, 'Let us set forth.' Then he said as they left the room, 'Hath it appeared today?' 'Yes, indeed,' said Henry, 'and it was ill content. It followed us as though it were angered.' 'Come,' said Father Thomas turning upon him, 'you speak thus of a thing, as you might speak of a dog—what is it like?' 'Nay,' said Henry, 'I know not; I can never see it clearly; it is like a speck in the eye—it is never there when you look upon it—it glides away very secretly; it is most like a goat, I think. It seems to be horned, and hairy; but I have seen its eyes, and they were yellow, like a flame.'

As he said these words Master Grimston went in haste to the door, and pulled it open as though to breathe the air. The others followed him and went out; but Master Grimston drew the priest aside, and said like a man in a mortal fear, 'Look you, Father, all this is true—the thing is a devil—and why it abides with us I know not; but I cannot live so; and unless it be cast out it will slay me—but if money be of avail, I have it in abundance.' 'Nay,' said Father Thomas, 'let there be no talk of money—perchance if I can aid you, you may give of your gratitude to God.' 'Ay, ay,' said the old man hurriedly, 'that was what I meant—there is money in abundance for God, if he will but set me free.'

So they walked very sadly together through the street. There were few folk about; the men and the children were all abroad—a woman or two came to the house door, and wondered a little to see them pass so solemnly, as though they followed a body to the grave.

Master Grimston's house was the largest in the place. It had a walled garden before it, with a strong door set in the wall. The house stood back from the road, a dark front of brick with gables; behind it the garden sloped nearly to the sands, with wooden barns and warehouses. Master Grimston unlocked the door, and then it seemed that his terror overcame him, for he would have the priest enter first. Father Thomas, with a certain apprehension of which he was ashamed, walked quickly in, and looked about him. The herbage of the garden had mostly died down in the winter, and a tangle of sodden stalks lay over the beds. A flagged path edged with box led up to the house, which seemed to stare at them from its dark windows with a sort of steady gaze. Master Grimston fastened the door behind them, and they went all together, keeping close to each other, up to the house, the door of which opened upon a big parlour or kitchen, sparely furnished, but very clean and comfortable. Some vessels of metal glittered on a rack. There were chairs, ranged round the open fireplace. There was no sound except the wind which buffeted in the chimney. It looked a quiet and homely place, and Father Thomas grew ashamed of his fears. 'Now,' said he in his firm voice, 'though I am your guest here, I will appoint what shall be done. We will sit here together, and talk as cheerfully as we may, till we have dined. Then, if nothing appears to us,'—and he crossed himself—'I will go round the house, into every room, and see if we can track the thing to its lair; I will abide with you till evensong; and then I will soon return, and sleep here to-night. Even if the thing be wary, and dares not to meet the power of the Church in the day-time, perhaps it will venture out at night; and I am prepared to face it. So come, good people, and be comforted.'

So they sat together; and Father Thomas talked of many things, and told some old legends of saints; and they dined, though without much cheer; and still nothing appeared. Then, after dinner, Father Thomas decided to view the house. So he took his Bible, and they went from room to room. On the ground floor there were several chambers not used, which they entered in turn, but saw nothing; on the upper floor was a large room where Master Grimston and his wife slept; and a further room for Henry, and a guest-chamber in which the priest was to sleep; and a room where a servant-maid slept. And now the day began to darken and to turn to evening, and Father Thomas felt a shadow grow in his mind. There came into his head a verse of Scripture about a spirit who found a house 'empty, swept and garnished,' and called his fellows to enter in.

At the end of the passage was a locked door; and Father Thomas said: 'This is the last room—let us enter.' 'Nay, there is no need to do that,' said Master Grimston in a kind of haste; 'it leads no-where—it is but a store room.' 'It would be a pity to leave it unvisited,' said the Father—and as he said the word, there came a kind of stirring from within. 'A rat doubtless,' said the Father, striving with a sudden sense of fear; but the pale faces round him told another tale. 'Come, Master Grimston, let us be done with this,' said Father Thomas decisively; 'the hour of vespers draws nigh.' So Master Grimston slowly drew out a key and unlocked the door, and Father Thomas marched in. It was a simple place enough. There were shelves on which various household matters lay, boxes and jars, with twine and cordage. On the ground stood chests. There were some clothes hanging on pegs, and in a corner was a heap of garments, piled up. On one of the chests stood a box of rough deal, and from the corner of it dripped water, which lay in a little pool on the floor. Master Grimston went hurriedly to the box and pushed it further to the wall. As he did so, a kind of sound came from Henry's lips. Father Thomas turned and looked at him; he stood pale and strengthless, his eyes fixed on the corner—at the same moment something dark and shapeless seemed to slip past the group, and there came to the nostrils of

Father Thomas a strange sharp smell, as of the sea, only there was a taint within it, like the smell of corruption.

They all turned and looked at Father Thomas together, as though seeking comfort from his presence. He, hardly knowing what he did, and in the grasp of a terrible fear, fumbled with his book; and opening it, read the first words that his eye fell upon, which was the place where the Blessed Lord, beset with enemies, said that if He did but pray to His Father, He should send Him forthwith legions of angels to encompass Him. And the verse seemed to the priest so like a message sent instantly from heaven that he was not a little comforted.

But the thing, whatever the reason was, appeared to them no more at that time. Yet the thought of it lay very heavy on Father Thomas's heart. In truth he had not in the bottom of his mind believed that he would see it, but had trusted in his honest life and his sacred calling to protect him. He could hardly speak for some minutes,—moreover the horror of the thing was very great—and seeing him so grave, their terrors were increased, though there was a kind of miserable joy in their minds that some one, and he a man of high repute, should suffer with them.

Then Father Thomas, after a pause—they were now in the parlour—said, speaking very slowly, that they were under a sore affliction of Satan, and that they must withstand it with a good courage—'And look you,' he added, turning with a great sternness to the three, 'if there be any mortal sin upon your hearts, see that you confess it and be shriven speedily—for while such a thing lies upon the heart, so long hath Satan power to hurt—otherwise have no fear at all.'

Then Father Thomas slipped out to the garden, and hearing the bell pulled for vespers, he went to the church, and the three would go with him, because they would not be left alone. So they went together; by this time the street was fuller, and the servant-maid had told tales, so that there was much talk in the place about what was going on. None spoke with them as they went, but at every corner people could be seen talking, and, as the Father approached a silence would fall upon a group, so that they knew that their terrors were on every tongue. There was but a handful of worshippers in the church, which was dark, save for the light on Father Thomas' book. He read the holy service swiftly and courageously, but his face was very pale and grave in the light of the candle. When the vespers were over, and he had put off his robe, he said that he would go back to his house, and gather what he needed for the night, and that they should wait for him at the churchyard gate. So he strode off to his vicarage. But as he shut to the door, he saw a dark figure come running up the garden; he waited with a fear in his mind, but in a moment he saw that it was Henry, who came up breathless, and said that he must speak with the Father alone. Father Thomas knew that some dark secret was to be told him. So he led Henry into the parlour and seated himself, and said, 'Now, my son, speak boldly.' So there was an instant's silence, and Henry slipped on to his knees.

Then in a moment Henry with a sob began to tell his tale. He said that on the day of the wreck his father had roused him very early in the dawn, and had told him to put on his clothes and come silently, for he thought there was a wreck ashore. His father carried a spade in his hand, he knew not then why. They went down to the tide, which was moving out very fast, and had left but an inch or two of water on the sands. There was little light, but, when they had walked a little, they saw the black hull of a ship before them, on the edge of the deeper water, the waves driving over it; and then all at once they came upon the body of a man lying on his face on the sand. There was no sign of life in him, but he clasped a bag in his hand that was heavy, and the pocket of his coat was bulging; and there lay, moreover, some glittering things about him that seemed to be coins. They lifted the body up, and his father stripped the coat from the man, and then bade Henry dig a hole in the sand, which he presently did, though the sand and water oozed fast into it. Then his father, who had been stooping down, gathering something up from the sand, raised the body up, and laid it in the hole, and bade Henry cover it. And so he did till it was nearly hidden. Then came a horrible thing; the sand in the hole began to move and stir, and presently a hand was put out with clutching fingers; and Henry dropped the spade, and said, 'There is life in him,' but his father seized the spade, and shovelled the sand into the hole with a kind of silent fury, and trampled it over and smoothed it down—and then he gathered up the coat and the bag, and handed Henry the spade. By this time the town was astir, and they saw, very faintly, a man run along the shore eastward; so, making a long circuit to the west, they returned; his father had put the spade away and taken the coat upstairs; and then he went out with Henry, and told all he could find that there was a wreck ashore.

The priest heard the story with a fierce shame and anger, and turning to Henry he said, 'But why did you not resist your father, and save the poor sailor?' 'I dared not,' said Henry shuddering, 'though I would have done so if I could; but my father has a power over me, and I am used to obeying him.' Then said the priest, 'This is a dark matter. But you have told the story bravely, and now will I shrive you, my son.' So he gave him shrift. Then he said to Henry, 'And have you seen aught that would connect the beast that visits you with this thing?' 'Ay, that I have,' said Henry, 'for I watched it with my father skip and leap in the water over the place where the man lies buried.' Then the priest said, 'Your father must tell me the tale too, and he must make submission to the law.' 'He will not,' said Henry. 'Then will I compel him,' said the priest, 'Not out of my mouth,' said Henry, 'or he will slay me too.' And then the priest saw that he was in an awkward position for he could not use the words of confession of one man to convict another of his sin. So he gathered his things in haste, and walked back to the church; but Henry went another way, saying 'I made excuse to come away, and said I went elsewhere; but I fear my father much—he sees very deep; and I would not have him suspect me of having made confession.'

Then the Father met the other two at the church gate; and they went down to the house in silence, the Father pondering heavily; and at the door Henry joined them, and it seemed to the Father that old Master Grimston regarded him not. So they entered the house in silence, and ate in silence, listening earnestly for any sound. And the Father looked oft on Master Grimston, who ate and drank and said nothing, never raising his eyes. But once the Father saw him laugh secretly to himself, so that the blood ran cold in the Father's veins, and he could hardly contain himself from accusing him. Then the Father read prayers, and prayed earnestly against the evil, and that they should open their hearts to God, if he would show them why this misery came upon them.

Then they went to bed; and Henry asked that he might sleep in the priest's room, which he willingly granted. And so the house was dark, and they made as though they would sleep; but the Father could not sleep, and he heard Henry weeping silently to himself like a little child.

But at last the Father slept—how long he knew not—and suddenly woke from his sleep with a horror of darkness all about

him, and he knew that there was some evil thing abroad. He
looked upon the room. He heard Henry mutter heavily in his
sleep as though there was a dark terror upon him; and then, in the
light of the dying embers, the Father saw a thing rise upon the
hearth, as though it had slept there, and woken to stretch itself.
And then in the half-light it seemed softly to gambol and play;
but whereas when an innocent beast does this it seems a fond and
pretty sight, the Father thought he had never seen so ugly a sight
as the beast gambolling all by itself, as if it could not contain its
own dreadful joy; it looked viler and more wicked every moment;
then, too, there spread in the room the sharp scent of the sea, with
the foul smell underneath it, that gave the Father a deadly sickness; he tried to pray, but no words would come, and he felt
indeed that the evil was too strong for him. Presently the beast
desisted from its play, and looking wickedly about it, came near
to the Father's bed, and seemed to put up its hairy forelegs upon
it; he could see its narrow and obscene eyes, which burned with a
dull yellow light, and were fixed upon him. And now the Father
thought that his end was near, for he could stir neither hand nor
foot, and the sweat ran down his brow; but he made a mighty
effort, and in a voice which shocked himself, so dry and husky and
withal of so loud and screaming a tone it was, he said three holy
words. The beast gave a great quiver of rage, but it dropped down
on the floor, and in a moment was gone. Then Henry woke, and
raising himself on his arm, said something; but there broke out
in the house a great outcry and the stamping of feet, which seemed
very fearful in the silence of the night. The priest leapt out of his
bed all dizzy, and made a light, and ran to the door, and went out,
crying whatever words came to his head. The door of Master
Grimston's room was open, and a strange and strangling sound
came forth; the Father made his way in, and found Master
Grimston lying upon the floor, his wife bending over him; he lay
still, breathing pitifully, and every now and then a shudder ran
through him. In the room there seemed a strange and shadowy
tumult going on; but the Father saw that no time could be lost,
and kneeling down beside Master Grimston, he prayed with all
his might.

Presently Master Grimston ceased to struggle and lay still, like
a man who had come out of a sore conflict. Then he opened his
eyes, and the Father stopped his prayers, and looking very hard at
him he said, 'My son, the time is very short—confess your sins.'

Then Master Grimston, rolling his haggard eyes upon the group, twice strove to speak and could not; but the third time the Father, bending down his head, heard him say in a thin voice, that seemed to float from a long way off, 'I slew him . . . my sin.' Then the Father swiftly gave him shrift, and as he said the last word, Master Grimston's head fell over on the side, and the Father said, 'He is gone.' And Bridget broke out into a terrible cry, and fell upon Henry's neck, who had entered unseen.

Then the Father bade Henry lead her away, and put the poor body on the bed; as he did so he noticed that the face of the dead man was strangely bruised and battered, as though it had been stamped upon by the cloven hoofs of some beast. Then Father Thomas knelt, and prayed until the light came filtering in through the shutters and the cocks crowed in the village, and presently it was day. But that night the Father learnt strange secrets, and something of the dark purpose of God was revealed to him.

In the morning there came one to find the priest, and told him that another body had been thrown up on the shore, which was strangely smeared with sand, as though it had been rolled over and over in it; and the Father took order for its burial.

Then the priest had a long talk with Bridget and Henry. He found them sitting together, and she held her son's hand and smoothed his hair, as though he had been a little child; and Henry sobbed and wept, but Bridget was very calm. 'He hath told me all,' she said, 'and we have decided that he shall do whatever you bid him; must he be given to justice?' and she looked at the priest very pitifully. 'Nay, nay,' said the priest. 'I hold not Henry to account for the death of the man; it was his father's sin, who hath made heavy atonement—the secret shall be buried in our hearts.'

Then Bridget told him how she had waked suddenly out of her sleep, and heard her husband cry out; and that then followed a dreadful kind of struggling, with the scent of the sea over all; and then he had all at once fallen to the ground and she had gone to him—and that then the priest had come.

Then Father Thomas said with tears that God had shown them deep things and visited them very strangely.

Then lastly he went with Henry to the store-room; and there, in the box that had dripped with water, lay the coat of the dead man, full of money, and the bag of money too; and Henry would have cast it back into the sea, but the priest said that this might not be, but that it should be bestowed plentifully upon shipwrecked mariners unless the heirs should be found. But the ship appeared to be a foreign ship, and no search ever revealed whence the money had come.

Master Grimston was found to have left much wealth. But Bridget sold the house and the land, and it mostly went to rebuild the church. Then Bridget and Henry moved to the vicarage and served Father Thomas faithfully, and they guarded their secret.

Now the beast troubled those of whom I write no more; but it is easier to raise up evil than to lay it; and it is said to this day that a man or a woman with an evil thought in their hearts may see on a certain evening in November, at the ebb of the tide, a goatlike thing wade in the water, snuffing at the sand, as though it sought but found not.

Witch In-Grain

by

R. MURRAY GILCHRIST

One of the chief pleasures of reading short stories with a view to compiling an anthology such as this, is the occasional thrill of discovery. It is occasional, too, perhaps once for every twenty books researched, obtained and read. Sometimes it may only be one story in a book that comes up to what I call my 'double standard'—quality and rarity. Very rarely is it more than two stories a book. Once in a blue moon it is a complete book, and such was the case with The Stone Dragon *(1894) by Robert Murray Gilchrist (1868–1917). This was Gilchrist's first book, and his only collection of macabre stories. That such a collection should have been apparently overlooked by anthologists for the last eighty years is both mystifying and gratifying—gratifying because it enables me to present for the first time a story completely unlike any you may have read before.*

Gilchrist began to write at an early age, and published several novels and collections of short stories. After spending several summers in Derbyshire, he afterwards lived for many years in a remote part of the High Peak District, studying the local people. The results of his studies were published in both factual and fictional form, factually in The Peak District *(1910) and fictionally in collections such as* A Peakland Faggot *(1897) and* Natives of Milton *(1902).*

'Witch In-Grain' is not from a typical Gilchrist book and one can only regret that he did not persist in writing more ghost stories. It is quite possible that he may have turned out to be one of the leading writers in this field. See if you agree.

Of late Michal had been much engrossed in the reading of the black-letter books that Philosopher Bale brought from France. As you know I am no Latinist—though once she had been earnest in her desire to instruct me; but the open air had ever greater charms for me than the dry precincts of a library. So I grudged the time she spent apart, and throughout the spring I would have been all day at her side, talking such foolery as lovers use. But ever she must steal away and hide herself amongst dead volumes.

Yesterday evening I crossed the Roods, and entered the garden, to find the girl sitting under a yew-tree. Her face was haggard and her eyes sunken: for the time it seemed as if many years had passed over her head, but somehow the change had only added to her beauty. And I marvelled greatly, but ere I could speak a huge bird, whose plumage was as the brightest gold, fluttered out of her lap from under the silken apron: and looking on her uncovered bosom I saw that his beak had pierced her tender flesh. I cried aloud, and would have caught the thing, but it rose slowly, laughing like a man, and, beating upwards, passed out of sight in the trees. Then Michal drew long breaths, and her youth came back in some measure. But she frowned, and said, 'What is it, sweetheart? Why hast awakened me? I dreamed that I fed the Dragon of the Hesperidean Garden.' Meanwhile, her gaze set on the place whither the bird had flown.

'Thou hast chosen a filthy plaything,' I said. 'Tell me how came it hither?'

She rose without reply, and kissed her hands to the gaudy wings, which were nearing through the trees. Then, lifting up a great book that had lain at her feet, she turned towards the house. But ere she had reached the end of the path she stopped, and smiled with strange subtlety.

'How camest *thou* hither, O satyr?' she cried. 'Even when the Dragon slept, and the fruit hung naked to my touch. . . . The gates fell to.'

Perplexed and sore adread, I followed to the hall; and found in the herb garden the men struggling with an ancient woman—a foul crone, brown and puckered as a rotten apple. At sight of Michal she thrust out her hands, crying, 'Save me, mistress!' The girl cowered, and ran up the steps and indoors. But for me, I questioned Simon, who stood well out of reach of the wretch's nails, as to the wherefore of this hurly-burly.

His underlings bound the crone and dragged her to the closet in the banqueting gallery. Then, her squawling being stilled, Simon entreated me to compel Michal to prick her arm. So I went down to the library, and found my sweetheart sitting by the window, tranced with seeing that goblin fowl go tumbling on the lawn.

My heart was full of terror and anguish. 'Dearest Michal,' I prayed, 'for the sake of our passion let me command. Here is a knife.' I took a poniard from Sir Roger's stand of arms. 'Come with me now: I will tell you all.'

Her gaze still shed her heart upon the popinjay; and when I took her hand and drew her from the room, she strove hard to escape. In the gallery I pressed her fingers round the haft, and knowing that the witch was bound, flung open the door so that they faced each other. But Mother Benmusk's eyes glared like fire, so that Michal was withered up, and sank swooning into my arms. And a chuckle of disdain leaped from the hag's ragged lips. Simon and the others came hurrying, and when Michal had found her life, we begged her to cut into one of those knotted arms. Yet she would none of it, but turned her face and signed no—no—she would not. And as we strove to prevail with her, word came that one of the Bishop's horses had cast a shoe in the village, and that his lordship craved the hospitality of Ford, until the smith had mended the mishap. Nigh at the heels of his message came the divine, and having heard and pondered our tale, he would fain speak with her.

I took her to the drawing-room, where at the sight of him she burst into such a fit of laughter that the old man rose in fear and went away.

'Surely it is an obsession,' he cried: 'nought can be done until the witch takes back her spells!'

So I bade the servants carry Mother Benmusk to the mere, and cast her in the muddy part thereof where her head would lie above water. That was fifteen hours ago, but methinks I still hear her screams clanging through the stagnant air. Never was hag so fierce and full of strength! All along the garden I saw a track of uprooted flowers. Amongst the sedges the turmoil grew and grew till every heron fled. They threw her in, and the whole mere seethed as if the floor of it were hell. For full an hour she cursed us fearsomely: then, finding that every time she neared the land the men thrust her back again, her spirit waxed abject, and she fell to whimpering. Two hours before twelve she cried that she would tell all she knew. So we landed her, and she was loosened of her bonds and she mumbled in my ear: 'I swear by Satan that I am innocent of this harm! I ha' none but paltry secrets. Go at midnight to the heath and watch Baldus's tomb. There thou shalt find all.'

The beldam tottered away, her bemired petticoats slapping her legs; and I bade them let her rest in peace until I had certainly proved her guilt. With this I returned to the house; but, finding that Michal had retired for the night, I sat by the fire, waiting for the time to pass. A clock struck the half before eleven, and I set out for King Baldus's grave, whither, had not such a great matter been at stake, I dared not have ventured after dark. I stole from the garden and through the first copse. The moon lay against a brazen curtain; little snail-like clouds were crawling underneath, and the horns of them pricked her face.

As I neared the lane to the waste, a most unholy dawn broke behind the fringe of pines, looping the boles with strings of grey-golden light. Surely a figure, a shape, moved there? I ran. Another moment, and I was in the midst of a host of weasels and hares and such-like creatures, all flying from the precincts of the tomb. I quaked with dread, and my hair stood upright. But I thrust on, parted the thorn boughs, and looked up at the mound.

On the summit sat Michal, triumphing, invested with flames. And the Shape approached, and wrapped her in his blackness.

The Tudor Chimney

by

A. N. L. MUNBY

Old buildings and the world of the antiquary have always been popular settings for ghost stories. Few living authors know more of this sphere than A. N. L. Munby, the Librarian of King's College, Cambridge. Dr Munby has a long background in the antiquarian book trade and his volume of ghost stories The Alabaster Hand *(1949) shows that same keen eye for the details of books and manuscripts which so enhanced the tales of M. R. James. In 'The Tudor Chimney' he turns his attentions to a standard piece of masonry. After reading it, you will no doubt think twice about unblocking any chimneys you find bricked over in your next house.*

I am an indefatigable note-taker. A life-time of antiquarian studies has led to a most formidable accumulation of material. Shelves of notebooks, cupboards and trunks of papers bear witness to my enthusiasms, and, I like to think, to my industry. Nor can I bear to throw anything away—I have too much of the magpie in me for that. So far I have successfully resisted the efforts of motherly women friends to 'clear out all that rubbish' and my commonplace books of what struck me as curious and interesting thirty years ago provide me with occasional reading matter of a particularly delightful nature. I have indeed one regret, When I was young and ambitious I vowed that I would conscientiously index all of my entries, a resolution which I kept for nearly three months. The task now is too Herculean even to bear thinking about. Luckily I have a memory above the average—particularly for what the more practical of my friends rudely dismiss as 'scraps of useless knowledge'; and one of these despised scraps once stood me in very good stead.

When Simon Venn first told me of his project. I supported it enthusiastically—for he is a very rich man. To restore a derelict house to its former glory is no occupation for the possessor of a modest income. Though the initial purchase of such a property may be effected for the proverbial song, the illusion of a bargain is soon shattered by the long face of the inspecting architect and by still longer accounts from the local builder. But considerations of this nature weigh little with a man whose fortune is based upon the secure foundation of a century-old whisky distillery. The finding, however, of a suitable house for renovation proved surprisingly difficult. He told me that he had explored perhaps a score of properties offered by optimistic agents. He had visited 'Tudor' houses, not a brick of which could have been laid earlier than the eighteenth century, and a 'Georgian' mansion which could hardly have been designed before the Great Exhibition. He had seen one or two perfect houses in settings hopelessly spoilt by modern developments, and not a few glorious sites with houses unworthy of them. In fact, Venn had begun to despair of ever being able to dissipate his surplus wealth in this delightful way, and in a fit of pique removed himself to the South of France.

It was in the following May—the year was 1924—that I next heard from him. He had returned to England, and had happened upon the ideal house for his scheme in Berkshire. The letter was written in an exultant tone that reflected the enthusiasm of the man. Nothing would suffice but that I came down at once to see it. The purchase had been completed and work was already beginning. He would make no attempt to describe the place—no words could do justice to its charms—and much more in the same strain. There followed minute instructions for the drive down. The letter was headed The Old Hall, Didenham, a village which lay, according to my friend's information, in the Downs between Wantage and Lambourn. Such an invitation was much to my liking. I consulted my engagement book, told several white lies over the telephone, and found myself possessed of four clear days. A telegram to Venn, some hasty packing, and my arrangements were complete. By noon I was speeding along the Great West Road, pleasantly deserted on a fine mid-week morning. Lunch at Reading delayed me for half an hour, but by half-past two I was on the last lap of my journey. Lambourn was behind me, and I climbed steadily up the second-class road on to the Downs. I have always loved these spacious chalk uplands, and Venn had chosen to settle in an area much favoured by ancient man. The prehistory

of the neighbourhood was fairly well known to me—the White
Horse, Uffington Castle and Wayland's Smithy had been visited
and revisited. but I had never before approached this stretch of
the Downs from the south side.

Some way short of the summit I turned up a side lane, breasted
a ridge and before me I saw what I knew must be my destination.
I stopped the car and gazed in appreciation at the scene before me.
Three hundred yards away was the house, set in a re-entrant of the
hill and sheltered on three sides. I could not see the village itself,
but the tower of a church just showed itself above some fine
beeches to the right. From the eminence on which I had stopped
I looked down upon the Old Hall, a building whose mellow red
brick glowed in the afternoon sun. I tried to guess its date, and
put it down as early sixteenth century, which I subsequently
learned was an accurate estimate. It was built upon an 'H' plan,
and at each end was a great multiple chimney-stack, displaying
those spiral brick chimneys which were so dear to the heart of the
Tudor builder. Round one of the stacks scaffolding had been
erected, from which I presumed that Venn had wasted no time in
getting to work. What I could see of the grounds was frankly
disappointing. To the front were a few acres of indifferent park-
land, but behind the house I could just perceive the angle of a high
wall which gave promise of a sheltered garden to the rear. The
general effect of the whole was somewhat dilapidated but by no
means derelict.

I restarted the car, and in a couple of minutes I was receiving a
smiling greeting from my host's manservant, an old acquaintance
of mine and a great chatterbox.

'Well, Dawson,' I said, 'how do you like your new home?'

'Very nice, sir,' he replied ,'and by the time Mr Venn's finished
with it, it should be a regular showpiece. But when he tells me
what he's going to do, I sometimes doubt if he will ever finish it—
in my lifetime—that is.'

'Oh, come,' I said; 'surely it's not as bad as all that?'

'Well, sir,' he responded, 'I shall be very surprised if we get the
workmen out this side of Christmas. I can't understand what's
come over the master. Take the dining-room, for instance—
it may be a bit on the small side, but it's cosy like—intimate,
if you know what I mean. Well, Mr Venn is not only joining it
up with the drawing-room, but, believe it or not, he's going to
take the first floor out so that it goes right up to the roof. I've

never heard of such a thing. Think of heating the place, sir, I said——'

He broke off suddenly as my friend appeared and became very busy picking up my bags.

'I heard you, Dawson,' said Venn, laughing, and added as the old man went off with my luggage:

'Poor old Dawson, I'm afraid he doesn't appreciate the excitement of tracing out exactly where the Great Hall used to be. I'm delighted that you've come. I do hope that you won't be too uncomfortable. We're camping out in the west wing during the alterations and having our meals in the library.' He glanced at his watch. 'We've got an hour before tea,' he said, 'just nice time to give you a general view of the place. I'll show you the plans for restoration after dinner.'

It would be unreasonable to inflict upon the reader an account of my tour of the house, especially as it has little bearing upon the events to come. I will, however, admit that Venn's enthusiasm was amply justified. The latent possibilities of the place were enormous. I saw it all—from the little walled sixteenth-century herb garden to the topmost attic in which were visible the hammerbeams that would become once more the roof of the hall when the intervening floors had been cleared away. In his bedroom Venn showed me with pride part of the original hall screen incorporated in some later panelling. The house was bigger than I had realised—there must have been quite fourteen bedrooms, and it was just on four o'clock by the time we reached the ground floor again.

'There's just one more thing I'd like you to see before tea,' said Venn, leading the way into a small room at the east end of the house. It seemed to be the room in which the workmen had made their headquarters, for it was full of buckets, ladders and the usual paraphernalia.

'What do you think of that?' said my host, 'isn't it extraordinary?' He was pointing to the fireplace, which appeared to be the oldest and was certainly the finest in the house. Above the great stone Tudor arch was a chimney-piece of carved oak, richly decorated with mythological figures and heraldic devices. The extraordinary aspect of this splendid relic lay in its being bricked up. The whole of the fireplace had been walled across.

'This room was one half of the small parlour of the Tudor house,' said Venn, 'and I intend to join it up with the housekeeper's room next door and use it as my study. But can you conceive anyone bricking up this magnificent fireplace and substituting *that*.'

With a wave of his hand he indicated an indifferent cast-iron stove on the other side of the room. 'Thank heaven, they didn't destroy it—one of my first jobs is to get it into use again.'

'That shouldn't take long,' I said, 'providing the chimney itself hasn't been tampered with.'

At this moment a workman entered the room and, seeing Venn there, he touched his cap respectfully. Venn nodded and said:

'How long would it take you to knock a few bricks out of this?' He tapped the walled-in area as he spoke. The workman cast a professional eye over it.

'Well, sir,' he said, 'if it's only one brick thick. I should say about twenty minutes. Would you like me to 'ave a go at it, sir? Just in the middle. I won't go near the stonework at the sides in case I damage it. That'll want 'andling careful.'

He seized a hammer and chisel, and as we went off the little room resounded with the ring of steel upon mortar.

We had nearly finished tea when the parlourmaid brought a message that the man working on the chimney would like to have a word with Mr Venn. He entered awkwardly, cap in hand and said:

'Beg pardon, sir, I didn't ought to trouble you, but I 'ope I 'aven't done wrong with that chimney. I've knocked an 'ole in them bricks like what you said, but there isn't 'alf a narsty smell coming out of it. I should say 'ooever bricked up that there fireplace 'ad got a reason for it, sir.'

'What sort of a smell?' I asked.

'Well, sir,' he said, 'it's what you might call a bit 'ard to give a name to. It isn't drains—at least I'd be very surprised if it was—but it's just narsty. It's as if something's burning what didn't ought to burn. Perhaps you gentlemen wouldn't mind stepping along and trying it for yourselves.'

We rose and followed him back to the scene of his operations. As we filed into the room the cause of his perturbation became apparent. There was a smell not very strong but none the less insistent; a kind of kitchen smell, but not the sort that any clean, well-ordered kitchen could produce—an infinitely stale reek of burnt fat and offal. The effect was, to say the least, disagreeable. Venn flung the windows open and some of the pungency was lost.

'I think it's just the stale air from the chimney,' he said. 'Just loosen some more bricks and let's see if it's blocked higher up.'

It was the work of only a few minutes to enlarge the aperture to a respectable size, and Venn cautiously inserted his head and shoulders. 'I can see the sky,' he said, and his voice sounded muffled and thin, as though it were far away. 'There's no other blockage,' he went on. 'I can't see anything that would cause a smell——' He gave a sharp exclamation, and withdrew his head sharply, not before a certain amount of dirt had lodged in his hair. From the chimney came the rustle and thud of falling debris. 'Damn those starlings,' said Venn ruefully, looking at his head in a wall mirror. 'I thought I saw something moving up inside the flue, quite a big bird by the look of it—more like a jackdaw than a starling, though I haven't seen one round the house. I expect there's a nest up there which wants clearing out.'

As he spoke something else came fluttering down inside the flue and stuck on the jagged hole in the brickwork. I took the tongs from the stove and pulled it out, but it was only a small bundle of rags, filthy and charred, and with an exclamation of disgust I dropped them back into the grate.

I don't think much else happened that day which is relevant to this narrative. After dinner Venn and I spent an interesting couple of hours in the library with his architect's plans, and there was much talk of butteries, solars and minstrels' galleries which I will spare the reader. We went up to bed at about eleven. At the foot of the stairs Venn said:

'It's a funny thing, but I seem to have got that damned smell in my nostrils; I could swear I got a whiff of it then.' I sniffed hard but couldn't be certain. 'I'll just see if the door of the room is shut,' he added; 'otherwise the whole house will reek of it.'

He returned in a few seconds. 'It *was* shut,' he said. 'I had a look inside and oddly enough I couldn't smell it at all in the room. Oh well, the whole chimney can be cleaned out in a day or two.'

He wished me good night, and I retired to my room, where I slept excellently.

I am a reasonably early riser, and the following day dawned so bright that there was no inducement to linger in bed. I resolved to take a short walk before breakfast, and was dressed by eight. It was thus that I inadvertently overheard a conversation at the foot of the stairs. I call it a conversation, though it was more in the nature of a monologue, delivered in somewhat petulant tones by the charwoman, a stout lady of about fifty, who had been pointed out to me on the previous day. The workman with whom I was already acquainted formed the reluctant audience.

'You men are all the same,' the charwoman was saying; 'eat your 'eads off and expect everyone to run about clearing up after you. I'll be glad to see the last of you, that I will. Mind you, I'm a reasonable woman, but what I say is that there's *necessary* mess and there's *unnecessary* mess. I know you can't carry out alterations without breaking the place up, though why it can't be left like it is, I *don't* know. But when it comes to strewing your nasty burnt rags up and down my nice clean passages that's another thing altogether. And I won't 'ave it. You've got a room, 'aven't you, to make your filthy messes in——'

'Now, look 'ere, Mrs Fisher,' interposed the workman. 'I tell you straight that them rags is nothing to do with me. There was a few old rags from the chimney, but they was left in the grate. Why should you think I want to go strewing them round the house? I got my work to do——'

'Well, you go and get on with it,' the acid voice of Mrs Fisher broke in; 'and if I 'ave any more trouble, I'll go straight to the master. And that goes for the 'ole lot of you. And if I sees the foreman, I'll give 'im a piece of my mind. About as much good as a sick 'eadache, 'e is.'

The workman made his escape and I descended the stairs. The aggrieved charwoman was engaged in sweeping a small heap of charred rags into her dustpan, an action which was punctuated by much muttering. 'Good morning,' I said. 'It's a lovely day.'

She agreed reluctantly, and I hastily passed by, in case she should start airing her grievances afresh. I remember wondering idly how it was that the rags, apparently from the chimney, should have found their way into the passage, but the whole thing seemed too trivial to worry about. I took a brisk walk up on to the hillside, and returned to breakfast half an hour later in high spirits.

The day passed pleasantly enough. At about ten my host's architect arrived, and the three of us examined in greater detail what I had inspected cursorily on the previous day. I liked Henson, the architect, a youngish man and a whole-hearted enthusiast for the scheme. Our pleasure was, however, slightly marred by one thing. In different parts of the house we kept getting occasional whiffs of the smell from the unblocked chimney. On two or three occasions the pungent, unmistakable reek came to my nostrils; then it was gone. Henson smelt it, too, and remarked on it, but all our efforts to pin it down to any particular place were unavailing. The chimney itself, which we examined, was quite free of it, and its source remained elusive. The flue upon inspection proved to be quite clear. There was no trace of birds or a nest—another minor mystery. I don't want you to think that we took all this very seriously at the time. But I am writing in the knowledge of what was to come, and these apparent trivialities then take on a more sombre aspect.

It was on the following morning that we got our first inkling of more sinister matters. After breakfast I took a turn upon the terrace, and then went to join Venn in the library, where it was his habit to read his morning mail. As I opened the library door I noticed his old manservant Dawson was seated in a chair—in itself an unusual occurrence—and was engaged in earnest conversation with his master. I was about to retire again, but Venn called to me:

'Come in,' he said, 'and listen to this. Dawson says he's seen a ghost!' His tone was light but his face, which he turned to me, was grave and I could see that he was worried. I knew Venn was genuinely fond of the old man, and he looked pale and shaken as he sat hunched into one of the library armchairs.

'Well, sir, that's how it is,' said Dawson. 'I couldn't stay another night in this house, not if you were to pay me a million pounds. Not but what I shall be very sorry to leave you, sir, and after all these years, too, and I will say that I could never hope to have a better master. But I'm not as young as I used to be, and another turn like the one I got last night would just about finish me. I didn't sleep a wink, sir, and I don't think I ever should under this roof. All night long I could see that figure standing there at the foot of the stairs, looking at me. It fair gives me the creeps to talk about it now.'

Venn interposed. 'What we'd better do is this, Dawson. You were going to take your holiday, anyway, in a month's time. Were you going to stay with your married sister at Hunstanton again?'

Dawson nodded. 'Well,' my friend continued, 'let's send her a prepaid wire and see if she can have you now. There's no hurry about your coming back—you can take an extra month if you like. And by that time we shall have got this place a bit more shipshape. I expect the upheaval of the move has upset you. But

I'm certainly not going to accept your notice straightaway. See how you feel in six week's time. What do you say about that?'

With apparent reluctance, Dawson allowed himself to be persuaded into accepting these arrangements. The wire was sent, a favourable reply was received, and by midday Dawson and his luggage had left for the station. Before he went, the old man drew me on one side.

'Look after Mr Venn, sir,' he said, 'if you'll excuse the liberty. I wouldn't like anything to happen to him. And believe me, sir, there's something downright evil loose in this house.'

He shook his head sadly, climbed into the car, and was borne away. At lunch I asked Venn what exactly it was that Dawson had seen.

'That's just the stupid part about it,' he answered. 'He either couldn't or wouldn't give any coherent account of it—all he did was to keep repeating some nonsense about a figure standing and looking at him. He was so upset that I didn't like to press him for any further details. The only thing he did say at all definite was that the appearance was accompanied by a fearful smell, which is of course suggestive. I'm beginning to think that perhaps I was a bit hasty in having that chimney unblocked. I've a good mind to have it boarded up again for the time being.'

'Let it wait for another day,' I said, 'and we may see something for ourselves. If you just brick up the hole again, you'll never really have any peace of mind here. We've got to try to find out more about it; a ghost isn't the sort of thing one can shut away and keep out of one's mind.'

There the matter was left, and by unspoken mutual consent we made no further reference to it during the day.

It is with extreme reluctance that I come to the next part of my narrative. I am aware that I cut no very heroic figure in it, though I hope I am old enough not to worry about that. But I do not even now like to remind myself of the horror and panic that seized me. There are certain human passions that strip from a man the veneer of civilised culture which normally encases him, that turn him into something primitive and elemental. I felt myself spiritually naked when face to face with the apparition that confronted me that night. But I am anticipating.

Venn and I spent the evening together in the library. He had some letters to write, and I was quite content to smoke and examine his books. At about ten-thirty he rose from his bureau and proposed going to bed. I said that I would read for a little longer, but I hoped that he wouldn't wait up for me. He looked a little dubious at this, but I assured him that I was quite happy to sit up alone. This was not mere bravado—I felt it unlikely at the time that I should actually see anything. Indeed, I became quite absorbed in my book after my friend had left me. I was sitting not far from the door, and the room was lit by a single reading-lamp. I was smoking my pipe, and after about twenty minutes I found it necessary to refill it. It was then that I first realised that the smell, which I was coming to know so well, was pervading the room. At the first whiff of that sickening reek I sat quite still and listened, but I could hear nothing. None the less, the atmosphere of the room had changed in some infinitely subtle way. The gloom outside the range of the single light seemed to have become more intense and to have assumed an oppressive malignant quality. The mild May evening seemed to have grown colder, for I was conscious of shivering. As I sat there, holding my breath, I was aware that I was not alone in the room. Something else was present, immediately behind me. How I detected this I do not know, but I was none the less certain of it. With an effort of will power I slowly turned my head, for I was intensely curious. I wish to God now that I had not given way to my curiosity. For what I saw still haunts me. Just on the outer edge of the lamplight a figure was standing—and I hope I never see anything again so monstrous and so repellent. It was a man, but it had the aspect of no living man. Its form was covered with the charred remnants of clothing, the bare legs were horribly thin: they were nothing but burnt skin and blackened bone. But it was the head that made my very blood run cold: it was hairless and scorched, and the face was nothing more than a featureless, seared, leathery mask. It was the face of a man long dead, but the eyes were alive. They glowed behind the mask with a baleful, infernal light that radiated malevolence.

In far less time than it takes to write these words I was on the far side of the door and fumbling with the key. The lock was stiff from long disuse, and I found it would not turn. As I struggled with it, something gripped the handle on the far side and pulled. Sick with panic I tugged with one hand and with the other I wrestled with the lock; with a sudden jerk the key turned and I was standing sweating and panting in the dark passage. On the panels of the door I could hear something scraping and scratching.

I ran as fast as my legs would carry me up to Venn's room. He was in bed, but jumped up when he saw me.

'Good heavens, man,' he said, 'what's the matter with you? Sit down.' I looked at myself in the mirror and realised the cause of his consternation. I was white and breathless, and my face was moist with beads of sweat. He poured me out a glass of brandy from his medicine chest, and as I gulped it down I told him what I had seen. His first reaction was to go to the door and lock it, then he seated himself on the bed again.

'You'd better sleep in my room,' he said. 'There's a spare bed in my dressing-room that we can bring in here. I can find you some pyjamas. I don't suppose you want to pass the night alone, and I certainly don't.'

Far into the night we discussed the matter. Venn decided that as the following day was a Sunday and the workmen would not be coming, he would move his belongings to the inn at Lambourn and stay there for a while. The two servants could easily be given a holiday. The work of restoration could continue by daylight for the time being, but no one would sleep in the house. I questioned him closely on what he knew of the history of the place, but he had little to tell me. He had purchased it in a great hurry, and it had been empty for some years previously. He believed that it had changed hands several times in the last fifty years.

'I do remember one thing the agent told me,' he said. 'It hasn't always been called the Old Hall—originally it had another name. He told me what it was, but I'm damned if I can remember it now.'

He thought for a few moments. 'No,' he continued, 'it's no good, I've forgotten—I'd know it if I heard it though.'

We agreed to follow up this line on the next day, and to enquire after any local traditions concerning the house. It was some time later that I had an inspiration.

'What about the heraldry on the chimney-piece?' I asked. 'That ought to tell us who one of the early owners was. As far as I recollect, there was a coat of three birds' heads—ravens, I think. It may well have been a canting device. Does the name Raven mean anything to you, or perhaps Crow? Or some combination incorporating either of them—Crowby?—Crowley?'

'Crowsley!' interjected Venn; 'that was it! Crowsley Hall was the original name.'

I was silent for a long time. The name of Crowsley had stirred some vague chord in my mind, and I lay pondering where I had heard it before. At last I thought I had it. It must have been nearly twenty years before, when I examined and catalogued a vast mass of manuscript materials relating to the counties of Wiltshire and Berkshire in the genealogical and topographical collections of an early nineteenth-century antiquary, which were still in the possession of his descendants. I was almost certain that embedded somewhere in my voluminous notebooks I had some information relating to the name of Crowsley, and I decided that it was worth a visit to London in the morning to see if I could find it.

I set off early, leaving Venn to arrange for the move to Lambourn, where I promised to join him in the evening. I spent the day delving among my accumulated papers, and cursed myself, not for the first time, for my failure to compile an index. The afternoon was well advanced before I found that my memory had not played me false. I *had* made extensive notes upon the family of Crowsley, and particularly upon that branch of the family to which Crowsley Hall had belonged. And certain passages which I had transcribed twenty years before seemed to have a considerable bearing upon our present troubles. I returned to Lambourn forthwith, and this is the gist of what I had to tell Venn after supper.

The fortunes of the house of Crowsley were founded, like those of many more famous families, upon lands acquired at the dissolution of the monasteries. A certain Thomas Crowsley was in a peculiarly favourable position at this period, as he was steward to the great Benedictine Abbey of Abingdon, and was thus able to sell to himself several of the Abbey's richest manors, upon exceedingly advantageous terms. Among these he purchased Didenham with its small manor house, which was largely rebuilt and named Crowsley Hall by its new occupant. Thus it was that almost overnight the steward of comparatively humble origin became a landowner. His elevation to the status of gentleman was not long delayed, as he received a grant of arms in 1547 and chose for his coat the punning device of the three birds' heads (*party per fess or and sable three crows' heads erased counterchanged*). This was embodied in the great oak chimney-piece, as we have seen. The majority of such parvenu families quickly adapted themselves to their new positions, and in a generation were indistinguishable from the long-established gentry—but this was not the case with the Crowsleys. In modern parlance they did not 'fit in'. They lived in constant friction with their neighbours, with whom they indulged in an orgy of bitter litigation. The Elizabethan records of the Court of Common Pleas leave no doubt upon this point, and their impudent arrogance is attested by a contemporary letter in which the writer refers to the whole family as 'a saucy over-weening contumelious brood'. Nor did the passing years seem to improve matters, for by the days of the early Stuarts they had become the most universally detested family in the county.

I have tried to sketch the background of intense local un-popularity because it had direct bearing upon the sequel. In 1640 the head of the family was a certain Julius Crowsley, a bachelor who lived alone at the Hall. He possessed all the unpleasant characteristics of his immediate forbears and his arrogance and insolence were a byword. He was, moreover, unfortunate enough to deliver himself into the hands of his enemies. One day he was out riding beyond the bounds of his estate. A closed gate barred his path and he shouted to a boy standing nearby to open it for him. Whether the boy made some impertinent reply or was merely slow in complying, history does not relate, but the horse-man lost his temper. He felled the child with the butt end of his whip and passed on. The boy, who was the son of a much-respected yeoman farmer, sickened and died. The smouldering resentment of the countryside broke into flame, and Julius Crowsley was apprehended by the sheriff's men, and brought to trial. In view of the high feeling that his action had aroused, the prisoner exercised his option to be tried, not at the Reading assizes 'by his country', but in London. Here he managed to produce medical evidence that the boy was already ailing, and in view of the conflicting testimony of the doctors he escaped with a fine. On May 1st, 1640, he returned to his manor in triumph. The county was in an uproar. Two night later a party of friends of the bereaved family broke into the house, intent on vengeance. What occurred is not recorded. Julius Crowsley disappeared and his body was never found, nor were his assailants ever arrested. A conspiracy of sullen silence hung over the area, and the missing man's servants appear to have been terrorised into holding their tongues. It is more than likely that the sheriff was half-hearted in his attempt to find the culprits, particularly as it was not certain whether the man was dead or had merely taken flight. The sheriff, too, would probably have shared the general approval which greeted Crowsley's disappearance, and in any case the Civil War would have turned men's thoughts into other channels.

These were the facts I had gleaned from my notes. It needed little imagination to supply the end of the story. I could picture Julius Crowsley in his house that evening, startled by the sudden arrival of armed men, his surprise turning to panic as he realised their mission. He would have sought about for some hiding-place. and some unlucky chance must have led him to climb up into the chimney of the small parlour. Perhaps his presence there was detected or revealed by some treacherous servant, and his merciless pursuers kindled a fire in the hearth. I could picture the man's feelings as the first spirals of smoke eddied round him, and the tongues of flame began to lick around his feet. He would blindly have climbed higher, desperately clawing at the sooty brickwork. The chimney was too narrow at the top to allow the passage of a man's body, but one hopes that he was suffocated by the smoke into merciful unconsciousness before the flames had done their work. So much one could guess. Yet why was the spirit of the tortured man not at rest?

Venn was deeply interested in my narrative. The rest of the story can be told in a few words—how we summoned Henson, the architect, upon the following day, how close examination of the chimney revealed a disused side flue, which with some difficulty was uncovered behind the wainscoting in the room immediately above. The pitiful remains which we unearthed there were given a decent burial in the little churchyard of Didenham. The sombre shadows of mystery and horror were thus dispelled and the old house was at peace once more. The work of restoration is now complete, and I am a frequent visitor. Dawson is in residence again, and is as talkative as ever—except upon one particular subject.

The Experiment

by

M. R. JAMES

And to close this anthology of rare tales, I am extremely proud to present a story by the great M. R. James, not included in his collected volume, as far as I can ascertain never before published in book form and certainly forgotten for over forty years.

M. R. James (1862–1936) did more for the ghost story than any other writer. He raised the art of writing tales of terror to a new high level, he brought the specialised knowledge of the antiquary and the English style of one of the country's leading academic figures to a genre that had suffered for too long at the hands of inspired amateurs, and he created a new style of ghost to match his new style of story.

The list of authors inspired by James is impressive, and includes H. R. Wakefield, Frederick Cowles, M. P. Dare, Sir Andrew Caldecott, Eleanor Scott, R. H. Malden, A. N. L. Munby and Sir T. G. Jackson. It is not hard to find traces of his style in the work of modern masters such as Robert Aickman and Ramsey Campbell.

Montague Rhodes James was born at Goodnestone Parsonage in Kent, where his father was curate, and later moved to Livermere in Suffolk. He attended Temple Grove School, East Sheen, and Eton, where he met A. C. Benson, with whom he formed a lifelong friendship. Benson was later to write of James, in his private diary: 'He is one of the few people to whom I can say, and do say, exactly what I think and as I think it. He never misunderstands, is always amused, always appreciative.'

While his brother Herbert pursued a military career, James became Provost of Eton, a post he held for nearly twenty years, until his death. His ghost stories were first written to amuse his friends, and read at Christmas time. He was persuaded to publish them and his first book Ghost Stories of an Antiquary *appeared in 1904. This was followed by* More Ghost Stories *(1911),* A Thin Ghost and Others *(1919),* A Warning to the Curious *(1925) and his* Collected

Ghost Stories (1931). He also wrote a children's fantasy The Five
Jars *(1922) and an amusing volume of reminiscences* Eton and
King's *(1926).*

*Though he is often compared to J. Sheridan le Fanu, it is in fact hard
to find any points of similarity between the two. Be that as it may, James
was so impressed with le Fanu that he researched and edited a volume of
his stories,* Madam Crowl's Ghost *(1923) and the popularity of le
Fanu today might well have been less than it is had it not been for
James's efforts.*

*But it is James's own ghost stories that made him famous to the
reading public and even now, half a century after they were written, they
are constantly finding new readers and spurring on others to try more
ghost stories. I owe my interest in the ghost story to James, thanks to a
wartime economy edition of his collected stories which was presented to
my mother and was one of the first books I ever read. It literally
frightened me so much that I was terrified of turning the light out at
night. Since then, of course, familiarity has dulled the edge of such fears
and it is a regrettable side effect of reading stories for such an anthology
as this that they no longer scare one. I envy anybody who has not read his
tales the pleasure of reading M. R. James for the first time.*

*And as a fulfilment of a lifelong ambition—to find new James
material—here is 'The Experiment'. It was first published in* The
Morning Post *(31 December 1931) and I have been unable to trace its
having appeared anywhere since. Though I would be the first to ac-
knowledge that it is by no means the best story James ever wrote, it still
makes an important addition to the available works of the undisputed
master of the ghost story.*

The Reverend Dr Hall was in his study making up the entries for
the year in the parish register: it being his custom to note baptisms,
weddings and burials in a paper book as they occurred, and in the
last days of December to write them out fairly in the vellum book
that was kept in the parish chest.

To him entered his housekeeper, in evident agitation. 'Oh sir,'
said she, 'whatever do you think? The poor Squire's gone!'

'The Squire? Squire Bowles? What are you talking about,
woman? Why, only yesterday——'

'Yes, I know, sir, but it's the truth. Wickem, the clerk, just left
word on his way down to toll the bell—you'll hear it yourself in a
minute. There now, just listen.'

Sure enough the sound broke on the still night—not loud, for the Rectory did not immediately adjoin the churchyard. Dr Hall rose hastily.

'Terrible, terrible,' he said. 'I must see them at the Hall at once. He seemed so greatly better yesterday.' He paused. 'Did you hear any word of the sickness having come this way at all? There was nothing said in Norwich. It seems so sudden.'

'No, indeed, sir, no such thing. Just caught away with a choking in his throat, Wickem says. It do make one feel—well, I'm sure I had to sit down as much as a minute or more, I come over that queer when I heard the words—and by what I could understand they'll be asking for the burial very quick. There's some can't bear the thought of the cold corpse laying in the house, and——'

'Yes: well, I must find out from Madam Bowles herself or Mr Joseph. Get me my cloak, will you? Ah, and could you let Wickem know that I desire to see him when the tolling is over?' He hurried off.

In an hour's time he was back and found Wickem waiting for him. 'There is work for you, Wickem,' he said, as he threw off his cloak, 'and not overmuch time to do it in.'

'Yes, sir,' said Wickem, 'the vault to be opened to be sure.'

'No, no, that's just the message I have. The poor Squire, they tell me, charged them before now not to lay him in the chancel. It was to be an earth grave in the yard, on the north side.' He stopped at an inarticulate exclamation from the clerk. 'Well?' he said.

'I ask pardon, sir,' said Wickem in a shocked voice, 'but did I understand you right? No vault, you say, and on the north side? Tt-tt! Why, the poor gentleman must a-been wandering.'

'Yes, it does seem strange to me, too,' said Dr Hall, 'but no, Mr Joseph tells me it was his father's—I should say stepfather's— clear wish, expressed more than once, and when he was in good health. Clean earth and open air. You know, of course, the poor Squire had his fancies,—though he never spoke of this one to me. And there's another thing, Wickem. No coffin.'

'Oh dear, dear, sir,' said Wickem, yet more shocked. 'Oh, but that'll make sad talk, that will, and what a disappointment for Wright, too! I know he'd looked out some beautiful wood for the Squire, and had it by him years past.'

'Well, well, perhaps the family will make it up to Wright in some way,' said the Rector, rather impatiently, 'but what you have to do is to get the grave dug and all things in a readiness—

torches from Wright you must not forget—by ten o'clock to-morrow night. I don't doubt but there will be somewhat coming to you for your pains and hurry.'

'Very well, sir, if those be the orders, I must do my best to carry them out. And should I call in on my way down and send the women up to the Hall to lay out the body, sir?'

'No: that, I think—I am sure—was not spoken of. Mr Joseph will send, no doubt, if they are needed. No, you have enough without that. Goodnight, Wickem. I was making up the registers when this doleful news came. Little had I thought to add such an entry to them as I must now.'

All things had been done in decent order. The torchlighted cortège had passed from the Hall through the park, up the lime avenue to the top of the knoll on which the church stood. All the village had been there, and such neighbours as could be warned in the few hours available. There was no great surprise at the hurry.

Formalities of law there were none then, and no one blamed the stricken widow for hastening to lay her dead to rest. Nor did anyone look to see her following in the funeral train. Her son Joseph—only issue of her first marriage with a Calvert of York-shire—was the chief mourner.

There were, indeed, no kinsfolk on Squire Bowles's side who could have been bidden. The will, executed at the time of the Squire's second marriage, left everything to the widow.

And what was 'everything'? Land, house, furniture, pictures, plate were all obvious. But there should have been accumulations in coin, and beyond a few hundreds in the hands of agents—honest men and no embezzlers—cash there was none. Yet Francis Bowles had for years received good rents and paid little out. Nor was he a reputed miser; he kept a good table, and money was always forthcoming for the moderate spendings of his wife and stepson. Joseph Calvert had been maintained ungrudgingly at school and college.

What, then, had he done with it all? No ransacking of the house brought any secret hoard to light; no servant, old or young, had any tale to tell of meeting the Squire in unexpected places at strange hours. No, Madam Bowles and her son were fairly non-plussed. As they sat one evening in the parlour discussing the problem for the twentieth time:

'You have been at his books and papers, Joseph, again today, haven't you?'

'Yes, mother, and no forwarder.'

'What was it he would be writing at, and why was he always sending letters to Mr Fowler at Gloucester?'

'Why, you know he had a maggot about the Middle State of the Soul. 'Twas over that that he and that other were always busy. The last thing he wrote would be a letter that he never finished. I'll fetch it. . . . Yes, the same song over again.

"Honoured friend,—I make some slow advance in our studies, but I know not well how far to trust our authors. Here is one lately come my way who will have it that for a time after death the soul is under control of certain spirits, as Raphael, and another whom I doubtfully read as Nares; but still so near to this state of life that on prayer to them he may be free to come and disclose matters to the living. Come, indeed, he must, if he be rightly called, the manner of which is set forth in an experiment. But having come, and once opened his mouth, it may chance that his summoner shall see and hear more than of the hid treasure which it is likely he bargained for; since the experiment puts this in the forefront of things to be enquired. But the eftest way is to send you the whole, which herewith I do; copied from a book of recipes which I had of good Bishop Moore." '

Here Joseph stopped, and made no comment, gazing on the paper. For more than a minute nothing was said, then Madam Bowles, drawing her needle through her work and looking at it, coughed and said, 'There was no more written?'

'No, nothing, mother.'

'No? Well, it is strange stuff. Did ever you meet this Mr Fowler?'

'Yes, it might be once or twice, in Oxford, a civil gentleman enough.'

'Now I think of it,' said she, 'it would be but right to acquaint him with—with what has happened: they were close friends. Yes, Joseph, you should do that: you will know what should be said. And the letter is his, after all.'

'You are in the right, mother, and I'll not delay it.' And forthwith he sat down to write.

From Norfolk to Gloucester was no quick transit. But a letter went, and a larger packet came in answer, and there were more evening talks in the panelled parlour at the Hall. At the close of one, these words were said: 'Tonight, then, if you are certain of yourself, go round by the field path. Ay, and here is a cloth will serve.'

'What cloth is that, mother? A napkin?'

'Yes, of a kind: what matter?' So he went out by the way of the garden, and she stood in the door, musing, with her hand on her mouth. Then the hand dropped and she said half aloud: 'If only I had not been so hurried! But it *was* the face cloth, sure enough.'

It was a very dark night, and the spring wind blew loud over the black fields: loud enough to drown all sounds of shouting or calling. If calling there was, there was no voice, nor any that answered, nor any that regarded—yet.

Next morning, Joseph's mother was early in his chamber. 'Give me the cloth,' she said, 'the maids must not find it. And tell me, tell me, quick!'

Joseph, seated on the side of the bed with his head in his hands, looked up at her with bloodshot eyes. 'We have opened his mouth,' he said, 'Why in God's name did you leave his face bare?'

'How could I help it? You know how I was hurried that day? But do you mean you saw it?'

Joseph only groaned and sunk his head in his hands again. Then, in a low voice, 'He said you should see it, too.'

With a dreadful gasp she clutched at the bedpost and clung to it. 'Oh, but he's angry,' Joseph went on. 'He was only biding his time, I'm sure. The words were scarce out of my mouth when I heard like the snarl of a dog in under there.' He got up and paced the room. 'And what can we do? He's free! And I daren't meet him! I daren't take the drink and go where he is! I daren't lie here another night. Oh, why did you do it? We could have waited.'

'Hush,' said his mother: her lips were dry. ''Twas you, you know it, as much as I. Besides, what use in talking? Listen to me: 'tis but six o'clock. There's money to cross the water: such as *they* can't follow. Yarmouth's not so far, and most night boats sail for Holland, I've heard. See you to the horses. I can be ready.'

Joseph stared at her. 'What will they say here?'

'What? Why, cannot you tell the parson we have wind of property lying in Amsterdam which we must claim or lose? Go, go; or if you are not man enough for that, lie here again tonight.' He shivered and went.

*　　　*　　　*

That evening after dark a boatman lumbered into an inn on Yarmouth Quay, where a man and a woman sat, with saddle bags on the floor by them.

'Ready, are you, mistress and gentleman?' he said. 'She sails before the hour, and my other passenger, he's waiting on the quay. Be there all your luggage?' and he picked up the bags.

'Yes, we travel light,' said Joseph. 'And you have more company bound for Holland?'

'Just the one,' said the boatman, 'and he seem to travel lighter yet.'

'Do you know him?' said Madam Bowles: she laid her hand on Joseph's arm, and they both paused in the doorway.

'Why, no, but for all he's hooded I'd know him again fast enough, he have such a curious way of speakin', and I don't doubt you'll find he know you, by what he said. "Go you and fetch 'em out," he say, "and I'll wait on 'em here" he say, and sure enough he's a-comin' this way now.'

Poisoning of a husband was petty treason then, and women guilty of it were strangled at the stake and burnt. The Assize records of Norwich tell of a woman so dealt with and of her son hanged thereafter, convicted on their own confession, made before the Rector of their parish, the name of which I withhold, for there is still hid treasure to be found there.

Bishop Moore's book of recipes is now in the University Library at Cambridge, marked Dd 11, 45 and on the leaf numbered 144 this is written:

An experiment most ofte proved true, to find out tresure hidden in the ground, theft, manslaughter, or anie other thynge. Go to the grave of a ded man, and three tymes call hym by his nam at the hed of the grave, and say. Thou, N., N., N., I conjure thee, I require thee, and I charge thee, by thi Christendome that thou takest leave of the Lord Raffaell and Nares and then askest leave this night to come and tell me trewlie of the tresure that lyith hid in such a place. Then take of the earth of the grave at the dead bodyes hed, and knitt it in a lynnen clothe and put it under thi right ear and sleape thereuppon: and wheresoever thou lyest or slepest, that night he will come and tell thee trewlie in waking or sleping.'